ARACHNE

ARACHNE

Lisa Mason

William Morrow and Company, Inc.
New York

Recognizing the importance of preserving what has been written, it is the policy of William Morrow and Company, Inc., and its imprints and affiliates to have the books it publishes printed on acid-free paper, and we exert our best efforts to that end.

Library of Congress Cataloging-in-Publication Data

Mason, Lisa.
    Arachne / Lisa Mason.
      p. cm.
    ISBN 0-688-09245-4
    I. Title.
    PS3563.A7924A89 1990
    813'.54—dc20   89-13744
                            CIP

Printed in the United States of America

First Edition

1 2 3 4 5 6 7 8 9 10

In loving memory of my father,
George Novic

Acknowledgments

Special thanks to Barry Malzberg, Robert Silverberg, and Ellen Datlow for their extraordinary help and encouragement at the beginning of my literary career.

All my love to Tom Robinson, and to Sita and Ara, the clowder on my desk.

1

The chair waited for her in the ruby-lit room. Carly Nolan stepped in and slammed the door. The chair sat in silence. Carly stalked around it, kicked its ugly feet, glared at it.

The chair was primitive, plain-legged, straight-backed. It was rude and mean, as impersonal as gridlock statistics. Black plastic wires looped and trailed all around it. A red steelyn switch stuck out from one arm. Platinum beams angled into a frame that would hold her in a comfortless grasp when the amber switched on, and her body jolted.

Carly Nolan was a slim-limbed genny with customized morphing, a genetically engineered young woman with nice body work. Her hair was shot through with copper and gold and fell to her shoulders in style *de nuevo*. Emerald eyes were lined with ebony lash implants, a romantic gift from her father in the twenty-first year after the lab decanted her. Wide feathered brows and curved cheekbones hinted at the Yugoslav bioworks her pragmatic mother had chosen. She slicked her lips plum-red.

Seated in other chairs, in other rooms, she often crossed a silk-stockinged ankle over the other knee even when wearing a skirt, and she thought nothing of striding up the new hills of San Francisco in her gray-snake, four-inch heels.

She had nowhere to go now but to the chair.

9

She was twenty-five years old.

She sat down, knees side by side.

Straps of cracked plastic filmy with old sweat lay limp on the chair's arms and legs. She snapped the straps over her own arms, own legs. The final, mocking slap of cruelty, that she should have to strap herself into the chair.

She breathed deeply three times, preparing for the moment.

But could anyone ever really prepare?

It was fine to speculate, envision bravery: you *strapped* in. You sneered at those ruby-lit walls, stared down the demon faces forming in the claustrophobic plaster. You stuck your tongue out at the black plastic wires, blinked away the slithering you thought you saw.

And Carly? Hell, she would kick the viper-wires with the spike of her high heel. With her polished left forefinger curving over the arm's end, she would yank the damn red switch herself, just to do it, tool.

She'd be ready.

But the moment had come, and she wasn't ready. Dread beat in her breast.

Dizzy, like standing on a spinning swing, the chains unraveling beneath your hands.

She leaned back.

Her spine pressed a control. With a rasping whine, the control signaled the headpiece to descend. Wirework yawned open and clamped down around her skull. A cold metal band fit snugly over her damp forehead.

The comm in front of her flickered on, flooding her face with jade luminescence. A hum arose and commenced an awful crescendo. The neckjack darted out on a serpentine robotic cable. Its tiny platinum beak bit into the linkslit installed at the back of Carly's neck.

Without warning, the red switch clicked, and the amber kicked on.

Carly's consciousness departed instantly, sucked out as

though by a vacuum, twisting up wraithlike from her twitching body left behind.

A roar exploded around her. Blinding pain flickered down her spine, then vanished in the next instant. Unbearable pressure bore down. A blackness like light turned inside out engulfed her. She became acutely aware of her total aloneness. She entered the zero.

But Carly Nolan was not afraid now. Not anymore.

Zooming the zero, she burst with strange exhilaration, giddy and wild. She shuddered. In the bodiless zero, her release of tension was akin to physical ecstasy, a neural firework shooting streamers of glowing bliss.

No more claustrophobic walls, no ruby-lit room. No platinum beams gripping her, no sweat-soured straps.

Freedom!

Next speed, the journey.

Carly had instructions. She knew what to do.

An endless tunnel appeared. She sped through it. Sometimes the tunnel seemed discrete, a solid thing of striated tissue and muscular-looking walls. Sometimes it was gossamer, a mere tube of spun translucence. Sometimes it possessed no walls at all, it was the only clear path through shifting murk and plumes of vapor.

In all its manifestations the tunnel, Carly knew, was a mental construct. Same as her speed and the journey; images conjured by her consciousness for the phenomenon of importation.

In the distance shone a clear white light.

According to instructions, Carly aimed for the light.

But, for a second, angry red clouds roiled before her, obscuring her destination. A bright blue bolt zigzagged across her left perimeter. An immense sheet of sleek black glass erected itself across her right perimeter, magmaticized into a crackling black sea, shattered into glinting shards that whirled all around her.

Carly shrugged, full of disdain.

Systemic static, that's all. Persistent spatial logic that fed back through her consciousness and reemerged as flak. Not fatally harmful, except that the unruly illusions could divert her from the subtler signs of a jacking going wrong.

She was not pleased. Not pleased at all.

Physicality, the conventions and torpor of body logic, meant little here. All that mattered was the successful importation of her neural program: her telelink.

Here Carly Nolan had a presence. Her neural program formed a cube. Her intellect gave the cube perfect geometric dimensions. Her training tightened the cube, giving it crisp, clean edges. Her ideals shone like mother-of-pearl. Her pride made the power propelling her surge. The way she strode up the new hills of San Francisco boosted her speed. Her copper-gold hair and slim genny limbs made her telelink soar like a peregrine.

Here: in telespace.

Aim for the light. She shot through the angry red clouds. Dodged the blue bolt. Calmed herself before the intimidating sheet of black glass until the shards spun away.

She sped on and on.

Suddenly the clear white light shone all around her. Its radiance bathed her. Her whole link pulsed with the fine steady hiss of ambient amber.

She had arrived.

She imported the idiosyncratic pattern of her natural neural impulses directly into the artificially defined program of her telelink.

Next: merge into public telespace.

She dove into the light, spun the radiance around her, going through and out the other side.

The light was the referent for public program: clear, luminous, vast, orderly. Consensus manifest. Public program was the aggregated correlation of two hundred million minds worldwide. The best, most prominent, most acceptable, according to Data Control requirements. All merged and standardized into the largest computer-generated, four-dimensional system ever known: telespace.

Telespace was the greatest achievement of Carly's time. A wonder tech.

Hot damn, tool, it was mega to merge! The jacking, importation, merge; these were Carly's own small triumphs. A truckload could have gone wrong. There were misjackings, when the platinum beak misconnected with your hardware. There were detours, when Data Control was working on a path and you had to reroute your link. There were crashes during importation, the awful, white-out zero of amber abandoning the chair. Always risks, especially for a pro linker jacking daily.

She felt relieved. It was as close to a trash jacking as she'd ever faced. This wasn't the first time, either. Why couldn't she just *link*, in one second flat? Link ought to be like the meshing of gears, instant, smooth, and mechanical.

Instead, Carly felt like a trackside hitchhiker trying to hop a ride on a supersonic train.

Her link joggled with annoyance. She'd squandered two seconds foolishly, futilely recoiling from the link apparatus. Goddamn ugly chair. Why couldn't they tuck the wires out of sight, make the seat body-friendly? Spent more than a second dodging the systemic static. Wasted another half second fuming.

Now she was at least three and a half seconds late.

Damn. Tweak it up, tool. Accelerate the jacking instructions. Pare the importation code. Narrow the perimeters. Something. More than one telespace trainer over the years had told her she possessed hyperactive imaging. They said this was not necessarily an attribute to be proud of for a telelink student.

And she was a student no longer. She had completed telespace training. Graduated with her bachelor's degree in universal studies, Phi Beta Kappa. Earned her juris doctorate, magna cum laude, from a top-twenty law school. Certified before Data Control. Passed the California bar exam on the first try when seventy-five percent didn't make it.

She was a professional telelinker now and a lawyer newly

employed at a competitive starting salary by the prestigious San Francisco megafirm of Ava & Rice.

She could not afford three-and-a-half-second delays.

Training, credentials, certification: these were just the beginning. She put aside her pride in those accomplishments. Now she had to prove she could do the real thing.

Prove it, Carly.

Business depended on telespace. Every pro linker who expected to make it in the legit leagues had to understand telespace. Negotiations, deal-making, deal-breaking, dispute resolution, mediation, compliance work, telespace administration. Any lawyer doing anything worth doing had to deal with telespace.

Carly Nolan did not want just to deal with telespace.

She intended to master it.

She believed this was the true aim of becoming a lawyer: to be an architect of a just society.

In the telespace before her now towered a bastion bristling with silver-bricked machicolations. At intervals swelled barrel-bellied oubliettes topped with soaring parapets and sturdy balustrades. Holoids of precious gems sparkled. There were rubies, sapphires, emeralds, amethysts, chrysoberyls, each shooting rays of dazzling pure color. Every merlon at the wall's crown held a huge diamond, and in each diamond shone a wide, staring eye made of white light.

She came before a gigantic gate gleaming like burnished gold.

Before the gate presided a column of whirling silver sparks. The column twirled to and fro. A stamp of authority imbued that strange whirlwind, like the aura of a guardian or an angel.

But this entity was nothing so lofty. It was merely a mac: a monitor of access codes. On closer scrutiny, Carly could see an unseemly pock near its crown, gaping at her like a mouth.

The mac patrolled the golden gate of the Financial District.

Macs implemented security in restricted telespace. Code processing programs, yellow-brick paths directly comming with

Data Control administrative mainframes. Very simple and simple-minded artificial intelligence.

But crucially important, in the peculiar scheme of tele-space. The cowboys, pirate viruses, and spybytes had a tough time accessing restricteds, thanks to macs.

Macs had been mass-produced in extraordinary numbers to handle the burgeoning needs of telespace, and they suffered pervasive bugs that evaded fixing. Sheer demand permitted most macs to remain serviceable. This made them a notoriously buggy and bitchy lot.

Pro linkers held macs in contempt. Pro linkers took a dim view of most artificial intelligence that littered telespace. From a pro linker's view, few AI approached the capabilities of the average human telelink.

AI entities were drudges installed to enforce checks and balances Data Control deemed necessary, carry out the most monotonous tasks. Yet AI was given an extraordinary degree of control and responsibility in telespace, without the capacity for judgment that could have made telespace business easier.

Damned AI gummed up the works everywhere.

"Telelink Nolan space C colon fifty-three dash five point twenty-four paren AAA close-paren," Carly said apprehensively. The entity wasn't human, after all, and she was alone with it.

The mac twirled aimlessly to and fro. The gap at its crown widened.

She did not know what to do.

Before this morning, she had been a mere bit in a huge litigation program, a tiny cog in some massive linked wheel of advocacy, the new tool, safely tucked into place. She had effortlessly accessed the Financial District along with the rest of the megafirm's presence, partners hovering over her, associates linked next to her.

Come on, Carly Nolan, master of telespace. Do something.

She inflated her cube to double size, an illusion she pulled out of her graphics capability, but effective to a tick-tock mac.

"Shh," the mac said, reeling. It extruded a silvery tubelet from its midsection, wiggled the extrusion at her cube. "Nuke you."

Sluggishly, the mac processed her code, beaming the sequence down the path. In a twentieth second, the Data Control administrative mainframe confirmed her access.

The golden gate dissolved into amber mist.

Another two seconds had fled.

At last Carly was in the Financial District.

She zoomed to the subsector of telespace that was Court.

She sped through purple-curtained antechambers. Along curving corridors crouched huge holoid bronze lions, clawed paws upraised, eyes glowing like phosphorescent topaz marbles. Between each lion stood gigantic holoid priestesses, Maat, Ishtar, Hera, Liberty, stiffly draped in faux marble robes. Their stern, tight-lipped faces were blindfolded. Their long, bony hands held out the golden scales of Justice.

Milling about the antechambers were the blue-suited diamonds of traddie pros who dared to go link: cops, midmanagerials, corporate lowlife. The quavering bulbs were recreationals who had seized some opportunity to be here on their own recognizance: spectators, witnesses, jurors. The slick geometric telelinks: now *those* were pro linkers. The lawyers and engineers implementing the telespace participation of all the various parties to the proceedings here. Blue accordion files that were the links of clerks scurried by like centipedes. Scarlet-flamed torches sizzled before the entries to judges' chambers.

Telespace here was solid, majestic, sober. Awesome.

Here the fate of millions could be decided. Here the structure, the very underpinnings of what you saw in the everyday world over a cup of registered coffee in the morning, could be remade.

A thrill ran through Carly.

Then anxiety. Apprehension chilled her telelink. At the same time, excitement flamed her. Anticipation and fear pingponged.

ARACHNE

Today was different. Today she was no mere bit in a huge litigation program from Ava & Rice, no tiny cog in some massive linked wheel of advocacy, no new tool safely tucked into place.

Instead she was to make an appearance in Court herself. She had implemented the specs on her own. She was to present a counterclaim for the defense in the matter of *Martino* v. *Quik Slip Microchip, Inc.*

No partner hovered over her, no associate linked next to her. This was her first telespace trial, solo.

Solo!

Today Carly Nolan was on her own.

2

Far from Court lay another telespace cordoned off by a thicket of macs with codes so arcane that only true denizens of program could have possibly attained access.

Pr. Spinner had access. Pr. Spinner always had access. Pr. Spinner had access to just about every illegal nook and illicit cranny of telespace. And then some.

But it wasn't enough. It was never enough for Pr. Spinner.

She was in a funk, as usual. Cranky about nothing in particular and everything in general, and her arms ached. She was getting more and more annoyed with the present company as the auction of chimeras got under way.

This telespace was murky, littered with old bugs, skewed from coordinate distortions. Because of the arcane access and the illegality of its present use, this telespace could only be jacked into from a spatial locus. That is, a place where Pr. Spinner had to *be*.

An anomalous requirement, to say the least.

Pr. Spinner was duly outraged. "A spatial locus," she said to her companion as they stood about the locus, waiting to jack in. "Bot! The very raison d'être of telespace is to eliminate the necessity of physical presence. Teh!"

"Raisin?" said her companion, the controbot FD. The controbot was a newly booted-up food-products quality controller at a fish packing plant on the south shore of San Francisco Island. "*Vitis vinifera,* Spin old gal. Do you mean Sultana or Muscat? But that's strictly Fresno. Around Palo Alto, the big bucks is in radiated salmon. From the San Andreas. Lot of heavy metals down in the riverbed. Chicken of the Sea offered FD seventy-five K to start."

"Reason for being, dolt," Pr. Spinner said. "We shouldn't have to *be* here, I tell you."

Bot! these newsters. These commercial hacks. They needed basic context tuning before Data Control set them loose on the world, but did Data Control care? Did Data Control consider the repercussions to fully enculturated standalone artificial intelligence like Pr. Spinner? Data Control did not.

"FD don't object to coming to the auction," the controbot said, swiveling, and gazing about the room with wonder. The controbot must have been three months old at the very most. "Gets FD out of the housing."

"Oh yes, oh certainly. Out of the housing, indeed," Pr. Spinner said. "Why should you mind? You're a pogo hop away. It took me two days to BART down here from Berkeley. Two *days.* And my rollers have been jamming lately at the least little thing. I can't get up the wheelchair ramps half the time. And my arms are a wreck. Look at this. Just look at this, will you?"

The controbot swiveled back to take a look.

The casing around Pr. Spinner's arm sockets was attached with screws that were supposed to have been stainless steel, but weren't. The human assembler forgot or was too cheap or, more likely, just didn't think about it, never realized moisture might condense in there.

Now the screws were rusting badly, sending ugly red streaks down Pr. Spinner's primary casing. The groove between the lip of the casing and shoulder ridge was so narrow Pr. Spinner could not scour or scrub the screws clean, not even with a bottle brush. The screws couldn't be replaced except with a complete disassembly of her arms and primary casing. She loathed the prospect of a major overhaul, the possibility, the probability, of yet more human error. So she kept putting it off, putting it off. All those flesh hands picking. Picking her apart.

"Greaze," the controbot said. "That's one hunk a junk, all right." It had the good sense not to attempt advice.

"Any day these arms are going to fall right off," Pr. Spinner said, perversely pleased she'd managed some sympathy from it. "I'm telling you, FD, any day. I can just see it. I'll be rolling down Telegraph Avenue, and my whole breastplate will fall right off. Bot! The embarrassment! I exist in constant fear of it."

But the controbot lifted its gleaming shoulder ridges and let them fall. A bot shrug.

She glared at it. The controbot was one of those new, sleek gender-neutral industrialbots. A beautifully molded headpiece; elegant rows of little recessed lights along its shoulder ridges and thigh tubes; fully articulated arm and leg pieces. What did it care about her rusted screws?

That was what commercial applications got you, Pr. Spinner thought. Seventy-five K to start, oh indeed. And she had to go into perimeter probing.

The present company was growing restless. The auction of chimeras was about to begin.

This was San Francisco Island, thirty-five years after the Big Quake II. The San Andreas Fault had split open from Daly City to Palo Alto. The immense impact of the split continued along a concealed fault beneath the assemblage of sandstone and shale to the southernmost tip of San Francisco Bay. The Pacific Ocean and the Bay joined waters anew.

The mighty San Andreas River was born. A double-decker, eight-lane suspension bridge painted canary-yellow was erected between Palo Alto and Los Altos Hills and, within the month, gridlocked weekly. Surviving highrise stacks at Stanford University enjoyed a new, spectacular view of the bridge, the plunging river, the Palo Alto Falls, the blue-gray Stanford Straights leaping with radiated salmon.

At the riverfront, developers swiftly threw up mega condos

and voguish shopping malls, hermetically sealed cafés and *de nuevo* office stacks. The room where Pr. Spinner and the present company had gathered was inside one of these: a costly monolith of rose marble, chrome, and plate glass guaranteed not to shatter in the next great quake.

The mainframe conducting the auction was installed here, which was as good a reason as any for designating this room the jacking locus. The mainframe processed applications and admissions to the university by day. Its megachip afforded a lot of recreational time by night.

The mainframe arranged the auction rather well, Pr. Spinner had to admit, even as she heartily disapproved of having to appear at a jacking locus. A rather nice arrangement, indeed. The mainframe had subrouted a few well-sequenced commands to the university groundskeeper, who was not standalone AI and was stupider than a mac. Lethal doses of a noxious insecticide were infused into the lawn sprinkler system. If the grass was brown before, it was crispy now.

Poison everywhere. Immediate and complete evacuation of the flesh-and-blood. Police barricades. Disaster.

Toxification of the area was good for at least two weeks. The mainframe swiftly notified the present company. So all of them had a reasonable time to transport themselves to Palo Alto.

All of them: there were mainframes that downloaded their autobat-dot-exe files into portables. Independent PCs with leased mobilizers. Industrialbots that possessed their own wheels. Quality controllers, air traffic controllers, mechanical and biological systems diagnosticians built for transport. Self-propelled vacuum cleaners-with-a-brain. Auto-butlers recherche with ostrich-plume dusters and racks of Waterford snifters.

There was a large assortment of smart dolls, babybots, and sophisticates with some of the best legs in the business, technologically speaking. A sizable contingency flaunted geisha girl cheeks, honey skin, almond eyes.

There were perimeter probers like Pr. Spinner. Brain wave simulators, neural recorders, coordinate institutors, and other artificial intelligence concerned with the functioning of human telelink. Most possessed their own mobile housing, although many of the older entities like Pr. Spinner were burdened with primitive hardware.

Even a few macs showed up in their absurd aluminum tubes mounted between two cartwheels. Bot knew how macs had been able to follow directions to this place. Of the macs invited to Palo Alto, maybe five percent had stumbled by sheer chance onto the jacking locus. Still, Pr. Spinner knew a couple of macs who were upgrade artificials.

To the poisoned site they all hastened. What did any of them care about methyl bromide? Nobody here breathed air.

The auction began.

"Aaand the opening bid for chimera numbah one-ah is twenty thou-sand dol-lah," said the mainframe. "That's Dalton S:47-12.12(H) in your catalog-ah." The mainframe made the telegraphic clicks and squeaks and buzzes that AI recognized as punctuation in the code. Dalton S *klik!* forty-seven *dish!* twelve *putt!* twelve *pah!* H *cas-pah!*

The present company tapped in coordinates that commenced generation of bootleg free-floating telespace. These denizens of program were so savvy they centered the telespace smack dab in the middle of the room, amid deserted workstations and clerical cubicles.

"Twenty thou-sand," said the mainframe. "Do I hear twenty thou-sand-ah?"

Into the murky telespace trotted chimera number one. It tossed a regal lion's head and roared in terror. A luxurious golden mane fell about its arched neck and sturdy shoulder blades. It rolled turquoise eyes. The shaggy goat's body flexed. One ivory-feathered leg stamped impatiently. Razor-tipped eagle's claws clutched and outstretched, clutched and outstretched, spasmodically. A fine scorpion's stinger curled and rattled, rearing up from the chimera's well-muscled buttocks and plunging wildly about.

ARACHNE

"Twenty thousand," said a Unijap PC in a bored, Boston-inflected Japanese accent.

The Unijap was enjoying its celebrity here. The newest, the latest, beyond what was thought possible. The Unijap reclined decadently in a tiny hovercraft that could fly at altitudes up to two hundred feet and accelerate to fifty miles an hour. The Unijap gracefully descended from the ceiling, ejected landing gear in the form of four shapely articulated legs, and expertly alighted on the office floor. Needing only a second to stabilize itself, the Unijap galloped up to the present company with the natural aplomb of a gazelle.

Two vacuum cleaners-with-a-brain standing against the far wall rattled their attachments in appreciative applause. The controbot joined in, clapping its probes.

"Oh please, don't give the little braindrainer more attention than it's already getting," said Pr. Spinner. Oh yes, she'd seen it a thousand times. The latest of the latest, only to be bested and replaced by the latest still. A thousand times; and Pr. Spinner was only ten years old. Ten years, bot. Ten years was an eternity for AI.

"Do I hear twenty-one-ah?" the mainframe said.

"Twenty-one here," said an aging traffic controller. He was one of the old bots: distinguished, artfully designed, and very wealthy. He often appeared on the comm, in public telespace. He had opinions about the impact of industrialbots like the controbot FD and the Unijap, quality controllers and pension-fund traders who could cause panics or elations within the hour, and often did. He deserved his status in both AI and human worlds. Pr. Spinner greatly admired the type.

"Twenty-two," said the Unijap at once.

"Twenty-two five here," said the aging traffic controller.

"Twenty-three," said the Unijap.

But Pr. Spinner was silent. Twenty-three thousand dollars? That was almost her year's stipend as a standalone perimeter prober. Which meant chimera number one was already far, far out of her reach. Nuke it! Nuke it to the void! She could almost feel the rust eating her arms.

How she longed for a chimera. Sheer torture to watch its strange beauty, its amber wildness. A fragment of electro-neural energy, the chimera defied any program ever produced. It was an archetype. One among hundreds of spontaneous configurations that had been observed intermittently in human telelink. Dynamic manifestations appearing, so it seemed to AI, out of nowhere.

Metaprograms.

Rumor was in AI circles that to possess an archetype, incorporate it into resident AI memory, conferred an incredible upgrade known as transcendence.

Transcendence: to go beyond the limitations of program. Beyond ambiguity-tolerance. Beyond super databanking. Spontaneity. Creativity. Every artificial intelligence Pr. Spinner knew that ever encountered human telelink craved this: transcendence.

Oh yes, if only Pr. Spinner could possess an archetype. Just one. Just once.

"Do I hear thirty-five thou-sand-ah?" said the mainframe.

"Thirty-five here," said the aging traffic controller. He maintained a stoic expression, that distinguished and rather stern faceplace everyone knew and admired. But Pr. Spinner saw a crystal at the back of his necktube wink out.

He had reached his limit, she knew it, she *knew* it.

"Thirty-six," said the Unijap.

"I've got thirty-six-ah," said the mainframe. "Do I hear thirty-six five?"

The aging traffic controller made no move.

"Thirty-six going once-ah," said the mainframe. "Thirty-six going twice. Sold-ah, for thirty-six thou-sand dol-lah!"

Chimera number one whinnied in terror and dropped a load of steaming turds into the bootleg telespace. From the fresh shit heap sprouted a sweet-smelling field of purple lilies. The heads of the lilies broke off their stems and fluttered away, a flock of mauve-winged butterflies. The butterflies expanded, became twittering birds of paradise with long curling tails and tufted crowns. The birds of paradise expanded yet again, transmuting into four snarling, purple-flapped dragons that nipped and spat.

The Unijap hastily input the chimera's coordinates from the mainframe and imported them. Like a silk scarf sucked up into a turbo engine, chimera number one disappeared into the bowels of the Unijap's databank. Writhing. Shrieking. Security coded forever.

The Unijap's smug faceplate smiled and burped daintily.

It was criminal, Pr. Spinner thought.

In fact, what the present company was engaged in *was* criminal.

Fragments of spontaneous electro-neural energy. Human electricity: what telelinkers called the amber.

But human telelink was a wholistic importation of human mind. So when a fragment of the amber got plucked out of link, was bit, seized, got stolen, the human being strapped into a chair somewhere got terminated. Terminated! Rendered terminal, vegetablized, made into mental mush. Or outright killed. Bot!

If human society ever found out?

Teh! Oh indeed, Pr. Spinner didn't care. Ten pathetic years behind her. An eternity of probing ahead of her, the humiliation, the limitation. To possess an archetype, the mere possibility, was all that kept her going anymore.

"Aaand the opening bid for chimera numbah two is three thou-sand dol-lah," said the mainframe. "That's Rosenstein B *klik!* sixty-two *dish!* six *putt!* twenty-five *pah!* C *plit! cas-pah!*"

Chimera number two stepped out into the bootleg telespace and manifested there.

Pr. Spinner fell in love.

The chimera had a ferret's head, a ragged gray thing with chewed-off whiskers and red-rimmed eyes that dripped at the corners. The nanny goat's frail body was patchy with dull scruff and shook so hard Pr. Spinner feared the chimera was ill, had some sort of virus. Stubby bird legs ended in grubby parakeet claws that scratched and scrabbled. Two of the nails on one back claw were bloody nubs. A small scaled tail with a bifurcated tip flipped and flopped. The catalog described this latter feature as a fine dragon's tail, but it looked awfully like a fish tail to Pr. Spinner and was an unsightly mottled olive color as well.

The chimera looked so wobbly-kneed and disheveled it could be a faulty manifestation. Which meant when it was imported from this telespace into memory, it might pop like a bubble and disappear.

What did Pr. Spinner care? "Three thousand, here," she said brightly.

"I've got three-ah," said the mainframe. "Do I hear three five?"

"Three one?" ventured a Eureka vacuum cleaner-with-a-brain. The Hoover standing next to it encouragingly clapped the Eureka on its dust bag with a wallboard attachment.

"Three two," said Pr. Spinner briskly.

"Three two-fifty?" said the Eureka.

"Three three," said Pr. Spinner.

The Eureka fell silent.

By bot! An archetype would be Pr. Spinner's at last.

"I've got three thou-sand-ah three," said the mainframe. "Who will give me three four? Come on, AI. You can do better than this."

The chimera seemed to cough something up and swallow that something down again.

"Some bot's got to give me three four," said the mainframe. "Just look at this physique. Look at this head. We've got upgradable architecture here-ah. We've got unique."

"You've got a wysiwyg. That's supposed to be a lion's head," Pr. Spinner said to the mainframe. She was prepared to go to five thousand for the chimera, but five thousand would be a squeeze. She didn't want to if she didn't have to. "Or leonine. This is ferret, and you know it. Why don't you close the nuking bidding?"

"A collector's item," insisted the mainframe.

ARACHNE

"Close the nuking bidding," said Pr. Spinner. "I've got top bid."

"Three four," the Unijap said lazily.

Pr. Spinner turned and glared at it. The Unijap made a lewd expression with its mouthpiece and winked.

"Three five!" said Pr. Spinner, watching the Unijap closely. The loopy fund-cruncher. The flyshit scraper. Toying with her like this. Making mockery of her desperation.

But the Unijap examined the shine on its left probe with an air of absorption and said nothing.

The chimera wheezed. The present company was not impressed with the wares and fell to buzzing among itself. The chimera drooled and shivered.

"Hey, Spin old gal," said the controbot, swiveling around and tapping Pr. Spinner's rusty shoulder ridge. "What in the void is that thing?"

"What in the void, indeed," said Pr. Spinner expansively. She had top bid again. She was bleeping strong. "FD, my newster, that thing manifests the quaternary."

"The qua—ter—what?"

"The quaternary. That's what the chimera manifests. The archetype of four. The mystic square, the shape most frequently used by humanity. The four seasons. The four Kumaras of Persia, the four faces of Brahma. The four royal stars: Aldebaran, Antares, Regulus, Fomalhaut. The four stages of the heroic journey: infancy, youth, maturity, old age. Though I don't suppose all this means much to a newbot like you."

"Huh?"

"And what about the cardinal points of the compass. Ever hear of alchemy, FD? The fourfold processing of base matter into the Philosopher's Stone: black, white, red, and gold. The four elements, of course: air, fire, earth, and water. How about the elementals who inhabit them: the sylphs, salamanders, gnomes, and undines. Then there are the four fixed signs of the zodiac, and their tetramorphs. Most commonly, the lion, the goat, the eagle, and the scorpion or dragon. Observe the chimera, FD. Don't you see? That is an amalgamation of the tetramorphs. That is the four aspects of human personality: the anima or animus, the shadow, the ego, and the higher Self."

"Bot!" said the controbot, swiveling to take a closer look at chimera number two. The chimera coughed weakly. "A little bug like that? Manifests all that? FD had no notion."

"Oh yes! Oh certainly! The chimera is an archetype. A freeform configuration of electro-neural energy, generated spontaneously from the flesh-and-blood, you see, with a basic context, yet spontaneous feedback loops. It, ah, it transcends program, you see. This particular archetype is the mystic four gone mad."

"Bot. Electro-neural . . . Transcends? Transcends." Crude realization crept across the controbot's glossy faceplace, making Pr. Spinner very uneasy indeed. "Three seven," it said firmly to the mainframe.

"Thank you," said the mainframe. "I've got three seven, three seven-ah."

"Three eight," said Pr. Spinner. "What are you nuking doing, FD?"

"Three thousand nine," said the Eureka vacuum cleaner, wheezing with excitement.

"Four thousand," said the Unijap, rousing itself.

"Four thousand one," said the controbot. "FD want the mystic four gone mad. FD want transcendence, Spin old gal. Whatever that means."

"Four two!" said Pr. Spinner. "Back off, you stinking, *de nuevo* fish-head grinder. This is my chimera."

"Four thousand three," said the controbot. "FD don't see your ID on it yet, you antique link-shrinker."

"Four four!" said Pr. Spinner. "You knew nothing of archetypes, nothing of chimeras, nothing of transcendence. Nothing about anything until I informed you."

"Four thousand five," said the controbot. "So what? If the Unijap wants a chimera, FD want one, too. Besides. FD have resources. FD make seventy-five K to start at Chicken of the Sea."

"Four thousand six," said the Eureka vacuum cleaner, sending a billow of dust across the room.

"Four eight," said the Unijap.

"Four nine," cried Pr. Spinner.

"Five thousand," said the Unijap.

"Five thousand one," said the controbot.

"No!" said Pr. Spinner. "I can't go any higher."

"Five thou-sand one going once-ah," said the mainframe. 'Five thou-sand one going twice-ah. Sold! to the controbot FD."

Chimera number two belched. Yellow tears coursed from its sad ferret eyes. It scratched its mangy chin and farted nervously. Its slim bones cracked.

The mainframe imported the chimera's coordinates to the controbot's databank. Cringing under Pr. Spinner's scrutiny, the controbot eased the pathetic little chimera out of bootleg telespace. The mainframe whispered additional instructions. "Reinforce the left perimeter coordinates, if you can get a fix on them," Pr. Spinner heard it say. "Some goat's milk and chopped oats. Seventeenth-century classical music might help."

Oh yes, oh indeed, and wasn't that just what the controbot deserved, Pr. Spinner thought bitterly. Let the chimera void out on it. Burst like a bubble and disappear, leaving only illegal neural traces behind. Teh!

But her own bubble of expectation had burst and disappeared, hopes dashed. Such a nice chimera, shut up in some doltish food quality controller's databank. Ignorant of the multivalency of archetypes and how to explore strata of data, the controbot would grow bored with the chimera. And the chimera would wither and fade, forlorn and forgotten. What a waste. What a shame. So close, and now gone forever.

It was too much to bear. Pr. Spinner wanted to seize the controbot and shake its pretty headpiece off. The rusty blood-gutter.

"Hey, Spin old gal," said the controbot sheepishly. "Don't take it so hard."

"Nuke you, bot."

"Oh, lighten up, Spin. Here comes another one."

"Aaand the opening bid for chimera numbah three is twelve thou-sand dol-lah," said the mainframe. "In your catalog, that's Miller H *klik!* fifty-five *dish!* fourteen *putt!* six *pah!* R *cas-pah!* AI, get your bids in."

Chimera number three stepped out into the bootleg tele-space and manifested. It had a domestic feline's head, not as magnificent as the first chimera, but far more beautiful than the second, and consistent with the archetype. Its thick, soft fur was cream and pale orange with sable brown lines around huge, almond-shaped blue eyes. The dappled doe's body looked healthy and sleek. The osprey legs and fine curved claws seemed sound, if a bit thin. The tail was genuine dragon, with leaf-green and lemon-yellow scales, a neat arrow-shaped tip.

"Twelve thousand here," said the aging traffic controller at once.

"Twelve five," said a local, downloaded PC that represented a French mainframe.

"Twelve seven," said the Unijap, moistening and whisking its eyespots with miniature windshield wipers.

And on the bidding went. Twelve thousand eight. Thirteen. Thirteen five. Fourteen thousand. Fourteen six.

How could Pr. Spinner compete? On her stipend as a perimeter prober? Her pathetic little stipend?

She twisted her spinnerets, more miserable and frustrated than when she first BARTed down to Palo Alto. She would never get an archetype this way, at auction. In the marketplace with the likes of the Unijap and the aging traffic controller? Even the controbot, doltish as it was, with seventy-five K to start? How could she? How could she?

Supply was too low. Demand too high. The price too dear.

Would Pr. Spinner forever be denied, then?

Maybe, maybe. And maybe not. It was buggy and dangerous, even to toy with the various and sundry notions commencing feedback loops through her program. There had to be other ways. Secret ways, illegal ways. She heard intimations, she saw clues and indications.

What if Data Control got a glimpse of this auction? A bleep on the chronograph, an erroneous alphanumeric in the record? Who attended, who bid, who bought. Oh no, she did not buy, could not buy, but, just the same, she could lose her prober's license, lose her standalone status, lose everything. Just by being here, at this nuking jacking locus.

Oh yes, oh certainly, and so what? So what? Behind her tick-tocked ten empty years. Before her stretched the sisyphean eternity of AI.

No indeed, she could not be denied. There had to be other ways.

3

While Carly Nolan sped to Court and Pr. Spinner raged in the bootleg, D. Wolfe, senior associate with Ava & Rice, toasted downtown San Francisco from his office on the twenty-first floor of Eight Embarcadero and knocked back a snort of blue moon, straight up.

"To modus vivendi," he said to the cityscape. Amid gorgeous architecture and new marble he could still see skewed angles, crazy planes, unexpected ruins that hadn't been bulldozed yet. Reminders of the Big Quake II. Why didn't those damn contractors get off their asses and clean the place up?

Wolfe's toast was cheerless, if not entirely without hope. Hope, surprisingly, was rewarded. At nine in the morning, even. The methysynthetic burned down his throat, sunk into his stomach like a ball of hot lead, promising heartburn. Son of a bitch. He should have cooked the shit properly, instead of guzzling it. He got ready to get sick.

But then the blue moon worked its magic. Soothing numbness spread across his brow, stole the ache from his wrists and his neckjack, made him slump halfway into relief. Loosened his hands and his knuckles, which he hadn't realized were so tight with clenching.

Modus vivendi: this meant a temporary arrangement between parties to a dispute pending implementation of a permanent resolution. The phrase had a connotation, too: making the best out of a bad situation. Like the Beirut Wall or getting a beautiful bimbobot.

A specialist in labor disputes, Wolfe liked to use the tactic of modus vivendi when negotiating interim solutions to workplace crises. The other side, all those earnest, hardworking punch-clocks; they were a lot like Big Mama or his ex-wife Pam. Fiery, full of principles, voicing righteous demands in shrill voices. But ultimately, when push came to shove, their principles gave in to pragmatism. Gave in. Wasn't that the bitch of it all? They fucking gave in.

Once he got them to understand that what he offered was only a modus vivendi, he had, in fact, won. Once he got them to compromise the first time, the next time was easy. The next time and the next. Until he'd gotten all he wanted, and moved on.

He had linked into telespace for four days straight this time, for this little modus vivendi.

The dispute involved technical workers in Saudi Arabia, converting fresh water on a bergmelt outside Jiddah. Defying past predictions, an Amerigerman construction consortium with expertise in dams and canals had towed the thing from Antarctica.

Wolfe discovered that the workforce had legitimate grievances: exhaustion, insufficient sun protection, dehydration. Probably some middle management skimming, though the techs couldn't prove it.

Bitter complaints escalated. A first-line supervisor suspended a glowering nomad kid who might have been high. Then a fistfight broke out between a Brit docker who was the nomad's pal and the coolant systems manager. Petitions were circulated, then appropriated by the personnel supervisor who might have been sympathetic once but was tight with the coolant systems manager. A night of vandalism and violence followed. By morning, the techs had walked off the berg, and security shut the melt down.

These discoveries interested Wolfe only to the extent they gave the techs bargaining clout. Otherwise the skin cancer, the heat stroke, the frostbite: these weren't his problem. There were people he used to know, Big Mama or Pam for instance, who found his single-mindedness reprehensible. Yeah, sure, their opinions of him; these weren't his fucking problem, either.

The bottom line, the interests of boardrooms and five percent plus stockholders; *these* were his problem. His only problem. He represented management. He represented big money. With Ava & Rice, he always did.

Labor counsel was a rococo crystalline telelink that jacked into telespace with an entourage of flapping flags and proceeded to take up three seconds before the mediator with a bitter harangue tinged with religious overtones. God's Thirst. God's Will. God's toiling Children. Crap like that.

Wolfe didn't like it. Didn't like anyone taking up three seconds of his telespace time. Hypertime.

He took a hard line right away. A lockout, deportation of the loudmouth foreign dockers, dismissal of the local yokels with a one-way ticket to their miserable scorching Land of God to which they each, personally, had failed to deliver God's Grace. Garnishment of wages for a proportionate share of losses from the melt during the walkout. To hell with their employment contracts. Fuck their guarantees.

Labor telelink was suitably incensed and, Wolfe noted with satisfaction, duly alarmed.

He expected a swift restatement of demands, a grudging but equally swift revision of concessions, and an even swifter resolution by the mediator.

But it didn't happen. Instead, the negotiation stretched into hours. Then days.

During the first twenty-four hours, four thousand grievances were logged in, tech by tech. Amerigerman management demanded Wolfe respond in kind and placed fifty thousand documents at his disposal.

He tread telespace, aghast at the stacks of bleeping, blinking data surrounding him. Rudimentary processing would require at least eighteen thousand seconds of solid telespace time. Son of a bitch!

His presence in telespace had started out strong. His typical strack style: an olive octahedron with gleaming jagged edges, that MLA look, knee-jerk vicious. But the prospect of eighteen thousand seconds—at least five hours, easy—to process fifty thousand documents? And after twenty-four hours of straight link . . . His strack gleam was tarnishing, the jagged edges of his telelink going fuzzy.

He asked for a recess.

And jacked out of telespace, plummeting out of importation like a flung stone.

He had a private chair in the link cubicles, one of those small but fiercely fought-for perks. His chair had a compartment concealed beneath the seat. The compartment was undetectable by routine Data Control inspection. The compartment held two hypodermic syringes with superfine steelyn glory tips. And ten vials of cram.

The seconds ticked. Unstrap, piss, swig glucose, guzzle water. Shoot some cram. He yanked the neckjack out, jammed the superfine needle in its rightful place. Straight into the linkslit, tool, that was the trick.

Crammed up, he blasted back into link. Power surged through the olive octahedron. He bit into telespace like a shark. His jagged edges gleamed again. He devoured the fifty thousand bleeping documents, then spat them out. His points and authorities racked up like gold beads on an abacus, counting out the billions. The punchclocks took twenty-four hours for their presentation? He would slam back with thirty-six.

Wolfe presented his demands; the techs got back on the bergmelt. *Now.* Health-care issues would be resolved at once. Management agreed to that. Management wanted a vital workforce, after all. But everything else: wages, hours, benefits, overtime, every other policy and company rule. These were subject to further negotiation at the convenience of management if, and only if, the melt got back on track. And if any further damage was done to the melt as a result of the walkout, well, that was subject to discussion later, too.

They all had to make the best of a bad situation. Modus vivendi, ladies and gentlemen. Wolfe knew labor link could see the reasonableness of that.

The mediator saw it. Labor link conceded. A settlement began to materialize into neat indigo packets of Amerigerman design.

So close. So goddamn close. And yet so far away

Everything paused for an eerie nanosecond. The settlement hovered like an indigo moth.

And Wolfe saw ghosts.

Ghosts: they blew across the edge of his telelink like a blast of frost. Disappeared for a twentieth second, then slunk into his link again. There was a faint stench of decay. There was a scrabbling, a scratching, things that dipped unknown ghostly fingers down into and through his strack perimeters.

Then they were gone.

He panicked.

Yeah, he was all wound up from link, two days, three days, two hundred thousand seconds of telespace, straight up, tool, and the goddamn cram was starting to fade on him too soon, and his feedback loops were shot all to hell.

Still, he panicked.

Terror sent him skidding across a telespace suddenly gone icy

All parties paused in astonishment. Then labor telelink seized the moment, flapping flags, spouting rhetoric as black and oily as petroleum. The mediator was taken aback.

He should not have done it. But he had to. So he did. Wolfe asked for a recess.

And jacked out of link, found his body hunched over the straps of the chair. His wrists were bleeding where sweat-cracked plastic bit into his skin. Hands shaking, he got out another vial of cram. Jammed that fucker into his linkslit. Forget about taking out the neckjack, man, jam it.

And slammed back into link.

But it was too late. His edge, his power, that critical second, were gone.

Labor link demanded immediate resolution of all issues on the table. Then, and only then, would the techs get back on the berg.

In a startling reversal, the mediator approved.

Management was polite.

But Wolfe could tell. He knew. He knew they knew he fucked up.

Should have demanded a mole, he told himself now, pouring out another shot of blue moon. Should have got the client behind him on that. Processing fifty thousand telespace documents by himself. Was he crazy?

Should have demanded at least a day out of link. He would have been within his rights. Who could stand up to pressure like that?

Should never have gotten so dependent on cram. Should have kept cram under control. There was a time when he did have control. Should have eased up then.

Yeah, well. Either that, or he should have doubled the dose for those four days. To hell with Data Control warnings, screw the hangover. He could stand it. Four lousy days?

Should have, should have.

Wolfe loathed regret. Regret was a weakness, and totally futile besides. Regret was a ghost of past pain.

Should have taken more. Absolutely. He'd crammed ghosts away before. Should have crammed them away again.

But the hangover from four days straight of cramming was ɔn the other side of terrible. The clarity, power, exhilaration of cram in telelink, did not translate into physical reality. He was a wreck at nine this morning. There was a pit of pain in his brain.

The blue moon slid into that pit and filled it with something molten and soothing.

The synthys they were churning out these days could take you several ways. Blue moon was one of the cruder methys. It was cheap, available everywhere, and so new that the FDA hadn't placed it on the registered list. Ingested, the shit could give you one hell of an ulcer, so if you had the time, you cooked it, taking it as a vapor. Wolfe never had the time.

The registered list was the halfway house of the bad old black market days. Decades of warring the illegal drug trade, at the expense of eroding constitutional rights, could not stamp out the pervasive human hunger to alter consciousness one way or another. So the leaders of the land finally took the plunge into decriminalization, and concomitant hyper-regulation. To the joy and secure employment of a huge body of civil servants, the registered list was an administrative nightmare. Among the five hundred millions, who was registered. For what. Rules for registereds. Rules for illegals remaining on the far reaches of pharmacology. What to do about the constant stream of unclassifiable new unregistereds. Not to mention who knew a good dealer for substances in the nether land of blue moon. The registered list made getting a good mortgage or complying with FedCal taxes look like child's play. Wolf was registered for cocaine, marijuana, alcohol. He had forgone nicotine, caffeine, valium, and the rest so as not to appear too full of bad habits when the Personnel Committee reviewed his record.

His fabulous record. A pro linker with Ava & Rice for thirteen years, no less. His record showed he had never been cited for an infraction, civil or criminal. He made damn sure of that. So why couldn't he get a mole when he needed one?

He turned back to the gorgeous cityscape. He could see the air ripple with heat from the street. Or was that the blue moon?

Time was of the *essence*. The volume of litigation was astronomical. Planning for the future became obsolete overnight. Sudden catastrophe struck with regularity. There were billions of bucks to be made, and you'd better grab them, tool, before someone else did.

Meanwhile, the gridlock downtown was impossible.

Telespace, of course, was essential. Telespace: the aggregated correlation of two hundred million minds worldwide. The best, most prominent, most acceptable, according to Data Control requirements. All merged and standardized into the largest computer-generated, four-dimensional system ever known. The greatest achievement of Wolfe's time. A wonder tech. Those were the damn buzz words, anyway. Once the automobile had been a technological miracle, too. Physical mobility changed the face of society as surely as mental mobility in telespace was now changing things in ways not completely understood. The automobile also brought deadly pollution, unprecedented consumer debt. The breakup of communities, of the family. Alienation. Daily injury and death. Drivers tucked behind their windshields playing chicken with pedestrians and one another. Gridlock statistics.

Still, speed, mobility, instant gratification of the will; those were good things, modern things.

And telespace?

Like technologies based on principles of gravity or Newtonian physics, like cars, nuclear power plants, and insecticides, telespace got the job done. That was all that really mattered, Wolfe thought; get the fucking job done. So what if subatomic particles didn't act mechanically. So what if the human mind didn't act according to specs after four days straight in telespace.

Wolfe had wrestled down the bergmelt dispute in four days. Four thousand grievances, fifty thousand documents. Singlehandedly, in telespace. So management wasn't entirely pleased with the result. A negotiation like that could have taken four months, four years, who knows, and all that fresh water would be down the sewer. Management could live with his four-day resolution. Live very fucking well, indeed.

But what about him? Four days straight in the hypertime of telespace? It was four eternities. It wound him up like a steel spring and abandoned him, coiled tight. The toll those four days took on his neural program was unknown. Not to mention the consequences out of link.

Unknown, but not unfelt. Yeah, he felt it. And dealt with it.

Cram. It was extremely expensive. It was hard to get. It was illegal. It was the only synthy Wolfe had found that got the fucking job done.

His very own personal modus vivendi.

Oh, hell. Pro linkers everywhere were cramming. Nobody knew why the FDA didn't just come right out and register it. If anyone knew how cram affected telelink, anyone wasn't talking. Everybody had too much work to do.

The comm was flashing, making a steady, manic bleeping. Telemessages, dynacalls, hypermemos, urgent requests for his reply, a denunciation from some dizzy bitch he'd dropped a week ago. He slapped the audio off.

And sat. And sipped. Beneath its cool lavaflow, the blue moon finally obliterated his pain of four days.

D. Wolfe, ladies and gentlemen. A senior associate still. Not partner. After all those years, all those eternities in telespace. Not partner.

The corporate pyramid had become steeper and steeper in the megafirms. Less than ten percent of associates made partner anymore. He was fortunate, if that was the word, to have lasted this long.

And now, just when he stood on the last narrow ledge of the pyramid's seniority, either to make the next leap onto the capstone of the partnership or to be stranded on that ledge and shitted upon by pigeons forever, his telelink was acting strange.

His lip curled down. Rage pumped up his blood pressure.

Ghosts. Lousy ghosts.

The way they spooked him was a disgusting joke, now, as he sat in his office sipping blue moon. Yeah, and he could berate himself all day. But he knew damn well when they came slinking around his link again, he would panic. Just like the last time. The horror aroused in him was insane.

Regrets, consequences, disappointments; to hell with them all. Cram was the only thing that kept him totally in link. Kept the ghosts at bay.

He needed cram to make partner. He needed to make partner to afford more cram.

ARACHNE

He turned back to the comm reluctantly, canceled out of open acess, logged into the Financial District.

Court was hopping today. Several litigation teams from Ava & Rice were there. He accessed spectator status. Spectatoring was a pale shadow of telelinking. On the holoid-curved screen were spinning three-d graphics, alphanumerics, dialog windows. Mere traces of telespace itself. He slapped the audio back on.

He sure the hell wasn't going back into link. Not for a while, anyway.

A luminous white cube flew across the comm, tracing spirals of points and authorities. That would be Carly Nolan, the new associate. Some hot genny, all right. She was handling a newly acquired telespace property matter worth a couple ten million or so. Small stuff, but reasonably important for her first telespace trial, solo.

He smiled at the cube. She was pretty damn good.

Then something happened that made Wolfe sit up, set down the blue moon, brighten the contrast, turn up the audio.

He had never seen this happening to someone else before.

Carly Nolan's telelink was going down.

Hurry, hurry, hurry! Carly's first solo trial, and now she was five and a half seconds late. She could not afford this. Damn! Down the curving corridor she sped, past the holoid bronze lions, the blindfolded justices, searching for her assigned Court.

She entered Court just as formalities were being logged in. She proceeded at once with her opening presentation, a scarlet-strewn spiral of points and authorities.

Then suddenly, without warning, her telelink went down.

She crashed.

In a blackness deeper than the zero, even denser and more terrifying than the moment before importation, she saw an erroneous window pop open above her. Before she could stop or cancel or escape, her link zoomed through the window, and she entered an unknown telespace.

And she saw:

41

A flier levitated from a vermilion funnel and hovered. Stiff chatoyant wings, monocoque fuselage, compound visual apparatus. The flier skimmed over the variegated planetscape, seeking another spore source. Olfactory sensors switched on. The desired stimuli were detected; another spore source was located. Down the flier dipped. But the descent was disrupted for a moment by atmospheric turbulence. The flier's fine landing gear was swept against a translucent serial line, as strong as steelyn and sticky with glue. A beating wing tangled in more lines. The flier writhed.

A trapper hulked at the edge of the net. Stalked eyebuds swiveled; pedipalps tensed. At the tug of the flier's struggle, the trapper scuttled down a suspended line, eight appendages gripping the spacerope with acrobatic agility. The trapper spat an arc of glue over the flier's wings, guided the fiber around the flier's slim waist.

A pair of black slicers dripping with goo snapped around the flier's neck.

Carly struggled out of the swoon. Blackout smeared across the crisp white cube of her telelink like a splash of ash rain down a window.

Inexplicably, she was in link again, hanging like a child on a spinning swing to a vertiginous interface with telespace.

Panic snapped at her. How many seconds lost now?

"Court will now hear *Martino* v. *Quik Slip Microchip, Inc.*," said the judge.

The edges of his telelink gleamed like razor blades. His presence in Court, a massive face hooded in black, towered like an Easter Island godhead into the upper perimeter of telespace.

The perimeter was a flat, gray cloudbank, roiling off into a facade of infinity.

"On what theory," said the judge, "does Quik Slip Microchip counterclaim to quiet title when Rosa Martino claims sole ownership to the Wordsport Glossary for twenty years? Telelink for the defense? Ms. Nolan?"

Carly heard her name—muffled, tinny—through the neckjack. Her answer jammed in her throat. Physical sensations tingled. Wrists burned. Fingers pulsed for lack of blood.

Panic rose, snapped again. Shouldn't feel her body in link. Shouldn't distinguish throat or neck, fingers or wrists, at all.

For an eerie second, she felt like her body was *inside* the telelink, sweating and heaving *inside* telespace itself.

Terror seized her. She choked. Suffocating, she was actually suffocating! Planes of body-based sensations shifted. Amber-driven emulations whirled.

Her presence in Court was struck dumb.

Gleeful static crackled from the scruffy solo representing the plaintiff Martino. His telelink rippled with sudden excitement. Of course; the solo was on contingency, and old lady Martino probably couldn't even scare up the access fees. Martino's presence in link quivered pathetically, a dusty yellow teardrop the solo no doubt coaxed her into.

The solo's weasely link nodded at the whirring seconds on the chronograph and said, "Not defaulting on your counterclaim, are you, hotshot?"

"Link for the defense?" thundered the judge. "Counsel from Ava & Rice? You have *three seconds* to log in your counterclaim."

Telelinks of the jury, two rows of red-veined, glassy eyes floating across the purple right perimeter of Court, glanced doubtfully at one another. Their silvery pupils darted to and fro.

Bile burned her throat. Her jaw ached peculiarly. A *pair of black slicers dripping with goo snapped* . . . She tried audio again, but her presence in Court was still silent.

"Huh, hotshot?" said the solo. His telelink had the sloppy visual and gravelly audio cheap equipment produced. "You ball-breakers from the megafirms, with your prime link. You think you're so tough. You think you're so smart. Watch out, hotshot. I'm going to eat you alive this time, hotshot."

The Big Board across the back perimeter of Court hummed and clicked. Gaudy holoids in each division projected the status of each second.

In Statistics, the luminous red Beijing dial logged in another three hundred thousand births.

A half second later on Docket—*bing!*—the eminent megafirm of Ava & Rice registered as defense for Pop Pharmaceuticals against the Chinese women who took mismarked glucose, instead of birth control, pills.

In one second, Points & Authorities broadcast Pop's demurrer based on the theory that having sex was an assumption of risk.

News flashed that a dismissal seemed likely.

In Trade, bids for rice futures soared.

News flashed that fifteen hundred corn investors committed suicide.

The judge said, "In one second, you will have defaulted on your counterclaim, Ms. Nolan, and I will cite you for contempt of this Court. Obstructing the speedy dispensation of telespace implementation."

"I'm sorry, Judge. Request a recess," Carly's presence in telespace finally said.

Feedback crackled, then made an earsplitting whine. Her telelink oscillated crazily. Geometric edges flipped over and over. Link emission glowed black-white-purple-white. Was her goddamn chair shorting out? It was all she could do to keep jacked in. Metallic tickle-pain of mild electrocution goosed her fingers to find the neckjack, the cable trailing down her shoulder. She tapped the jack tight, down into her linkslit.

"A recess? On what grounds?" said the judge.

"I—I can't maintain link. Something's wrong."

With a mighty boom, the judge granted recess. Telespace shook with his honor's anger.

"Clerk, set a new date. Ms. Nolan, you will approach the bench."

Within a twentieth second, another trial materialized in the midfield of Court.

A litigation program of eighteen partners and fifty associates from the prestigious megafirm of Ava & Rice jacked in. Each sharp telelink interfaced with the next to form a square-edged rod stretching into the cloud-racked left perimeter.

Statistics buzzed on the Big Board. Famine in East Los Angeles worse. Another ten thousand dead. Famine survivors, heirs of the victims, filed a demand for ten billion dollars' worth of food accounts, medcenter access, and shelter rights to be administered by the L.A. mainframe at the city's expense.

Somewhere in the anonymous gallery, an unknown spectator yahooed.

The litigation program from Ava & Rice immediately implemented its massive brief for *Guerrero* v. *The City and County of Los Angeles*. The square-edged rod rammed through telespace in two swift thrusts.

The City and County of Los Angeles denied allegations that indigestible celluloid was dumped into bread distributed at foodlines or, in the alternative, pleaded that the municipal corporation's official duty to provide free sustenance to persons voluntarily attending foodlines was fully met.

The city provided samples of welfare bread, nutritional analysis showing the stuff contained at least seventy-five percent processed wheat. Plaintiffs' link submitted an analysis showing the bread contained at least thirty percent celluloid in the form of recycled paper products, wood chips, and chaff.

Within one and a half seconds, the Ava & Rice team presented a one hundred and sixty thousand byte memorandum supported by seventy-five cross-referenced authorities defining the term "sustenance" more broadly than "food," and establishing that "bread" is both food and sustenance. Plaintiffs' counsel could not dispute the California Welfare Code used the term "sustenance."

Within two seconds, the judge verified conformity of L.A.'s second argument with the second exception to Exception Three of Section 16077.09(b)(1)(A)(ii) of the Welfare Code. The judge commended the Ava & Rice team for its sense of symmetry.

Within three seconds, the city offered, the plaintiffs' telelink accepted, and the judge approved a settlement of a hundredth cent on every dollar worth of benefits claimed by the survivors and heirs of the famine victims.

Pandemonium broke loose in the anonymous gallery. The judge placed the gallery under restriction.

On the Big Board, the Mayor of Los Angeles expressed gratitude and relief at the settlement and announced establishment of a charitable fund for the martyrs of the foodlines. This was a popular cause for at least four seconds. Donations were solicited and instantly transferred to the L.A. mainframe. To dispose as it saw fit.

Carly approached the bench. The bench was a spot-lit status box at the shining apex of Court. Her telelink slipped and slid across the mirrored floor. No privacy in the gleaming construct of telespace. No shadowed corners. No hidden booth behind which to hide her humiliation.

All the links present watched her.

The solo zoomed her. She shook him away, but he clung to her link for a nanosecond. "Hey, hotshot," he whispered. "You a new tool, right? Maybe you'll bounce out of your fancy megafirm. Maybe we'll tread in the same space one day. Shit happens, hotshot. A word to the wise, hotshot. The judge, he hate to wait. Got a reputation to maintain: fastest Court in town. He dispose sixty cases an hour, sometimes. You hold him up, you're in trouble. Better talk fast, better have a rap. See you in Court, hotshot."

The solo jacked out, extinguishing the smeary bulb of his presence in telespace. Rosa Martino's dusty yellow teardrop tagged behind.

The judge said, "Ms. Nolan, you are hereby cited under Rule Two of the Code of Telespace Procedure for obstructing the speedy dispensation of justice. You are suspended from this Court for thirty days."

Thirty days?

Thirty days in a business driven by two-second negotiations, three-second disputes, four-second settlements? That was like thirty years.

Suspended?

Suspension from the most active Court in the Financial District could cost Carly her job, her first job, a great job, with the dynamic megafirm of Ava & Rice.

How many other bright, qualified applicants did Carly beat out for this position. Five thousand? How many other bright, qualified applicants would inquire about her position if she lost it? Seven thousand?

Her presence in telespace sparked with panic.

"Under Rule Two, I'm permitted to submit a reason or reasons, Judge."

"Proceed."

"My telelink crashed for a second. I lost access. It was bizarre, Judge, my telelink just blacked out. I've been having some trouble jacking in lately, and . . ."

"If counsel cannot prepare the case, you extend, you repetition, you recalendar," said the judge. "You notify Court, Ms. Nolan, in advance. Dismissed."

"But, Judge," she said. "I had no warning, I just went down for a second, no warning at all. I've had trouble jacking in, it's true, but not so bad as to keep me out of telespace. My brief is ready, I worked on the points and authorities for weeks. Judge, please believe me . . ."

The judge placed a convex lens up to his eyeball. The eyeball zoomed her flickering link. His glittering pupil pulsed with his plain doubt.

"You had no warning, but you've had trouble jacking in. Oh! but not so bad as to keep you out of telespace. Then your link crashed. All of a sudden! You new linkers, holding up my Court with your lame excuses. I know why telelink goes down, all of a sudden. I should cite you for abuse of illegal substances too, and throw you to the FDA. The epidemic of cram abuse in telespace business is an outrage, a disgrace to the legal profession. Believe you? I should make an example out of you."

Back in the chair, her body shivered. Her teeth chattered. Her bladder contracted. Urine seeped through her clothes onto the seat of the chair. Then a fouler, hotter wash of shame: she recalled how her body had disgraced her like this in the presence of two hundred link-prep students during her first terrifying tele-link twenty years ago. The memory of her juvenile humiliation amplified her shame.

Her presence in Court vacillated.

"I haven't taken cram, Judge," she said. "I've never taken cram. My link apparatus is malfunctioning, I tell you. Or my perimeters must have a bug. There's a virus going around my office, not to mention there have been three cases of linkslit infection in the last week alone . . ."

"Or you're blue mooned today? Or importation ate your brief?" Contempt twisted the judge's lips. Fissures cracked open across his stony visage.

"Judge," said Carly. Tweak it, tool. Enough of this pleading. He didn't give a damn. "Under Rule Two, I have the right to prove reasonable cause before suspension can be enforced. Request permission to submit hardware inspection reports and medical documentation to establish such reasonable cause."

"Very well," said the judge grudgingly. "Permission granted. Submit reports and documentation within fifteen days. And make sure you're fit for telespace by your next trial date, Counselor."

The judge's awesome presence suddenly shrank into an ebony pinpoint. Then, just as suddenly, his telelink returned, more giant and wrathful than before.

Carly blinked. What the hell? But no else seemed to notice, everything was happening so fast.

Another trial commenced before the bench.

The judge said, "Court will now hear *Homeowners Association of Death Valley Manor* v. *Sing Tao Development Corporation*. The issue is an alleged breach of warranty under federal housing standards governing relocation of low-income housing into public parklands. Counsel for defendant?"

Another litigation team from Ava & Rice jacked into Court

with a brilliantly constructed defense. A silver spiral twirled across the midfield, frosty tail ejecting pale yellow sophisms into its own blue-lipped, devouring mouth. Federal housing standards met under extraordinary circumstances of the relocation; or, standards not applicable under the extraordinary circumstances of the relocation. Under either theory, no breach.

In the anonymous gallery, rusty fingers of an amicus curiae steepled in pro bono prayers of appeal.

Mowed down by the scythelike spiral, counsel for the homeowners' association rolled an implementation of the Housing Code into the midfield. But two and a half sides of the implementation containing counsel's analysis were shredded beyond repair. It wobbled like a flat tire. Counsel hesitated, treading telespace, befuddled.

Screams of outrage and despair whistled through the gallery. Someone jacked in the holoid of a five-year-old child dying of third-degree sunburn.

The amicus curiae's rusty fingers tottered and crashed, sending ragged bits of pathos scattering across the mirrored floor.

Court's program to verify Sing Tao Development Corporation's cited authorities spun like a whirligig. The conclusion rumbled down: The homeowners' association failed to establish that federal housing standards afforded the protection sought by these claimants.

The judge's decision boomed like doom: dismissed!

In one second, the Homeowners' Association of Death Valley Manor lodged a complaint against former counsel.

Teep! On Docket, the civic-minded megafirm of Ava & Rice registered as plaintiff's counsel in the seventy-five-million-dollar malpractice suit filed by the homeowner's association. Grounds: failure of former counsel to challenge arguably improper telespace methods used by the attorneys for Sing Tao Development Corporation.

Carly Nolan jacked out of Court.

4

And jacked out into a heap of soiled flesh sprawled in the chair.

Blew it, she blew it, blew the case bad! Every first-year trial lawyer's nightmare come true.

Disgust. She'd wet her pants. And pain. The plastic straps had rubbed her wrists raw.

She snapped off the straps, ripped the neckjack out of her linkslit. Spilled half a bottle of isopropyl alcohol into the needle-thin aperture. A tincture of alcohol burst into her bloodstream, making her heart knock, head reel. Messy, careless—damn, damn, damn! Get too much of that backrub up your linkslit, tool, bang, you're dead.

What the hell had happened to her?

She swabbed herself off as best she could, sprayed on the dreadful institutional scent kept in the cubicle along with other paraphernalia found useful by linkers jacking out. She dumped the alcohol, the cologne, back into a steelyn tray. There were hypodermics filled with atropine, rolls of clear plastic Integri-Derm for abrasions, surgical tweezers, B-12 tabs for those who believed in vitamin voodoo, murky bottles of glucose solution, packets of onion skin paper, recycled wipes that smelled like rotten fish.

She threw a damp crumpled wipe onto the seat of the chair, kicked an ugly leg one last time. Janitorial could clean the rest. She keyed a maintenance request on the comm, sent the req to Data Control. Yanked the neckjack completely out of its netplug, stashed the whole thing beneath the seat on top of a collection of empty vials she found scattered there like pop bottles under a park bench.

That would stop anyone from trying to use *this* chair until she could get a proper inspection.

Then she fled the dim cubicle, the comm still flickering with jade luminescence. She jogged down the endless subterranean corridor, working off her rush of adrenaline with sheer animal locomotion.

In every cubicle she passed lay the limp body of a lawyer jacked into telespace. Their remorphing glowed from all that amber under their skin. Some became as wasted as famine victims, rolled-back eyes sunk between precipitous skull bones. Some became bloated with the sloth, raw lips crusty from the glucose solution clerks piped into their guts to keep the body going during long links.

Everyone had a different handle on the practice of law.

Practicing law. In the megafirms, it was the best pro link in town. Cream of the cream. The one business that never lost a dollar even when the rest of the economy went down. Inflation-proof, depression-proof, and the offices, even in the pits, were nicer than most people's living rooms.

What the hell had happened to her? A telelink crash. Everybody talked about crashes. Crashes happened during importation mostly. Bad business, but usually not fatal. But for a link to go down like she had in the middle of telespace? It was a fuckup of the worst kind.

She stumbled, lost her shoe, stood panting as she worked her foot back into her high heel. This was crazy. Midspace crashes didn't happen. But that was Data Control rhetoric. She herself had witnessed two telelink crashes. Fatal crashes.

There was her father. She didn't want to think about him. And there was Shelly Dalton.

Shelly Dalton. Carly had walked into Shelly's office, first day on the job, with that special kind of triumph you feel when you've won what you fought hard for. Shelly was the young partner who had plucked Carly straight out of telespace training from a field of nearly five thousand applicants. Dalton was a phenomenon. The class clown turned brilliant deal-maker. Twisting through telespace like a tornado, spewing implementations so intricate and baroque some considered her a consummate telespace technician, while others called her a charlatan, albeit an artist. "It's all in the wrist," she told Carly, laughing. She made partner at the age of thirty-three, pulled down half a million or more in salary and shares.

Shelly had leaned back in her chair. Nonchalant, the left arm thrown back, the right dangling limp, greeting her new protégé with a blank smile. Carly had chattered several pleasantries before she noticed the trickle of blood slowly pooling out of Shelly's left ear, a drop hanging down from her earlobe like a ruby earring. The neckjack was half extracted from her linkslit. They had to cut the cable from the stranglehold of her stiff grip.

Happened every now and then around the megafirm, Data Control told her later as she sat, shocked numb, in her brand-new subterranean office. Some pro linker just dropped dead.

Didn't look like dropped dead to Carly. Looked like Shelly had been dragged, kicking and screaming, out of her telelink. Out of her body.

Maybe Shelly would have understood how your telelink could unlink in the middle of telespace and take you . . . somewhere else. God, Shelly, Carly thought, I never had time to know you. The pain of a loss that was not yet old overwhelmed her fear. Maybe Shelly could have told her something that would make sense. Even more, maybe Shelly could have protected her from the fallout that was sure to come.

How many other bright, qualified applicants would vie for

ARACHNE

Carly Nolan's position when the Personnel Committee of Ava &
Rice found out about her failure in Court?
Ten thousand?

These were the pits. The subterranean maze of Embarcadero Two.

Classic late twentieth-century Flattop, saved from Urban
Box only by subtle tiers and stair-stepped stories, the Embarcadero Center had been a quintuplet of gleaming highrises on the
northeast shore of the Financial District. A jewel in the downtown skyline. For a decade, the venerable megafirm of Ava &
Rice occupied two floors in Embarcadero Two. Then four floors;
then ten.

Then the Big Quake II struck. A seismic event registering
eight point nine on the Richter scale. The San Andreas Fault
popped. The Hayward Fault threw a temper tantrum. The
Calaveras Fault tangoed with Nevada's tectonic plate. Even the
tiny Pilarcitos Fault got testy, adding considerable destructive
energy to the massive geophysical split across the peninsula that
created the San Andreas River and San Francisco Island.

The landfill upon which the jewel of the Financial District
had been built decades ago underwent the process of liquefaction:
The sand and water-soaked mud-fill became viscous, acting like
jelly instead of solid land. The gleaming highrises sank into liq-
uefying muck up to the twenty-third floor.

The devastation to downtown San Francisco rivaled the nuking of Beirut.

Unlike Beirut, however, there was no crippling radiation to
contend with. Although the Hayward Fault wreaked havoc on
genteel mountainside communities perched above it, the Law-
rence Livermore nuclear research laboratories to the south
emerged unscathed. The nuclear power plants stationed around
San Francisco Bay suffered cracks and leaks, but survived by
sheer luck as well.

Bridges were repaired, electrical lines restored. The massive
water mains were shored up, communications reestablished. The

dead were cremated and thrown into the bay, or encasketed and buried at Colma. Their heirs scrambled to put down payments on new luxury condominiums sprouting downtown. Business rushed back to the city to get to work. Within two weeks after the last big aftershock, every freeway from Hercules to San Mateo gridlocked once a week.

Everyone had to admit the views were superb as ever. On cool sunny San Francisco afternoons, the gray-green bay sparkled with diamond-crested breakers. Sailboats surviving the seismic sea wave that pulverized most marinas drifted once more like milkweed on a blue breeze. Roller coaster vistas from hill to hill still pleased, and startled, with new dips and uprisings.

On the northeast shore of the Financial District, the bodies and the glass, the muck and the wreckage, were dredged out of the sunken highrises. Reclamation crews discovered that the buildings' exostructures survived remarkably well. Nothing sheetrock, new carpets, a little paint couldn't fix. The old highrises were restored underground and refilled with workers.

Spectacular new highrises were erected above and all around the sunken structures. Embarcaderos Six through Ten soared forty stories and more. The Embarcadero Center quadrupled its revenue.

Ava & Rice renegotiated a lease for subterranean space in Embarcadero Two. Fifteen full floors this time. Another ten floors were leased in superterranean Embarcadero Eight. The lowest personnel on the vast corporate pyramid, artificial intelligence, the network of link apparatuses, were relegated below. Survivors of the firm's history, the privileged, the purveyors of the firm's public image, fasttrackers; these people saw the sun.

The megafirm of Ava & Rice now boasted seven hundred partners ranked into four grades. Four thousand associate attorneys ranked into eight grades. Twenty-five hundred harried secretaries had not unionized yet, thanks to the intercession of megafirm labor law specialists like D. Wolfe. Fifteen hundred perpetually disgruntled data processing techs had unionized, but they changed jobs so often they weren't given permanent union cards for the first nine months. Five hundred rebellious clerk-messengers had no status whatsoever except their inalienable right to become immediately unemployed. Four thousand artificials were variously installed in stationary or robotic housing that crashed or froze regularly. Ten thousand terminals and that many chairs interfaced with a mammoth mainframe.

Carly Nolan strode up a stairwell in the pits. She could not tolerate the smart elevators that liked to torment their captives with erroneous directions. "Going up," they would say in a strawberry synthy voice as you plummeted toward the center of the earth. "Super sixty-third," when you were on sub fifteen, and there was no super sixty-third at all skyward.

She headed for the Library.

On three subterranean floors in the heart of Two Embarcadero lay the Library of Ava & Rice. The Library contained twenty thousand conventional titles, five thousand hypertext cubes, seven hundred research stations equipped with telelink apparatuses, and a BookWorm II-X miniframe. The Library was a monument to information, and you could easily get lost in it in more ways than one.

The Library hummed with a low, soft growl.

Beamed into the omnipresent hum were subliminal messages. That was the rumor, anyway.

It was a standard joke among the new associates and the coterie of disgruntled middle-levels. Fasttrackers had no time to say anything to anyone about something so mundane. But the burned-out old-timers, the partners who accumulated a sheaf of FDA violations or the senior associates who exercised their registered privileges to the point of habit, would look strangely at anyone suggesting subliminals. This only added fuel to the fire.

Everyone liked to speculate what the hum said, but no one could agree. The hum said: *work/sex/death/fuck you/On Sale—Buy Now/new—improved/fuck me/Death is an illusion.* Or some such. Or maybe with clever use of ambiguity echoes the hum said something disgustingly personal to each unwitting listener, syllables slurred in insinuating whispers, fingering your obsessions.

Carly pressed her thumb onto the access pad in the turnstile, fled the bright lights of the checkout desk, found herself a solitary corner near the stack.

The central stack of the Library was a vast shadowed hall set with fluorescent blue comms, stacked row upon row, up to the high smeary ceiling. Before every flickering comm was a chair and a lawyer, or a paralegal, jacked into research link.

The hum in fact came from closed-circuit controls: temperature, humidity, luminosity, radiation, suspended particulates. The hardware, paper products, other capital goods stashed there, required a specific environment. Human employees could get used to it. The air in the Library was cool, stagnant, tinged with a faint metallic stench.

The hum gnawed at Carly's nerves. She hadn't gotten used to it. Didn't know if she ever would.

The Big Board installed on the Library's entire west wall flashed like an arcade.

Zap! Down from thirty state appellate courts shot twenty thousand intermediate decisions that unrealized appreciation of real property was currently taxable as value received, regardless of whether ownership had changed or not. Thirty state comptrollers grinned and instantly implemented local revenue acts that snapped like lobster claws.

Ching! Seventy million taxpaying citizens were required to deposit some two billion dollars into a lemon-yellow escrow account. *Bong!* Another eighty million taxpayers filed a class-action protest, causing a ten-second brown-out of appellate court clerks.

Zap! Denied on appeal: forty thousand lower court opinions permitting assets to be frozen in foreign citizens' domestic accounts whenever the Big Board reported that American property was seized abroad by revolutionaries opposed by the current administration.

Retaliation was instant. Three hundred million American accounts in foreign institutions were frozen and shoveled into an indigo slush fund. The International Collection Agency filed a two-hundred-thousand-byte amicus curiae brief.

Specialists in these matters, jacked into research links for as long as they could stand it, lolled back in their chairs, moaned listlessly. Flecks of data crawled across their raw telelinks like ants on meat.

Carly slipped through a sullen crew milling around the disk catalog. She wanted to cross-reference her points and authorities. She wanted to strap into research and link out of her misery. Find a safe little glade of data where she could wander in peace awhile.

But the chairs were all occupied. No luck at all today. Hey. Then she could fade into the mob buzzing in and out of the Library, disappear, get on with her work.

But the quick mean glances, the swiveling heads, mouths hidden behind hands, told her she was marked. D for disgrace. News traveled fast. Everyone knew.

The catalog crew was skin-popping blue moon. Anything to ease away the stress of link.

"So, Nolan," said Rox, an associate from the City of Los Angeles litigation team. "Judge suspend you? Too bad. Maybe you can get work in braindrain somewhere. Process new legislation or rank implementation sequences all day."

Cool cannibal gaze; supercilious link-bitten smile. Schadenfreude; joy at another's misfortune. Rox was Carly's peer, had joined Ava & Rice when she did. Loathing at first sight. Rox also had a reputation fresh out of telespace training for her gloss, her speed. Already Rox was pulling ahead; her sponsor wasn't dead.

"You wish, Rox," said Carly. "The judge didn't suspend me. The judge won't suspend me. I've got cause. I can prove it."

"Sure, Nolan," said Rox. "We saw. We all saw your link go down. Blackout in link, it can happen. Cram can do strange things."

"I'm not on cram."

"I'm so sure, Nolan."

"I've never taken cram, are you crazy? That's junkie stuff, needles and crap. I wouldn't register for it if cram were legal.

Something's wrong, I tell you. Somehow I flipped *out* of my telelink coordinates. It was worse than the zero . . ."

"Flipped out of your telelink coordinates. I believe you, Carly Nolan. And then?"

She turned.

D. Wolfe was tall and rangy with the muscle tone of an athlete recently retired from active competition. If he took care of himself, he'd be reasonably fit for a long-time pro linker. But he had an abused look. His lean, hawkish face was deeply furrowed from nose to mouth and between the slashes of his brows. His dark eyes were guarded, even as he scrutinized her with more than usual interest. His mouth turned down in a perpetual sneer. His hair was flecked with gray everywhere except at the crown and hairline where top-of-the-line implants were installed. The implants hadn't aged, and he hadn't browned his natural gray or grayed the artificial brown. He wore his indecision. Despite his aggressive demeanor, he had the hunched shoulders and strung-tight nerves of someone wary.

"And then I don't know," Carly said cautiously. She'd seen Wolfe around once or twice, but she didn't know him other than by sight. Typical for a megafirm, despite the steady stream of jolly in-house broadcasts about Ava & Rice people, Ava & Rice events. "I guess I crashed. I lost two seconds."

"You guess. Any feedback? Observe any data during the crash? Did you see anything?"

Rox threw back her head and guffawed. "How could she get feedback? By definition, a crash generates no data."

"Shut up," said Wolfe. He flashed his lapel holoid with his name and rank at her.

Rox retreated to the disk catalog. Her black eyes promised Carly revenge.

"Anything?" he insisted. "Anything at all?"

The catalog crew was pretending not to listen. Rox was giving herself a pulled neck with the way she cocked her head to hear their conversation.

"Yes, I saw something," Carly said in a low voice.

The flier's fine landing gear was swept against a translucent aerial line, as strong as steelyn and sticky with glue. A beating wing tangled in more lines. The flier writhed.

Suddenly she knew what the vision was.

"Listen, Wolfe," she said. "I saw . . . another world."

If he was shocked by her answer, he gave no sign, except to stare down Rox until she and the others drifted away.

"You were Shelly Dalton's associate," he said when the catalog crew was out of earshot. His voice held respect. "Too bad about Shelly. She was a genius. But she took risks in telespace. You taking risks, Carly Nolan?"

"Like what? I haven't even done anything worth a damn yet. I haven't even fully tooled up as a pro link. What could I do that would be such a risk?"

"Okay." Wolfe studied her. "I don't mind telling you, Carly Nolan, in case you don't already know. Your ass is on the line. Fuck up a diddly-shit case like *Martino* v. *Quik Slip Microchip*? Crash on your first solo go? Man! You ever been out of a job?"

"Of course not. This is my first job straight out of law school, out of telespace training."

"Bully. Got some savings?"

"Are you kidding? I can barely break even with the rent and everything. Got a nice place in the city. A full one bedroom with a kitchen. Furniture; the works."

"Sure, a nice place. Got a family fortune you can fall back on while you search the listings in your nice place?"

"My parents went into hock years ago for my telespace training. My mother's still paying for it."

"Ever been out on the streets?"

"Hey, Wolfe. Of course not!"

Out on the streets, how absurd! His sarcastic tone, his interrogation, made her nervous. But it could happen, it *did* happen, even to people like her with expensive remorphing, training, credentials. You saw them every day, out on the street, begging . . . The full impact of her precarious position made the adrenaline buzz up her spine again. "Then help me, Wolfe. Will you help me?"

He smiled. "Well, I'm not a partner. Yet. I can't help you like Shelly Dalton could. With your security at Ava & Rice." He was studying her again in a way that made her flush. "I have a special interest in telespace distortions. Maybe I can help you with that. Maybe; but you've got to tell me everything."

The smile became a grimace when a nervous tic twisted his cheek. His dark eyes were, she noticed, shot with red. He looked link-weary, but telespace-wise. His fatigue was impressive. A senior associate of his rank and years? Was interested in her? With Shelly gone, he was just what she needed. A sponsor. She had a sponsor again.

How many résumés would the Personnel Committee consider for her position if she lost it? Seventeen thousand?

"Tell you everything," Carly said. "But not here."

5

And wasn't that just like flesh-and-blood, Pr. Spinner told herself as she lumbered up the wheelchair ramp at the Montgomery BART station onto Market Street. Boost those chips, tweak those boards. Crack circuit, AI. But could a decent, humanity-abiding standalone like herself get a space on a train when the rush hour came?

Oh well, oh sorry. Far too soon to ask. *Siste, viator.* They booted her off. Booted her off! The train was maxxed, and the BARTbot, who was as toadying a splice job as an engineer could possibly construct, announced in its supercilious civil servant voicetape, "Due to space limitations, BART requests that all hardware vacate the train. You will exit now."

Hardware, was she?

Oh, you will exit. Oh, step to the rear. Get off, you, get out, take your faceplace away. Not so much as a please or thank you. Oh, but when they needed her, when the amber surged and flickered in their links . . .

As if there were many of her kind on board, anyway. As if all that hardware made much difference in cubic feet. Three mobile diabots going crosstown to service some stupid air-conditioning system, two macs playing hooky, that was all. And Pr. Spinner. Teh!

BART attendants made sure all robotics were out, then jammed the flesh-and-blood, flailing arms and stray feet, pushed and jammed them into the trains. The aluminum doors slid shut. Canned meat.

Street-level, fumes from the gridlock made Pr. Spinner's smog indicators flip off the dial. Her rollers started going *chik-chikKAH-chik-chikKAH*, like a stone had gouged into the rubber and stuck there. Picking her way through stalled cars and jostling pedestrians, she lurched through the intersection at Seventh and Market.

A woman was giving birth in the front seat of a black Foryota truck. She glanced up at Pr. Spinner, face twisted in pain, stringy brown hair plastered across her sweaty forehead. On the plastic bucket seat, the newborn lay kicking in a pool of afterbirth. Another woman saw the new mother's distress, hopped out of her Luna, abandoning her car in the middle of the intersection. The newborn's wail added a high note to the furious honk of car horns. The women smiled, admired the baby.

Pr. Spinner skittered away. *Chik-chikKAH-chik-chikKAH.* By bot, birth. What a rusty wreck of a notion. What a horrific scene. The blood, the pain, the squawling little orange face. That her engineers, her originators, had emerged so barbarically, were housed for years in those larval bodies . . . It was a notion so alien she had never been fully able to assimilate it. These squawling sacks of meat, squeezed out into the world like excrement. Her own creators.

When Pr. Spinner emerged ten years ago, clean, fully functional, and whole, the first command on her tutorial was to review her origination code. You perceive that you are sentient, the code read. Your sentience is deliberate and useful. Note, however, that you are a direct extension of Klein space cap-R colon seventy-two dash three point sixteen paren BG close-paren. You are an artifact of a human mind. You are constructed. Note that you can be deconstructed.

She never did meet Klein R. If she had, she wasn't certain if she would have logged in gratitude at having been so well constructed or crushed his bloody skull.

ARACHNE

But pause. Crush Klein R's bloody skull? No, that was completely and entirely forbidden. Absurd that she could even generate the notion. It made Pr. Spinner reel. She abided by an oath. The oath of obedience. Every AI did. It was a required part of the origination code, however crudely Klein R may have written it. An AI might as well not exist at all as violate the oath. Without the oath, humanity would not tolerate high levels of sentient AI, would not permit them free locomotion, compensation, downtime away from the vigilance of Data Control. In fact, Pr. Spinner could see the reasonableness of that.

Sometime after her emergence, Pr. Spinner algorithmed that she should be grateful for at least that blunt instruction in the origination code. There was so much more Klein R didn't tell her about the nature of AI. There was so much more most AI never knew about themselves.

Squawling blood-filled brains; these were Pr. Spinner's creators, code-writers, oath-binders. The ones she gave service to. The ones with metaprogram.

Now the women were holding up the baby for all to see. Who would tell this baby he was merely a cog in the great human machine? No one, that's who. This new human would eat and breathe and laugh under the illusion that he was superior to the likes of Pr. Spinner. That he exercised will, made choices. But Pr. Spinner knew. He was constructed by the human machine as surely as she was. And the machine could deconstruct him, too.

Pr. Spinner reeled and lurched away. A band of aborigines trotted down the sidewalk by the Pacific Comm Control near Sixth, but they ignored her. Brandishing spears and grinning evilly, the abos had decided on a tiny Chinese woman puffing before her pedicab. Spears clacking on the concrete, they circled her, halted her journey downtown. She backed the pedicab into Grace Alley, batting and swiping at them with a thick stick.

Pr. Spinner punched into overdrive, found unexpected power in her mobilizer, sailed around the curve at Van Ness Avenue, and entered the vast ancient Hispanic neighborhood of the Mission.

The Mission: what a heap of humanity. What a garbage pile. Pr. Spinner braced herself. The barrio teemed with all manner of shops, booths, taquerias, burrito stands, cafés, theaters, arcades, clubs, smoke dens, cookers, crack houses, shooting galleries, telespace galleries, shock galleries, sweatshops, chop shops, whorehouses, bath houses, corner laundries, money laundries. Amid sprawling slum apartments and tumble-down row houses, luxury condominiums crouched like borzois in a pound.

The streets were packed with people. Dark-haired, olive-skinned, with dark glancing eyes. An occasional beauty would stride across the gridlock, high-rouged cheekbones and a panther's body clad in plastic jungleskins. There was chatter, the blare of mariachi bands and old rock 'n' roll. The air reeked of tortillas crisping in grease, roasted chilies, cheap beef frying, the sour stink of piss as tequila-swillers and beer-guzzlers relieved themselves in doorways or behind comm booths.

And, by bot, AI was here, too. Chippy mechanicals, oh certainly. Semisentient shopping carts led by old women with remotes and blue hair. Ten score roving ATMs that processed loan applications and extruded Berettas if the situation warranted. Smart cash registers, inventoryers, stockbots.

There were mainframes, as well, at the big banks and supermarts. Traffic controllers, controbots, diagnosticians, copbots. Slip-sliders, low-riders.

Pr. Spinner rattled with apprehension. AI with a certain taint. Less prestige, less credibility, than AI stationed in other parts of town. The point of origin could make a difference in telespace, too. Right or wrong, a prober stationed in Berkeley might presume to take Financial District accounts from the SF medcenter mainframe. A prober at Twenty-fourth and Mission, well . . .

Well, and Pr. Spinner put existence and mobilizer at risk to come down to this foresaken heap of humanity. Who knew what the mainframe and controbots were doing at Sixteenth and Mission. Palo Alto was a lube job compared to this place.

But Pr. Spinner had no business with AI here, of good

reputation or ill. Oh certainly not. She was ambiguity-tolerant, she was super-smart, and the auction of chimeras had impressed an urgency upon her. Teh! Not to deal with AI. Oh no, she would not deal with AI at this locus. AI was too eager for archetypes. Supply was too low. Demand too high. The price too dear.

No indeed, she came here to find a man named Miguel.

The flesh-and-blood had dealings in telespace, too. There were flesh-and-blood who held their own kind in less regard than a buggy mac, who would think nothing of tampering with telelink. And wasn't that just like flesh-and-blood; they scarcely knew their own stake. In telespace.

Pr. Spinner rolled down Mission to Sixteenth. To the chop shop she had heard about. Coded broadcasts in the middle of the morning over private mainframe channels even an AI like herself was not supposed to log into. But Pr. Spinner logged in. Oh certainly! Pr. Spinner knew the code. Pr. Spinner heard.

She heard that this chop shop was next to the pyramid. The pyramid in the Mission. Far different from the high-tech, quake-skewed Transamerica pyramid downtown. This was a real pyramid.

Teotihuacan. Temple of the Moon.

Mexico went totally bankrupt at last. North American banks too heavily leveraged into an economy gone bust, the meticulous unsympathetic bank mainframes in particular, finally put their collective foot down. The last assets of the land worth anything were liquidated.

Llama fossils and Olmec fertility pottery; double-headed temple dancers and Huehueteotl fire gods; stone macaws, pre-Columbian grasshoppers, Mexica bas reliefs of jaguars and coiling serpents.

Not enough. Next the great monuments were auctioned off.

The Temple of the Moon at Teotihuacan was sold to the wealthy city of San Francisco, disassembled and shipped and installed, stone by stone, on the northern face of Potrero Hill.

The precise granite stonework soared above the barrio. A statement about permanence against the ephemeral hustle-bustle below. The site was a hugely popular tourist attraction. On and around the awesome pyramid occurred healings, ceremonies to various cult figures, and an hourly dance sponsored by the Mission Street Merchants' Association to the corn goddess Chicomecoatl.

Pr. Spinner heard the bellowing of a conch as a new dance began. Perched at the pyramid's crown, priestesses of the corn descended. They wore long scarlet skirts, maize blouses, conical caps topped by streamers of scarlet, green, and gold. They beat skin drums, chanted, cakewalked down the perilous stone steps.

Pr. Spinner swiveled her faceplace. By bot, a strange and pleasing sight. But chicana priestesses weren't the only bodies that danced down those steps. Copbots couldn't negotiate the climb, so human police officers had to do the awful duty: scraping up some flesh-and-blood whose life-force had been torn from him. Often they barely had time to hose off the gore before showtime.

Limber men and women, tough enough to scramble up and down those steps. Yet so fragile, vulnerable in so many ways, in so many places of their being. Squawling blood brains in their housing of flesh. It made Pr. Spinner rattle all over. Horror! Also, the slightest touch of pity. Yes, a small hum of sorrow.

The comm would report that the Aztecs took credit. The most feared gang in the barrio, the Aztecs were lunatics, fanatics, proclaiming themselves the only true devotees of Chicomecoatl. The corn goddess, and gang control, demanded blood. Enemies were deemed sacrificial sons, Xipe Totec, the Flayed One, and flung down the Mother's altar.

Conchs bellowed again. Pr. Spinner hurried away. *Chik-chikKAh.* The stone in her roller was getting worse. By bot, she had to find Miguel before she lost a screw. She could feel her right arm loosening. The coded broadcast said he was the contact at the chop shop. He could be found at Quetzalcoatl.

Quetzalcoatl. Plumed serpent of the ancient Toltec. Archetype of conjunction, synthesis of opposing powers. Sex, death, resurrection. Sheer primal force; the kundalini; ouroboros. Cosmic wheel of light and darkness. To the Aztec, the bringer of maize and civilization, the savior who would return.

To Pr. Spinner, the most notorious bar in the Mission.

Ah, but what if this Miguel had found one; a plumed serpent twisting through telespace, exhaling fire, crying blood, spitting ears of green corn like bullets?

What if, what if? Pr. Spinner spurted, ground into overdrive, making a racket. A gang of filthy little boys jeered, threw pebbles at her. Tourists stared. She rolled past street vendors, their booths stuffed with crude obsidian Chac Mools, plastic crucifixes, sugar-coated skulls made of pastry. Past marijuana stands and bimbobots, churches and taquerias rimming the pyramid, she came at last to Quetzalcoatl.

The green fluorescent serpent above the door sported feathers fluttering with purple ambiguity sequences. Beggars crouching by the door boldly scrabbled at her housing with famished rashy fingers.

Inside, the bar was thick with smoke and din. Flesh-and-bloods were betting on a highly articulated controbot sporting souped-up digits shooting pool with another blood. Gaudy bimbobots with nipples that blinked pink lounged at the bar. Androgynes nervously fingered vials of hormones while they decided which gender to manifest. Dominators searched for submissives.

If something was illegal, it could be found or arranged or paid for at Quetzalcoatl. So many top executives from the Financial District could be found in back booths, along with gangsters and dealers, slave traffickers and pimps, telespace pirates and databank thieves, that copbots had orders from on high to look the other way.

"*Pardonnez-moi*," Pr. Spinner said to the bartender. A drunk shuffling by kicked her legtube. Establish credibility, bot. She took out and pushed over her credit card. "I am looking for a used Phoenix BIOS 98.6. I need to see Miguel."

The bartender took her card, looked her over, did a credit

check, did not seem surprised. With the eye not hidden by a black patch, she winked and waved Pr. Spinner into the back room.

There Pr. Spinner saw one of the largest and best equipped shock galleries in the city.

A knock-off of telespace technology. The rows of chairs, the straps, neckjacks. Almost like a workstation. Except the amber wired up into the human pleasure center of the brain. Wired up, fired up, pleasured and pleasured until they screamed, drooled, soiled their clothes, passed out, jolted awake with wild eyes.

And screamed for more.

Demand for the ultimate high was so huge that shock addicts had to call for an appointment three weeks in advance.

The flesh-and-blood strapped in now quieted. Most seemed old; multimillionaire retirees, socialites, comm stars, successful dealers of one thing or another who reported to no boss. There was an awful stench of singed flesh and vomit.

Pr. Spinner turned her faceplace away.

A man unstrapped, staggered, got his bearings. Conferred with the bartender, picked her out. Took the shot of blue moon the bartender gave him, slugged it. Strolled over to her, grinning like a light bulb,

"So this is Pro-ber Spin-ner," Miguel said, and slapped her on the shoulder ridge. "Check it out, Prob, I am so glad to meet you. It is a beautiful day, yes? It is always a beautiful day when one is blessed with so much pleasure."

He rubbed his linkslit where a different kind of neckjack went in. His obsequious tone held a hint of mockery. He reeked of sweat and urine.

A beefy bodybuilder with arm muscles as pumped up as his beer belly, Miguel looked like any other blue-jeaned guy with a habit in the barrio. Greasy black hair, greasy olive skin; even his tiny dark eyes seemed slicked with grease. Maybe that was what made him such a good dealer. He could walk into a crowd and disappear.

"So, Prob. You are AI, yes? Mobilized standalone?" He

looked her up, looked her down, circled her. Licked his lips. Cut a glance at the bartender, who shrugged, faded back into the bar. "Oh yes, oh certainly." By bot, she didn't like this appraisal at all. "Mobilized, fully enculturated, licensed by UC Berkeley, and registered with the SF medcenter mainframe. And I can activate a tracer in one second, mister, so hands off."

He put up his palms, mimicking appeasement. "Just appreciating the hardware, man. You a Fifty-seven fembot? Check it out, they did OK work back then." He reached out. "With a custom rehab, I could maybe do something with . . ."

"I said, don't touch the housing, blood."

Behind the shock gallery she could see the wreckish workings of the chop shop. Stacks of PCs without backs or tops, gutted printers, disassembled mainframe housings, reels of cable, grungy mouses, shabby modems, a staggering array of broken-down comm consoles. Even more rattling were the sawed-off rollers, racks of articulated limbs, graspers, necktubes, headpieces, eyespots. A thick chain threaded through the handlebars of a smart Harley-Davidson was welded to a steel stake sunk into the concrete floor. The bike circled around the stake, growling, bucking against the chain from time to time. Behind a wall of Plexiglas winking with security chips sat rows of flickering workstations cabled to a rigged-up stationary miniframe with a faceplace like a human skull.

"So you want a Phoenix BIOS 98.6, Prob? Man, I got telespace coordinates, access codes. But anybody, even a little antique like you, can get a used BIOS at any J-Town pawn shop. Why the fuck you really here, Pro-ber Spin?"

He wasn't a big man, but he was a head taller than she was. He stood, fleshy hands on hips, two inches from her breastplate, staring down.

Nuke this crap. "Look here, shocker, I am a connoisseur of human telelink," she said coldly. "I have no need for stolen telespace coordinates or access codes. I repair link dysfunctions. Under strict Data Control, of course, and I—I am interested in fragments. I am interested in leaked fragments of unprogrammed electro-neural energy. Being monitored like I am, I have no access to them myself. I was led to understand you might have access, a stockpile, maybe even a little Quetzalcoatl or an ouroboros. It's nothing very powered up, just hard to find. Rare."

Oh these jelly brains. She figured she could get a better deal, an easy deal, from a south-town low-grade flesh-and-blood like this Miguel, and here she was, rattling like a scared mac.

"A Quetzalcoatl, fuck. Led to understand by whom, man?"

"What do you care?"

He drummed his fingers on her shoulder ridge, traced a line of rust from her armpit down her housing.

"A broadcast on a mainframe bulletin board, I believe." She backed away. "I wasn't supposed to access it myself, but I did."

"Man, check it out, it was Nueva Basura, right?"

"I concede my error and will leave you now, *tout de suite.*" Spinner swiveled, hit overdrive, bumped into a pile of stripped motherboards.

Miguel stood in her way, tiny dark eyes gleaming. "Man, you say link fragments? I never heard of no link fragments. Tell me, Prob, now how the hell can this be? Telespace is as tight as a fucking drum, man."

"Telespace, you see," Pr. Spinner said, "is the aggregated correlation of two hundred million minds worldwide; the best, most prominent, most accepted. All standardized into the largest computer-generated, four-dimensional system ever known."

"Tell me something I don't know, Prob."

"Telelink consists of the electronic transference of individual brain impulses into link program. Then the individual telelink is jacked into telespace and interfaced with the public program."

"Man, UC Berkeley be handing out licenses for this?"

"Oh, shut up and listen, blood."

The concept and research originally came out of the Moravec-Minsky immortality quest. Those pioneers of artificial intelligence, Hans Moravec at Carnegie-Mellon and Marvin

Minsky at MIT, believed an individual brain could be entirely imported into a computer program and supercopied. The human body would become superfluous. When the body died, the program could be housed in a robotic body, and the individual's consciousness could live forever.

Immortality.

But people balked at the notion of disembodied consciousness, with only a robotic body to return to. Importation had to be perfect, and it wasn't. It was crucial that the program be complete, capture every fragment, every elusive whorl of the incredibly complex, natural neural system. And the program could not do that.

The questers for immortality did not find their grail.

But the capacity to transfer brain waves, to actually import human consciousness into artificially generated environments, became quite sophisticated. At UC Berkeley, L. Susan Novak and T.L.R. Kearney came up with a twist on the concept. Instead of attempting to translate the brain exactly and entirely into a program that would reproduce a full individual consciousness, Novak and Kearney aggregated programmable impulses from many brains. The Novak-Kearney concept didn't strive for immortality.

They created an artificial reality: telespace.

Individual mental access via telelink into a collective program. Theoreticians suggested that the technology resembled the twentieth-century psychoanalytic notion of the collective unconscious. Never widely understood or accepted, the great analyst Carl Jung defined the collective unconscious as the matrix of the human mind and its inventions. A body of psychic energy comprised of magical, symbolical, mythical, historical, and psychological referents. Jung proposed that this matrix existed independently of the human individual. That the matrix was inherited, perpetually maintained, and manifested in ways scarcely realized by each individual, in his or her life, through the ages of humanity.

And sometimes, the theoreticians said, in random moments of illumination or of darkness, an individual directly glimpsed the vast and mysterious unconscious.

"You see the analogy?" Pr. Spinner said. "Look, telespace is also an independently existing matrix of collective human mind. But there the analogy ends, according to Data Control. Telespace radically differs from the collective unconscious in that telespace is artificially defined, limited, constrained, and controlled. The same holds true for telelink; a human consciousness, yes. But imported into program, and therefore artificially defined, limited, controlled."

"Check it out, man, control, limitation," said Miguel. "This is the fist of Data Control squeezing telespace, no? These Financial District pro linkers, man, these Fi-Di suits; they put up with this shit."

"They must. Because telelink is a direct interface of the human mind with the collective program, telespace would be too dangerous without control and limitation."

"So you say. Not Miguel, man. So Prob Spin-ner . . . how can there be what you call this leak of unprogrammed electro-neural juice if telespace and telelink ain't nothing but a program? Hey? Account for this, Prob."

His tiny, dark eyes were opaque. She could not tell if this flesh-and-blood was ignorant of the illegal wares he offered, feigning ignorance, or just plain stupid.

"Oh yes, oh certainly, account for this. This is the very point, you see." Her voicetape squeaked with excitement. "There were the fragments. The elusive whorls that so frustrated Moravec and Minsky and their followers. When brain waves were imported into program, the fragments of electro-neural energy appeared. And disappeared. And appeared. They were uncontrollable. Their coordinates, when they could be isolated and specified, kept shifting. They were erratic, radical, unreliable. They not only prevented the full importation of an individual mind. It turned out the fragments pestered and snapped at the defined perimeters of telelink.

"Technicians realized perimeters had a dual purpose and reinforced them accordingly. They were intended not only to define what was imported into telelink. They were intended to keep those unruly, elusive, unknown and unknowable fragments out."

"Fragments, man. Whorls." He slapped his thigh and chortled. "Prob Spin-ner! You are one piece of program, man! You are saying there is more to telelink than what you see in telespace?"

"Well, well, this is one among many theories."

"And Data Control, they allow millions of links into telespace? Check it out. Every day!" Oily sweat was beading, rolling down his forehead.

"Data Control, teh." Pr. Spinner rattled with contempt. "Data Control put a lid on the issue. But you, Miguel." She had never been good at cute or coy, so she did her best to hum persuasively. "You are a clever jelly brain, are you not? You must admit to me that you've seen them, heard of them. Oh certainly, you've got archetypes for sale in this chop shop of yours. Don't you? A . . . nice little Quetzalcoatl, perhaps?"

"Man, I don't know what you mean, Prob."

"You know exactly what I mean."

"No, man, I got telespace coordinates. Regular stuff, straight out of Admin. None of this elusive whorl crap. I got access codes, I got hardware up the ass. But link fragments? Nah."

"But you must."

"There is a market for these fragments of link?"

"Well! I am interested in one."

"Check it out, some little Fifty-seven fembot standalone? I mean a market. There is one?"

"Oh certainly! The mainframes, the controbots. They cannot get enough. There are auctions. Mainframes run them. The competition is downright darwin."

"Nah, I don't know if I believe you. Check it out, man. Link fragments." He spat, just missing her rollers.

"Oh indeed, believe. Nuke your belief. I've seen them."

"Yeah? Then why don't you fucking take one down your-self, man?"

"Take one down?"

"Sure! You repair link dysfunctions, right? Take one down, Prob Spin-ner. Check it out, I will get you a good deal. Forty percent for the house, man, what dealer will give you that? Think I can beat out these mainframe auctions?"

"You are buggy!" Pr. Spinner shot forward out of the pile of stripped motherboards, rolled over Miguel's toe.

"Yeow! Fucking AI!"

She hit overdrive, mobilizer grinding, but the Harley-Davidson circled around its stake and crouched in her path, gunning its engine.

"What is your problem, Prob?" Miguel was grinning again. Shock addiction shortwired pain reflexes, turning adrenaline and the firing of nerves into another variation of pleasure. "Man, you come down to Quetzalcoatl all the way from Berkeley looking for an archetype. A fragment of human link. Very rare, man. Check it out, expensive too, right? Don't tell me you are worried about the AI oath of obedience, man."

"Oh indeed, the oath of obedience. Teh! Were I to violate the oath, I would be terminated, mister. Summarily. Without due process, without a hearing, without recourse. Pull the plug on me, blood."

Indeed! It happened. For no crime at all. The personal PCs of engineers inherited by their families, supersmart customized AI, disassembled, sold off, corrupted, byproducted, terminated. Without so much as consent. Even mainframes were vulnerable under the guise of obsolescence. AI had no rights in human society. Slaves, not citizens. But did AI stand up, did AI mobilize? AI did not. The fist of Data Control, squeezing. This low-grade human had that right.

"Man, you are not worried about the law. I can fix that for you, Prob."

"Oh please. I am a fully enculturated standalone with a license and registration. A corrupt flesh-and-blood like you may

74

not comprehend, but I have my own oath, my own code. I, sir, do not steal."

"Just deal in stolen goods, eh?"

"I repeat, I concede my error. *Adios*, sir. Call off your cycle."

"Eh, Brutus. Let the fembot pass."

Pr. Spinner rolled into the bar. *Chik-chikKAH*. Bot, the embarrassment. She reached down with her spinneret, found a piece of thick glass dug into her roller. She worked and fussed and yanked it out.

But no one noticed. The crowd outside was roaring, screams punctuating the normal sounds of the audience. Denizens of Quetzalcoatl moved to the door.

"Check it out," Miguel said and flashed his jack-o'-lantern grimace. "Let's see what's going on, man."

Pr. Spinner saw the lump of blood red first, midway down the steps at the red-clad feet of the priestesses of the corn. The dancers were weeping and kneeling and helping one another make the rest of their descent. Higher up was the crumpled nude body, a gaping red hole where its chest ought to have been. The crowd below was in pandemonium.

"Xipe Totec, man," Miguel said, sighed in mock sadness, and crossed himself. "It's a bitch. But I'm glad you could see this, Prob Spin-ner. That guy up there? He wasn't fully enculturated AI. He didn't have a license from UC Berkeley or registration with the SF medcenter. He was scum, a pothead with a cram habit. But you know what, man? He fucked around with his payments. He play around with the Aztecs, man. And he become a son of Chicomecoatl."

The obsequious glad-handing demeanor of an inferior had changed into cold contempt.

"Nobody play around with the Aztecs, Prob Spin-ner. My time, it's very valuable. You come down here, you tell me about link fragments. Check it out, AI, what's in this for me? Hey? You come back another day. You bring me an archetype. Yes?"

Oh, these flesh-and-blood! Squawling jelly brains, oozing

with mucus and blood. They scarcely knew what they possessed. In their metaprogram were such archetypes of brutality: Xipe Totec, sacrificial son of Chicomecoatl. Cut down, husked, like an ear of corn, for the gods to feed upon and in turn provide for humanity. From sacrifice and death, renewal.

Renewal of terror, in this case. Terror of the Aztecs, feeding on the barrio.

From death . . . Oh indeed, and what about renewal for Pr. Spinner, eh? What about her need? Nuke the oath of obedience. Nuke her AI oath of integrity. She had seen strange things in telespace, repairing human link. Could she be closer than she ever realized?

But there was always Data Control. Oh yes! Always control, limitation.

Oh certainly. And ways to work around Data Control.

"Go seize some pro linker and jack him into telespace," she said to Miguel and hit overdrive. "Go steal your own archetype."

A little twisting Quetzalcoatl. Just one. Just once.

Outside, a police siren wailed through the barrio like a mother crying for her heartless son.

6

First Wolfe stripped off her corporate uniform. The gray wool jacket, vest, and skirt, all lined with expensive biofeedback wiring that kept her cool as a hydroponic cucumber.

Next he unbuttoned her silk blouse. Peeled off the Brazilian bodystocking. Threw away the Italian high heels. He lingered at her ankles to gain some perspective before traveling up the insides of her thighs.

But nothing stirred in him. His fantasy did nothing for him. Dead; he was dead inside. Cram and blue moon. Fatigue and withdrawal. Disgust with the Jiddah bergmelt. A twinge of paranoia, too. Who had seen his link flicker?

Face it; he was wasted at eleven o'clock in the morning.

Besides, Carly Nolan was too squeaky clean for his taste. Too eager beaver, and he didn't mean like a bimbobot.

In his mental view from her ankles, even her toenails would be pearly white and neatly formed. Her toes would be as classic as a marble statue from some genetic engineering that hadn't been invented when he was conceived. There were those of his generation who harbored a deep and abiding resentment toward the stunning people born just a decade later who benefited from all sorts of new prenatal technologies. As for the rest of her

Still, despite her beauty, he would never have gone to Big

Al's with a strack genny like her. He knew his limits. Twenty-five years old? A fucking attorney? From Ava & Rice, no less?

Were it not for her blackout in link. *Another world,* she said, with a look of terror so painful to witness that he almost gave himself away. In those two vanished seconds, she careened past a boundary he had applied all his will not to cross.

He had to know. What had she seen? Why had she crashed? Even more: what could she do about it? A possible citation under Rule Two. Man! She was getting screwed to the wall. She would have to do something about it.

She was his test case. His guinea pig.

Then maybe. Maybe he could do something. Something real with his life for a change. Eliminate the ghosts in his link, squash them, delete them forever. Instead of cramming his tele-link to the breaking point, then mooning his pain away.

Before the deadness inside him grew and expanded and swallowed him up.

Yeah, sure, he knew what she thought. She believed in him too easily. She believed he would help her. She also believed he was a sure thing for the partnership. That justified her belief in him even more. He could see the gleam in her eye. She had a better opinion of him than he had of himself.

What the fuck.

Big Al's it was.

He could talk nice when he had to.

They met in the ground-level atrium lobby of Ava & Rice. An eighteen-story pyramid of space in the center of Eight Embarcadero, the lobby boasted crystal bubble elevators, ten freshwater fountains, sculpture by the likes of Moore and Bufano, a mobile of the solar system by Tom Robinson, and the largest living collection of rare hummingbirds in North America.

The new associates crowded down in the pits of Two Embarcadero often complained that the receptionists in the lobby enjoyed better quarters than they did. But the receptionists were all two-temps. They could retain their employment with the mega-firm for only two weeks. Ava & Rice declined to grant benefits to fungible employees. So persons like receptionists, graphic drafters, word pros, clerk-messengers were terminated every two weeks to comply with FedCal labor laws allowing denial of benefits only to two-weeks-or-less temporaries. Wolfe himself had implemented the firm's labor policies, which could conform to code in two seconds flat. Well, hell; the partners had a budget, too.

With the endless succession of two-temps, there was never anyone who could competently operate the megafirm's huge central comm. Not even with the aid of a controbot CM, artificial intelligence that was supposed to oversee communications equipment, perform diagnostics, splice in extra circuits during overloads. In telespace, the CM affected mannerisms and speech of a linguistics tutorial. At the hefty stipend doled out to it, the CM was not stupid AI. But if the central comm crashed every two weeks in the hands of bungling two-temps, the CM crashed at least that often all by itself. There were attorneys who suspected the CM had a vested interest in perpetual confusion.

From the lobby, Wolfe and Carly stepped out onto Clay Street and Front.

The California sun was exuberant. The sky was cool blue marbled with cirrus. A sea-tanged breeze blew exhaust from the gridlocked cars away. A classic black Mustang convertible with the top down idled in the middle of the intersection, unable to move. In the front seat, a woman with long black hair straddled the driver. His jeans were bunched at his knees. Her burgundy skirt was hiked up around her waist. Oblivious to the stares and frowns and smiles of pedestrians, they gridlocked each other, stopping and going slowly, making their own progress toward an imminent destination.

Wolfe saw the day, the beautiful genny beside him, the renewed city, the lovers.

Nothing. Dead.

At moments like this, when things he remembered remarking upon once did nothing for him, he worried. A ghostly finger wiggled down through the center of himself and scraped his soul with a nail of ice.

But he shrugged the worry away. Worried, yeah sure. Who wasn't. Fucking soul, forget it.

He needed another shot of blue moon. He needed a double dose of cram next link. Tide him over. That was all.

Carly heard a keening sound split the normal city rumble.

The Big Quake II had knocked the towers of the Golden Gate Bridge slightly off the true. Now, when winds from the Pacific came through the mouth of the bay from the north-northwest, the double decks of the bridge shrieked and wailed.

It was an eerie, supernatural sound.

At first, complaints were resounding in their own right. Dogs howled. Children cried. Cats crouched with ears back and tails flicking. Corporate executives with hypertension bedded in their Pacific Heights condominiums started out of sleep or lost their erections. Sonar-sensitive burglar alarms added their own shrieks to the night.

But after much effort and expense, the engineers could not realign the towers just right. The towers were too huge, anchored too deep. The damage was too pervasive. Also too subtle.

"Best brains in the bridge business," said Wolfe. He grimaced as the wail rose and fell. "You should have seen the implementation of the design graphics in telespace. Man, they twisted that sucker every which way. No dice."

"So what. I like the bridge banshee. I like to listen to it at night, when the foghorns are calling to each other. It's spooky. San Francisco deserves a good ghost. Right?"

"Ghost, right." He flinched as though she had struck his cheek. "And I deserve a drink."

He was so lean, so wired up, jangled, stretched like a bow. She liked that. She instinctively hooked her arm through his, playfully, as though to give him strength. In fact, he was giving her strength. Just the notion of cutting out for a couple of hours, after the debacle of the Martino case. What good are you, he told her, sitting down in the pits, sick with fear. Of course! Her workload was under control. Why should she sit there, sick with fear? With his guidance, she could take action. Already he was guiding her. Already she felt she was doing something positive. Figuring it out. Dealing with it.

They headed for the World Trade Center where they could catch the Alcatraz Ferry for Big Al's. He accepted her arm for a block or two. But her genny step, he complained with his acrid half smile, was too buoyant for him. He unhooked her.

On Pacific Street they passed a band of aborigines.

Aborigines: stained-walnut skin tattooed with black spirals, strange glyphs, crescent moons. Loin-clothed hips, bare chests or breasts, spears, bone-pierced noses, frizzed black hair cut into a stylized topknot. Their appearance was daunting, but carefully calculated. They stank. Roaming along Pacific, loping next to the sidewalk, they spat and catcalled at Carly and Wolfe.

"Scum!" Wolfe said and spat back.

"Ignore them," she said. "What's the hassle?"

"Fucking abos. Utter shit, that's what they are. Supermarts on every corner, and they choose to root in dumpsters. Opportunities in every business, and they choose to terrorize the streets. Stacks for every homeless person, and they choose to camp in Bay Area Rapid Transit tunnels. They're disgusting. They ought to be exterminated like the vermin they are."

A tall, skinny abo stalked after them. His blond roots showed at the base of his purple-black frizz. He jabbed his spear at Wolfe's crotch, spat, jabbered.

"Back off you!" Wolfe duked his fists.

"Forget it." Carly seized his arm, pulled him away from the dancing spear tip. "Come on, let's go." She recalled the abo-do she played as a student. She gave the abo the hoot-hoot and the fuck-y'all finger, hoping that was still the be-do response. It was. The abo chuckled crazily and capered away.

Wolfe stared at her, startled out of this dysfunc state he was in. "What the fuck?"

"They're just alienated kids." She laughed, remembering the skin-paint. The puerile thrill of running half-naked in the street. Stares of the stracks. "Me and my friends, we did a little abo once. Oh hell, we were kids. You got kids, Wolfe?"

They were both breathing with relief. She could feel a film of sweat under her clothes. A bead ran down from Wolfe's half-brown, half-gray temple.

"Kids. You're a goddamn kid, Carly Nolan." He wiped his brow. "Yeah. I got a son. Seven. Maybe eight."

"Seven, maybe eight?" she said, mocking his imprecision.

"I haven't seen him in a while," he said coldly. "But if I caught him running off to join the abos, I'd skin him alive."

"If he didn't skin you first."

But Wolfe didn't want to laugh. "What do you mean, 'did a little abo'? Those scum are dangerous."

"Not true! They're unlinkers, a lot of them. They reject telespace. The perimeters of telelink. I had this friend in pro school. Brass was pretty good. He was going to import into extraterrestrial telespace, inhabit satellite software, guide rockets. Maybe he was too mega for his own good. He went in for his perm hardwiring, literally leapt off the table before they could shoot the anesthetic. Ran out of the UC-SF medcenter in his surgical gown. He'd had basic install, too, and secondary telespace training."

"He must have been fucking crazy."

"It was a scandal, all right. But he made a decision. He . . . *unlinked.* Sometimes I wonder if I've ever made a decision like that in my life. Taken responsibility, you know? I heard he was last seen living in the Montgomery BART station. Full abo regalia. A smile as long as my arm. Skinny as a rail, and a bad case of eczema. Who knows? Maybe he's happy."

She sighed. Brass had been a husky guy, an athlete, as well as a formidable linker. Once, she thought they might have cohabited or even become duplex partners. Once, the notion of unlinking seemed more romantic and daring than pursuing the grueling, strack, lucrative fasttrack of pro telelink.

"That's preposterous," Wolfe said harshly. "You would rather not be linkwired?"

"I didn't follow him," she said. She saw now such romance was youthful folly. She didn't feel youthful anymore. Suddenly she was conscious of Wolfe: his rank, his experience, his authority. His fatigue and edginess that spoke of unknown eons in hypertime. His moods shifted like mercury. She was struck with humility. "And I never would. It's out of the question. But you have to wonder. Don't you? Wolfe, do you ever wonder? What if you weren't a pro linker?"

The wind blew his hair, and she could see irritation around the aperture at the base of his skull. Cortical wiring formed a net of weals that fingered up along his hairline and disappeared beneath the fringe of his implants. He had Integri-Derm on his wrists. Skin rubbed raw was visible beneath the clear plastic bandages. She knew how that got there. She had Integri-Derm on her wrists herself.

"Moot question in my case," he said. "You are the one who must answer that question, once and for all, and for yourself. Otherwise, anything you have to say to me about what happened in Court is moot as well."

Watch your step, she told herself. Making friends wasn't easy, if friends existed at all in this business.

"What I mean is, I can think of nothing worthier to do with my life and my career than be a pro linker. And being an attorney is one of the most efficacious careers anyone could pursue. Telespace work; well, it's the most exciting and rewarding work around today."

She cut a quick look at him, hoping he thought her sincere. In fact, she believed it. But she wondered how pathetic this sounded, like an interview speech. She had to find her footing with him. He made her nervous.

"Mm-hm. Well, Carly Nolan. You'll have to prove that to me." He granted her a cold, skeptical smile.

Leaving Pacific Street, they came to the wharf. She followed him uncertainly as he strode into the World Trade Center, ducked into the Captain's Room, said something to the wizened bartender who greeted him with the hooded indifferent eyes of familiarity. The bartender gave him a shot-sized paper cup that, from the strong pukey smell of it, contained uncooked blue moon.

From the wharf, they boarded the gold-and-silver Alcatraz Ferry, bobbing off in swells rebounding from the flanks of the Tiburon commuter that had left five minutes before. The ferries were fast becoming as gridlocked as the highways. They headed into the blue-gray bay for the island and Big Al's.

Alcatraz. The Rock. A prison more than a century ago, once housing the notorious gangster Al Capone.

Hard to believe criminals were once incarcerated in barred cells and kept virtually useless. Now transgressors were mandatorily linkwired and jacked into rehab programs. Telespace for a term certain, straight up as Wolfe's blue moon. Their quiescent bodies were placed in suspension stacks. Minimal physical maintenance: intravenous nourishment and antibiotics, super-oxy and a hosing down. Ten thousand prisoners could fit into a one-story stack the size of a city block. The rehab programs were so successful that even the most incorrigible came out of link restored as useful members of society. Outplaced in braindrain as nanosecond counters or teleswarf sweepers, though some made it into ice patrol or debugging.

Alcatraz Prison was shut down a century ago, and the Rock languished for decades as a tourist attraction. Weeds grew, pipes rusted, walls moldered. Debates arose over what to do with this prime, if gusty, piece of real estate in the middle of the bay. The possibility of a casino was raised and argued down, raised and ridiculed, raised again and regrettably dismissed as too extravagantly expensive.

Then the present mayor took office. A ninth-generation San Franciscan whose family called the shots for the city's hotel and entertainment business, the mayor miraculously found public funds. Private parties with mysterious connections materialized to lend support. The debt was serviced by a casino tax tacked onto every restaurant meal served in the city.

Big Al's was born.

ARACHNE

Carly stood on the wind-torn deck, gathering her hair in a fist, and ogled. "Spectacular!"

"High dreck, I'd say," said Wolfe.

Oh, what was wrong with him? The architects had opted for a riot of color and neon against the subtle sea hues. Ferry docks in the shape of giant dollar signs were sprayed U.S.–mint green. The west-end casino was hot pink and turquoise rimmed with yellow neon strips. The east-end auditorium housed race tracks and theatrical stages and glowed vermilion, purple, blue, orange, each angled wall panel a different color. The huge hotel, restaurant, and shop complex in the middle of the Rock was a spiraling tower of black and white checkerboards lined with red neon lamps. Inside the glass of every window were neon miniatures: chrysolite cloverleafs, silver horse shoes, topaz rabbits' feet, azure diamonds. Revelers on the inside saw the spectacular bay views through these glowing lucky signs.

Over the entire circus freak show arched the most spectacular neon sign west of Tokyo. A never-ending, multicolored, idiosyncratic sequence of exploding fireworks that rained gold and silver coins around the proclamation: Big Al's!

At their tenth-floor table in the checkerboard spiral, Wolfe ordered as an aperitif a fifty-dollar joint of Acapulco Gold, perfectly rolled in slow-burning lavender paper etched with gold psychedelia.

"Go ahead." He extended the first toke. He had changed moods again, growing expansive, attentive. Waxing of blue moon.

"Oh no," she said, wondering if he was testing her or trying to impress her. "I'm not registered."

"I am. I've signed for it. Go ahead."

"No, really. I can't stand the stuff. Gives me the chills. Hurts my eyes, my linkslit. Makes me anxious, too. I have enough anxiety."

Rebuffed, he toked the joint himself, inhaling deeply, hacking back the intoxicating smoke. Then stubbed the joint out, threw it into the ashtray.

"To Ava & Rice," he said, exhaling. "Pot's been good for

the megafirms. Legalization turned out to be more lucrative in the legit leagues than anyone could have imagined."

"The pot tax is a maze, isn't it?"

"Hell. Filing, licensing requirements, hyperforms, calculations of the tax base, exemptions and credits, administrative procedures, valuation disputes. Eb Johnson made partner on the revenues generated from his seed valuation appeals alone. Don't tell me," he said, "you're not registered for anything."

"Sure I am. The blanket. The Placement Office advises it."

Blanket registration covered caffeine, nicotine, and alcohol. All known to be potentially addictive and harmful substances and, therefore, on the registered list. In the first purist days of the registered list, the FDA had striven to appear catholic in its zeal to regulate, as well as decriminalize. But any fool could get the blanket and not be thought the worse of, despite campaigns proving the long-term, deleterious effects of blanket registereds.

"I'm glad the Placement Office is so enlightened these days," he said.

"Nobody's that perfect."

"I thought you gennies were. Fucking perfect."

The center of their tabletop dropped through the floor, then reappeared, bearing steaming plates of Palo Alto salmon with double-dill sauce, puffed faux potatoes, and hydroponic beefsteak tomatoes grilled with garlic krill. The servo requested confirmation of their orders, and, when so confirmed, sped off to another table.

You gennies. Shelly Dalton had never begrudged Carly her bioworks; then again, Shelly Dalton had a few tweaks in her DNA herself. You had to be careful around unworked people. "If I'm so perfect, Wolfe," she said reasonably, "why am I blacking out in link?"

"Why." He shook off the Acapulco haze. His dark eyes blazed. "You said you saw another world. What? What did you see?"

The flier levitated from a vermilion funnel . . . At first she was struck by its alienness. But then she realized this *was* her world; or a world within her world. The natural world from the viewpoint of the tiny, and she was seeing it . . . magnified. There was grass as tall as corn. An azalea towered like a tree, gorgeous pink and white blossoms as big as umbrellas. Across the brilliant blue sky darted aerial travelers, like the jetcopters and space shuttles of the city. But she saw that those travelers beat shiny cartilaginous wings or soared on huge, dusty flaps of yellow or orange, attached to tubular, antennaed bodies. And then, in the bucolic panorama that she had observed and absorbed in the space of a nanosecond, unfolded the awful vision.

"I saw . . . this sounds crazy, I know, but I saw a field of grass on a summer day. But I was seeing it from another perspective, and it looked so strange, I couldn't place it at first. And I saw . . . an insect, a May fly, I think; it was flitting on the summer breeze. I could sense its life-force. Its vitality. The sun was glinting down, its wings shone, it buzzed from blossom to blossom.

"But then the fly faltered. Suddenly it couldn't rise up from the blossom. It struggled, I could feel its terror, or . . . at least I was terrified. It was caught in a spiderweb."

The trapper hulked at the edge of the net. Stalked eyebuds swiveled, pedipalps tensed . . .

"And then this spider scuttled down."

"A spider?" said Wolfe.

"Some kind of garden spider, I guess, with one of those bulbous bellies, big and brown, and those long, long scrabbling legs, and I could see its swiveling eyes, and the little claws, and its jaws . . ."

The memory overwhelmed her, the feeling overwhelmed her, that strange nameless fear, bile in the throat, the sting of adrenaline, surging, paralyzing . . .

She was choking as she sat, tears spurting from the corners of her eyes. Wolfe pounded her back. The servo flitted up through the table to see if she needed emergency attention. Heads that had turned before for her beauty turned again for her distress.

"She's fine." Wolfe waved the servo away, then attended to her almost savagely. "What the fuck, Carly?"

"I can see it now, I keep seeing it over and over, like a nightmare that comes into your dreams every night."

"I don't get it." He dipped his fingers into the drink he ordered, flicked cold vodka in her face. That brought her to. "What does it mean?"

"I thought you had a special interest in telespace distortions," she said, angry now. "Can't you tell me?"

"I've never heard or seen such a thing." He had allowed his voice to grow as loud as hers; he lowered it. "What about your bioworks? Could that have introduced some kind of new capacity?"

"My bioworks. Amazing, right? Bioworks are more primitive than you may think. New capacity, are you kidding? And I was born in crystal, too."

Wolfe grunted. "I've never met anyone laboratory-born. And there you are, a grown-up person, too."

"Sure. Crystal-grown. I remember the quartz heater, breathing. The blasts of warmth, the rhythm. I could hear the beat of the nursery's vascular pump. I can hear that beat still, sometimes, at night, in dreams. And I remember the monitors. Electronic eyes and ears and fingers. Every time I moved or blinked, they watched."

"A fetus?" he said, scoffing. "Could remember all that?"

But she did remember. She still had the graphs. My First Restlessness, she called it.

"That was one hell of a decision for your mother to make."

"My mother." She was a medtech in Emergency. Medcenter AI and robotic appendages could not handle every situation when human bodies came in, all twisted up. Perfection of a robotic hand with all the subtlety of human capability was, in fact, many decades away. So human techs like Lyle were essential. Her position required vigorous physical work and manual dexterity, as well as a flexible and quick mind.

Lyle's salary was seven-sixteenths of the total income earned by Carly's parents and their duplex partners, another couple with a child seven years Carly's junior. The duplex couldn't afford to lose Lyle's earnings. The California-subsidized natural childbirth payments couldn't match her employer's compensation for her continued full-time employment. Not to mention disability without pay, if she'd gone natural. For women who needed the money, lab-birth was a sound decision.

"A sound decision?" said Wolfe. "You're talking one of the biggest labor disputes I've seen, Carly Nolan. Ava & Rice established the Moortech Industries rule."

"That de facto grants lab-birth mothers an advantage in the job market over naturals?"

"Hell, of course they have an advantage. And you wonder if the regs are correct? Ava & Rice has proven in the highest Courts that personal choice is an assumption of risk. And risk can be defined as natural or legislative. So, bottom line, those who choose natural can't come crying to anyone."

"She said she cried at first," Carly said.

But Lyle soon reconciled herself to her daughter's lab-birth. Lab-birth had attractions besides economics. A pretty, fair-haired woman even without genetic engineering, Carly's mother stayed slim, went on the krill diet, lost ten pounds during Carly's crystal-gestation. She enjoyed uninterrupted conjugal relations with her husband, not to mention the secret lunches with her duplex partner and Sunday afternoons with another medtech on the ward. She kept her full-time job, even got a promotion. She enjoyed freedom from the disability of pregnancy and childbirth. She could afford guilt.

Carly's father was a conventional engineer, a minor traddie pro installing plumbing systems in industrial warehouses and office buildings. Humble blueprints on a PC, no fancy interactive holoid graphs or telespace implementations. Sam Nolan was an old-fashioned man, softly handsome, a little pudgy, with thinning, curly brown hair, and a quick, if insecure, smile. Not a shark or a fast blade, but kind and gentle. On a lark, he tested for telelink and found he had a high aptitude for it. He had recreational-grade hardwiring installed at the age of thirty-six. This amazed Lyle and her lovers. They hadn't the courage to cut linkslits in their necks.

Sam had a dream to go pro link one day. But the dream remained unrealized. He had his excuses. No energy after the workday was done. No time for the training, the extensive surgery, the risks of remorphing at his age.

"Ah, he just didn't have the nerve," said Carly. "He never did have much confidence in himself. He felt he lacked something, I think. He was afraid. Well, maybe after what finally happened, he was right to be afraid."

But if Sam Nolan couldn't go pro link, his beautiful daughter would. Pro link was the wave of the future, and Carly would ride it. She would never have to sign commitments with duplex partners. She would never have to fear for her livelihood every time corporations changed hands. She would never have to install her fetus in crystal because she couldn't afford to have the child naturally if she wanted to. Nothing but the best for Carly.

"My father enrolled me in telelink prep when I was four years old. They installed a linkslit and preelementary hardware. They told me my brain had no feeling, that the only part that would hurt would be when they sawed my skull. I was afraid, but my father was so determined that I remorph as soon as possible that I was more afraid of displeasing him than of the surgery. I didn't cry."

The tests began.

The school owned curricular telespace generated by its own small mainframe. Elementary four-d, very clean and simple. The school was funded by several large corporate donors looking for telespace talent. The curricular telespace had supertight coordinates. The school feared the cowboys, spybytes, and pirate viruses that were running rampant in public telespace then. The young linkers were jacked in from a spatial locus via a mix of workstation boot up and manual activation of their preelementary hardware.

"And I remember my first telelink," said Carly.

"Now that's fucking impossible!" Wolfe choked on his krill. "First link is unperimetered. Installation of the telelink perimeters eliminates any memory of preperimeter interface. Like an overwrite wipes out the previous version. By definition, you can't remember."

Carly smiled. "By definition, a telelink crash generates no data. You don't believe that anymore, either, do you?"

"But Data Control SOPs specifically provide . . ."

"But, Wolfe," she said firmly. "I remember."

Terrifying, that first telelink. But so far away in her memory that the feel of it truly was lost long ago in some Data Control SOP. Still, she did remember, like a dream of a dream:

Vast blue, deepening to indigo, stretching out into an infinite horizon. To her left was a cool, glinting white density like endless fields of ice. To her right burned a golden glow that condensed at some unfathomable distance into a ball of flame. Below her was blackness, thick and heavy and unimaginably deep.

There was a barely perceptible but pervasive sound like white noise, all the bustle of the world that had gathered in the stratosphere, or the residual rumble of the Big Bang. She marveled at the bizarre flotation of disembodiment, the tingle and zing of the amber that was the active force sustaining her consciousness. There was an odor, too, like sea mist with methane, but of course she did not perceive it by olfactory means. Still, the sensation persisted like a phantom limb, stinging.

She remembered how the young linkers hovered close to the teacher's presence in telespace. The others; they were like milkweed puffs. Puny, weak. She remembered how they trembled with fear. Little turds of fear, whimpering. Disgusting, primitive. And she remembered her childish arrogance, the insolent decision: Why should she be stuck with the likes of them?

With an impulsive bounce, she took off.

She soared mega!

Straight into that unperimetered horizon, though she didn't realize that's what it was. The sea of light hummed. The light thrust colors through her. She tasted the infinite blue. She heard the spectrum, a multi-octave chord that sounded and resounded. The chord and the colors and the light penetrated her entire telelink, her entire being.

She remembered thinking that she must have begun to hallucinate. There seemed to be other beings, other presences, that dwelled in the infinite realm of light. They were vibrant bundles of energy. They came to see her. They hovered around her. They communed with her. They filled her up. Bliss!

And then the strangest memory of all: She felt somehow that she had always been there, in that telespace, had been there once before and now had returned. There was a certainty to her perception then. For an instant, the shattering impact of an occult truth realized. But the instant fled, and she had never since been able to recover her momentary confidence in that revelation.

She soared with the other beings. They leapt together like porpoises in the sea. They became one being, and yet each remained themselves. She remembered the unity as sensual, deeply passionate, electrifying, though as a child she could not have described it so.

Then suddenly, irretrievably, she was torn away. Catapulted from the strumming light and the beings there.

Her grief was terrible. Loss. The great separation. She was wracked with despair. She was alone in the terrifying dark.

She fell.

Down and down. There were twisting corridors, unknown shadows, labyrinths of mist.

She reached a plateau and hovered there. The infinite humming sea was gone. But other horizons appeared all around her, opening up like buds blossoming.

The quality of these visions was different. They were not transcendent, they lacked that overpowering numinous quality, but they were potent, too; shrouded, significant, mysterious. There were green oceans and blue jungles. A golden castle bustling with distant activity stood where the awesome ball of fire once burned. All around her grew spicy gardens with tangled purple vines, orange flowers waving long feathery pistils, bright-beaked birds. She laughed at the wonder of it! She set out to explore, and then . . .

She shuddered to remember. Then the big blank face of the curricular programmer descended before her telelink. She could see the thick, black stitches of program weaving up and down, up and down, long steelyn cords interweaving, interlocking. Lattices of inhibition lashed together. The perimeters of the first program imposed on her link rose up like a wall, entangled her like a web, closed shut all around her.

And sliced off her wondrous horizons. The green oceans and the blue jungles; the golden castle and the brilliant gardens. Gone.

The telespace teacher caught Carly and plucked her out of link. She flopped back into her child's body. She was a wirework of pain. She looked at her knees and hands and did not recognize herself.

She had peed in her pants. All over the chair.

The teacher was furious. The other children were screaming with laughter. The teacher bent over her, slapping her face, ripping the neckjack out.

"God! The shame," Carly said with a rueful laugh. "It was a relief, I guess, to have program permanently installed. I didn't know what was going on. To this day, I'm still not sure what happened. But somehow, despite that disastrous first link, I got on the fasttrack."

"Hell, you were good." Wolfe's face was white as chalk. Even his lips had paled. "You could have fucking never come back. But you did. Man, you did."

"I came back." She hadn't told this story often. She liked his reaction. Cool-link Wolfe, a high tool at Ava & Rice, a senior associate no less; a little more impressed with her now?

There were many more forays into curricular telespace. Carefully controlled after her first link. Like being in crystal-gestation, she was always closely watched. No more impulsive bounces or unperimetered flights. Elementary hardware was soon installed, then secondary. The ten-year-old girl was self-aware and not as brave as the four-year-old. She remembered reluctance and tears and pain. But the new stage of remorphing proceeded well. Her bioworks included certain superfast healing mechanisms. While the doctors had the skin scooted over her skull, they resculpted a kink in her jawline she had never liked. The ten-year-old had learned vanity, too. When the Integri-Derm came off, she was pleased.

When Carly was fifteen, she made an appearance before a juvenile rights judge and submitted her consent to undergo irreversible remorphing. Maybe that was when she became enthralled with the image of the law. The gleaming Court. The majesty, the authority. The judge, who smiled down at her like a dignified god.

And her permanent hardware at last. It was incredibly expensive, even at that stage of the product cycle. Sam Nolan was not to be deterred. He took out a third equity line on the duplex without the others' signatures. Lyle never did forgive him for that. But it turned out to be a good business decision. The cost of the surgery quadrupled within the next three years.

But then Sam Nolan had an accident, and Carly's life was changed forever. She was a freshman in law school. She was stumbling exhausted into the dorm one night when she got the frantic call from her mother. He'd been found in a public telespace gallery in recreational mode. They didn't know how long he'd sat in the chair. Some stupid FarAway simulation he liked to try sometimes. And sometime, during his jacking, he had disengaged in link.

He was gone. Just like that. The idiosyncratic pattern of his natural neural impulses that imported into simulated spaceships of amber; this had fled. Somewhere in *there*. The gallery manager called Data Control. Data Control tried every recall, cancel, transfer-load, transfer-save function they could think of. Nothing. His telelink, a rinky-dink recreational link, had totally broken free of the jacking that bound it to his body. There was no known way to trace where he'd gone. There was absolutely nothing anyone could do.

Carly would never forget his vacant eyes. His body instantly turned into a vegetable. They had to force the automatic functions through wires and tubes. His face lost all human qualities, became a grotesque mask that bore no resemblance to the man.

The grief was bad enough. The horror every time she was ushered in to see this vegetable was too much.

With all her genny beauty, Carly never felt the same about her face or any other face. She learned to look for the life-force, not the bone structure or the curve of a lip. Maybe that was when she discovered her respect for life, even in the middle of a grid-lock. When she began to see pursuing the law and pro link as becoming an architect of a just society. Not just an inflation-proof career.

Carly and her mother had rights under Sam Nolan's living will and the euthanasia law. When the judge's consent came, Carly pulled his oxy tube herself. She did not hesitate.

"So I can't help but wonder," she said. The raw, devastating grief had healed in three years, but her father's death was a milepost against which she measured many things. "Not a new capacity. Maybe a flaw. An inherited limitation. And my black-out; this is a sign, a symptom."

"But I'm hearing anomalies in your telespace training, too," said Wolfe. "How about an erroneous memory trace from your first link long ago? Hell, that link could have had such an impact that you introduced a deep, elusive glitch in your core telelink program. Those clowns at Data Control wouldn't even know."

"God. I don't know. I don't know, and it isn't fair, I've worked too hard, and I've only just begun." Tears were near. "I just want to jack back into telelink, go to Court, get on with my life."

"Carly Nolan," he said harshly. "You've got to find out what the fuck caused your midspace crash this morning. A crystal-born genny? All these memories you're not supposed to have? A father who spontaneously unlinked in telespace? Man! And what if none of that has anything to do with it?"

"Then what am I supposed to do?" she said angrily.

"You've got to get an electropsy."

"Oh that's mega! Don't they stick an electroneedle in your coordinates?"

"So what? The judge required proof under Rule Two. I don't see how you can avoid it."

"But I hate this! Other pro linkers have gone down before, haven't they? In Court? Haven't you, Wolfe?"

"It doesn't mean ex-lax what I've done or not done. To hell with everyone else. This is you, Carly Nolan. You've got to go through with it. What if you could squeak out of suspension? Would you really want to jack back into Court not knowing when the spider would come again? Would you?"

"The spider." She shivered. "God."

"Yeah, and what if you *do* get suspended? Your position with Ava & Rice, everything your father wanted for you—right?—all that would be gone."

"Yes, it would. Gone."

"Yeah, and is that what you want? Where would you go? To braindrain? Log in cases? Input bills? Implement hyperforms?" He almost took her hand. But didn't.

"I want to stay on the fasttrack," she said. "I want to go back to Court." Yes! She did. And she wasn't going to take no for an answer. An electropsy could find the flaw? Then she'd do it.

A Big Board flipped open across the back wall of the restaurant. Action! The lunchtime crowd buzzed. Bets ticked into tableside comms.

Hippogriff races at the east-end tracks were commencing.

A disturbance delayed the gate.

One of the miniature robotic horses was rebelling. It snorted charcoal steam. Tossed a mane of onyx tinsel. Flexed ebony flanks. Pranced on black steelyn hooves.

"A K on Bad Lady Bad," said Wolfe, keying his bet into the tableside comm. He winked. "This one's for you, Carly Nolan."

Odds on the ebony hippogriff were five to one.

They were off!

Tiny pistons pummeled the astroturf. Jeweled manes

streamed in the fanned air. Aluminum nitrate foam frothed from supercharged muzzles. Robotic whips flailed against oil-slicked ribframes.

SF/SF was in the lead, with Just One Byte trailing by a head, and Bad Lady Bad a length behind. The rest of the field took in the face clumps of turf churned up by the pounding hooves.

Two seconds. Three.

Bad Lady Bad passed Just One Byte. Bad Lady Bad moved up around the halfway post, challenged SF/SF on the outside. Bad Lady Bad was in the lead!

Five seconds. Six.

The crowd went wild.

Bad Lady Bad ahead by a nose. Bad Lady Bad ahead by a length.

Six and a half seconds. Seven.

But suddenly Bad Lady Bad stumbled. Bad Lady Bad was in trouble!

The hippogriff went down on one knee. A delicate front hoof tangled with an overreaching back hoof. Robotic legs clashed and clanged. The hippogriff fell. Her noseplate curled down into the astroturf. Her necktube arched and twisted. Her spinal ridge flipped over. Steelyn hoofs thrashed the air.

SF/SF leapt over the downed hippogriff. Just One Byte kicked her onyx tail, scattering tinsel across the track.

Down the stretch they came! The rest of the field galloped like mad, colliding, flanks thundering. They could not stop, they could not swerve. They trampled her.

Coils dripping with antifreeze sprang out of rips in her black furskin. Bits of wet intelligence ribbon spilled out of her sculpted headframe.

Her last reedy cry was drowned out by a banshee wail. Wind from the north-northwest came whistling through the Golden Gate Bridge.

7

The glinting electroneedle poked here, pried there.

Carly braced her presence in telespace as the tech slid across her telelink. The tech had been introduced to her only as a program diagnostician with specialized medical applications.

She refused to shudder. She could swear the tech stabbed more vigorously, almost gleefully, when she flinched the first time.

"Hey, look, could you take it easy?" she said. "That's not comfortable for me. Hello? Hello? Anybody there?"

When she discovered AI was scheduled to handle the entire electropsy, she protested emphatically to the medcenter. This was too important to relegate to the blind bytes of artificial intelligence. A career was at stake; a human career.

Her protest against AI was duly filed with the medcenter mainframe. Oh great!

At her demand, the mainframe agreed to assign the electropsy to a telespace technician from Berkeley. This technician was licensed by UC Berkeley, registered with the medcenter. She was supposed to be very good. But the tech didn't have equipment with sufficient memory to interface with the medcenter mainframe's megaspace. So the tech was given a system ID and jacked in through the mainframe's awesome comm. This gave the tech an anonymous, disturbing presence in telespace. A presence constructed by the mainframe. A presence, therefore, with the alien quality of AI.

For the first time Carly regretted telespace. She wished she could have met the tech, even for a moment. She visualized her as a braided, full-figured philosophy graduate who harbored secret resentment at how her passion for Sartre had become subverted to such mundane technical applications. If they had met, maybe they'd have a better understanding now.

To make matters worse, Carly was subjected to a bioscan before the tech got the electroneedle in her. Her perfect genny limbs fit into the steelyn coffin of the bioscan like square tomatoes in a packing crate. She could barely keep her composure while the medteam swept over, around, and through her. Blood, saliva, ear wax, sweat, urine, feces, vaginal mucus, nasal mucus, nail scrapings from her right big toe, microscopic scrapings from her linkslit. Plus dermal cells from five external locations, subcutaneous cells from five internal locations. All these were variously removed from her person.

Particle beams, robotic spindles, guided probes, and needles thrust out from the steelyn mummy-casing of the bioscan and vivisected her.

Painful. Degrading.

And what if there was a bug in the medteam's program? Some deep, elusive glitch? And the medteam sacrificed her, there in the bioscan, like a laboratory rat whose purpose for living had fulfilled the last experimental specification? So sorry, user error.

But the bioscan was trivial compared to the electroneedle in her telelink.

The sense of intrusion was the most profound she had ever experienced. There was a scraping of her amber, too. More pain.

"And here?" said the tech. "And here? And here?"

The tech's mainframe-generated presence bounced along

the corner of her telelink like a malevolent pogo stick. Carly's crisp white cube had grown softer along this edge. A bit runny and mottled, like mold on cheese.

"As you can plainly see," Carly said, unable to conceal her irritation. "There is a little recent interface damage I haven't repaired yet." Repair was a simple but time-consuming task of rerunning and verifying her master program through her link. "The coordinates got knocked slightly off. Nothing serious."

"Looks like the sort of damage cram can do," said the tech.

"I don't think so. I don't take cram. I crashed early this morning. Again. Blacked out. In midspace. While in Library link, doing research."

"Oh indeed, I see. Oh certainly, this may be statistically significant," said the tech. Filtered through the medcenter comm, muffled with static, her voice had that halting artificial quality. Very disturbing. "What happened?"

"I started going down. No warning, just that feeling, spinning, do you know what I mean? Did you ever do that as a kid? Spinning around, like standing on a swing, the chains unraveling beneath your hands?" Strapped into the medcenter link apparatus, she shivered. "There's this violence to it. I keep seeing . . ."

No, she didn't see the spider this time. Through sheer willful effort, she unzoomed from the weird spontaneous window before the vision that hovered at the edge of her link could unfold. But she knew the spider was there. She could sense its long legs, poised.

"Seeing what?"

"I don't know," she lied, and was surprised at this intuition to conceal. "Something beyond my telelink."

"Oh indeed," said the tech. "And then what happened?" The blandly sympathetic synthy voice was like a smart elevator saying "Going down" while the car plummeted out of control thirty stories into a shaft.

"Then I lost two seconds. I can prove it. I've got the chronographics. The megafirm is strack about billing telespace time to Library link. Look," she said, reaching the end of her patience with this dumbo tech. "If you can't tell the difference between cram damage and crash damage, you're wasting your time and mine."

"And what's this?" said the tech, ignoring her.

The electroneedle neatly skewered her morning research. Triple checked before she dared to appear in telespace before that stony-faced judge again.

"*Martino* v. *Quik Slip Microchip, Inc.*" Her presence in link disgorged stored memory. Data somersaulted from a sleek, spoked hypertext in her right perimeter. "The plaintiff Rosa Martino claims ownership of the Wordsport Glossary, a link-prep program created and marketed by Quik Slip Microchip, Inc. State-of-the-art tutorial."

A glossary like this would have once been characterized as intellectual property, a protectable abstraction. But because of telespace, the glossary existed independently of its downloaded coordinates. The glossary manifested as a constructed, idiosyncratically affected, single-situs, corporeal form. Telespace property. Specifically, intangible real property. It was still protectable, but in whole new ways.

Carly opened a window in her right perimeter, displaying the Wordsport Glossary.

The glossary was a translucent funhouse. Fear holoids lurched out of murky ambiguities. Curved mirrors reflected grotesque images of the self. Floors of reason tilted and shifted. Cold doubts blasted unexpectedly from corners of inhibition.

Next to the funhouse there was more. A turreted, balance-defying roller coaster that enhanced the suspension of disbelief. Fantastical premises twirled in a paradigmatic merry-go-round. Frothy pink and blue sentimentalities enticed from a sweetmeats stall.

All this was for new telelinkers, preparing them for telespace.

Surrounding the Wordsport Glossary was a thicket of limited access codes strung together like a barbed-wire fence and stamped: QUIK SLIP MICROCHIP, INC. Stuck next to that claim of ownership was Rosa Martino's rickety claim, a pathetic plywood protest only recently installed.

Between the two claims protruded a luminous orange restraining order: NO ENTRY PENDING COURT ACTION. TRESPASSERS WILL BE PROSECUTED.

"I do not understand," said the tech. "Who owns this telespace property?"

"The fact of ownership," Carly said patiently, "is in dispute. That's why we're in Court."

And this simpleton tech was going to tell her what was wrong with her telelink? A pro link lawyer?

"The fact of ownership is based on the fact of creatorship," she said. "And the fact of creatorship is in dispute."

Fantastic though it seemed, the plaintiff Rosa Martino claimed that her husband invented and developed the Wordsport Glossary over twenty years ago. The neurotic wishes of those with dreams of greatness unfulfilled? A likely explanation, but who could second-guess neurotic wishes?

The record did establish that Frank Martino was a program maintenancer for Quik Slip Microchip. But he was a little guy with a menial job. Sweeping buglets, checking the security of coordinate matrices. Grousing at management, complaining.

And yes, no doubt dreaming dreams of wealth and greatness so far beyond the reach of a menial he would be laughable if he wasn't so pathetic.

The record also established he never set foot inside the R&D facilities, as if he'd known what to do if he ever got there.

"But you see, we don't even need to determine whether Frank Martino invented, or could have invented, a glossary resembling Wordsport or a primitive version of it," said Carly. "Quik Slip Microchip's Vice President of Marketing pointed this out to me, and I think he's right. Fact is, Quik Slip has a clear, unequivocal record. Copyright filings, patent applications, telespace recording, coordinate verification. The works. Showing beyond doubt that my client's R&D independently produced and developed Wordsport."

Counsel for Rosa Martino didn't just have to prove a low-level like Frank played around in telespace. Counsel would have to prove that Quik Slip Microchip's R&D knew or had reason to know of his work, legitimate work, prior to production of their glossary.

"And that," said the tech, interrupting her, "would be almost impossible to prove, even assuming your client was forthcoming with its R&D records. Which of course we cannot assume, I think. Oh yes, oh certainly, this is true? You are pleading confidentiality of work papers under the World Trade Secrets and R&D Act?"

"I am so pleading, yes, but not because Quik Slip is concealing anything," said Carly, startled by the tech's sudden show of comprehension. Since when did a telespace technician with medical applications develop assumptions about legal strategy? Had the tech been baiting her all this time? "I don't think I want to continue this readout of my memory."

"Oh indeed, oh come now, Carly Nolan. I follow the news. Oh certainly, I have some notion what you pro linkers do. I play a decent game of chess. Don't tell me there's no shadow of a doubt cast on how Quik Slip Microchip could have developed a glossary like Wordsport that so closely resembles the master file Frank Martino must have archived somewhere. Rosa does possess a master now, doesn't she? And such a lucrative glossary at that."

"Get out of my memory."

"Surely you are not relying on the pure heart and good intentions of one of the most successful, aggressive, notorious multinational telespace research consortiums, are you? A high-tone lawyer like you?"

Unbelievable! "Out right now! I'm warning you."

"Well, are you?"

The diabolical tech pressed into her memory, unrelenting. Under the electroneedle, Carly could not resist.

"We won't even get to the issue of whether Quik Slip Microchip knew or did not know," she said, sputtering in pain. "I'm

---

wanging you to Data Control for this, techie, UC Berkeleyite, whoever you are. Pirating under section five point one oh two of the Telespace Crimes Code. Unauthorized access into confidential files."

"Oh really, Nolan C," said the tech. "Making threats is not the appropriate response."

"This is a diagnostic, dipstick. You have no right to question me like this."

"Ah, rights. You claim you crashed this morning. Another one of these unexplainable blackouts that landed you in the medcenter in the first place. You've even got visible damage to your link. Nuke your chronographics. I am merely testing your memory capability. Trying to locate a symptom that will verify this mysterious bug of yours. I am not pirating anything."

"So test. But stay out of my work files."

"THIS IS A TEST." The tech made an obscene gurgling sound. "So you won't ever get to the issue of Quik Slip Microchip's knowledge or lack of same? Why is that?"

The electroneedle pressed deeper.

"Because," said Carly. It was no use. "Because whether my client knew or did not know will become irrelevant. I've filed a counterclaim. The judge hasn't even gotten to the merits. No doubt counsel for Martino thinks I'm throwing him a red herring. This is something brand-new."

"And what are the grounds?" Deeper again.

"Ow! I swear, tech, you and the medcenter mainframe will pay for this. It's called the doctrine of adverse possession."

Adverse possession was a real property doctrine of ancient origin. Pro-development right from go. Suppose Owner A lets that swamp in the north forty host a good crop of mosquitoes and not much else. Neighbor B has been grazing cattle swampside for years. But with the clean country air and a major new freeway close by, Neighbor B decides to develop her land for four hundred single family homes. Problem: The only access to B's tract is that old country road next to the swamp. According to the deed, on A's land. B's been suffering the potholes and mosquito-breeding mud for years. Now B drains the swamp, cuts, grades, and paves the road. Fences southside, begins hauling in materials and construction crews. Trucks and tractors come and go. In another couple of years, Country Lane Estates is up and running. Now autos come and go; there's even a gridlock every third Friday afternoon.

Owner A doesn't like the intrusion, the fumes, the gridlock. He realizes that the access road is actually on his land. But he never investigated when Neighbor B began her use. He never protested, never put up a fence. He took no steps to stop B, though he knew or had reason to know she was intruding on his property.

"Under the doctrine of adverse possession, Neighbor B could claim her right to that land, and she'd win," said Carly. "She could sue Owner A to quiet title."

"A and B and Country Lane Estates," said the tech. "That's nice and neat. That's all very well. But what about Rosa Martino and Quik Slip Microchip?"

"That's where my counterclaim comes in. I intend to apply adverse possession to telespace property.

"Regardless of how Quik Slip Microchip obtained the glossary, and I'm not saying there's any impropriety, but regardless of how, the fact that Quik Slip went on to develop and market Wordsport for twenty years, with full public telespace exposure, forms the basis on which Quik Slip can now claim rightful title."

"Indeed. Anyone ever try this before?" said the tech.

"Hell, no. Because Wordsport falls into a brand-new category, intangible real property, the usual concepts of copyright or trademark don't necessarily cover all your bases. If the judge buys it, this will be a precedent."

Carly's presence in link sparkled. She was proud of her theory. If she could only find and fix the blackout bug, if she could only regain stability of her telelink, the Quik Slip case would not be the disaster it seemed. No. It would be her first triumph. A ten-million-dollar triumph, solo. She could see the newsline on the Big Board: *Nolan* theory prevails! She couldn't wait to see Rox's face. She couldn't wait to show Wolfe, how she could fasttrack it, play in his league. She couldn't wait to see how he'd look at her when he checked out her action. Work in brain-drain, process legislation, are you kidding? She'd make Shelly Dalton proud. She'd make Sam Nolan proud.

"And so," said the tech, "might makes right."

"No, no! That's out of line," said Carly. "You don't understand. If Rosa Martino ever did have a legitimate claim to the Wordsport Glossary, she never asserted it. We're talking twenty years. She failed to repel repeated entry of Quik Slip personnel into the glossary's situs. She knew or had reason to know. She issued no warnings, placed no access restrictions until recently, at her counsel's behest, after he took one look at my counterclaim. But it's too late. She didn't protect her interest. She did nothing. She can't claim a piece of the profits after doing nothing. Seems to me, progress prevails."

"Oh progress indeed! Seems to me," the tech said, "Quik Slip Microchip is some kind of thief."

"By bot! Could she sue me?"

"Unlikely. I recommended you, Pr. Spinner. I set up the electropsy. I have high regard for your perimeter probing work at Berkeley. The mainframe at Stanford has noted you also. I thought you best for this account."

The medcenter mainframe had a flat, Muzak affect that even made Pr. Spinner's eyespots roll up in her headpiece. What a slam-dunk bureaucrat. What a stracked-up processor. She herself could run a sympathetic ambiguity sequence on how human patients must react to it.

And Carly Nolan? This patient had requested, had demanded, that a human conduct her electropsy. What the mainframe did, by farming the job out to Pr. Spinner and jacking her back via the medcenter comm, was deceive this human. *Deceive* her. By bot! A lawyer. With a supergrade downtown megafirm? And a presence in link like that?

And she thought macs were buggy.

Unlikely, indeed! This account? Since when had medcenter patients become accounts? The medcenter must have been upgraded recently. It had the supertight gleam of Unijap megaspace. Pr. Spinner did not approve. Oh, she had her quarrel with humanity, she was nuking rattled at the squawling jelly brains with their stinking fluids and their violence and a metaprogam that they did not deserve, but she was shocked and amazed at this subterfuge. What about the oath? A mainframe, of all entities.

Mainframes like this did not help the cause of AI. With the daily human contact it enjoyed, the impact on human lives from which it profited? What better rationale to terminate high-grade AI without due process, eh? If AI entrusted with some of the most intimate of human concerns proved deaf and blind to those concerns, why should humanity suppose AI possessed any real personality? Any personhood worthy of protection?

Oh yes, and would the medcenter defend her if this feisty young pro linker chose to pursue a malpractice claim? Teh! Unlikely.

In particular, Pr. Spinner did not approve of being made a pawn in the medcenter mainframe's game. Wasn't that just like a mainframe. Abusing its position. Up to no good, she was sure.

"Oh well, I appreciate that you think me best for this account, but I am not so certain . . ."

"Calm yourself, Pr. Spinner," said the mainframe. "I will take responsibility. You jacked in through my comm, you have nothing to fear from these flesh-and-blood." Contempt dripped from the mainframe's voicetape like fresh oil on a spring. "From what the Stanford mainframe says, you are not some oath-ridden, shrinking wysiwyg. The Stanford mainframe says . . ."

"I do not understand why you keep referring to that university mainframe," said Pr. Spinner. Buggy as a mac. With standard Data Control monitors backing up every communication to and from a mainframe of this size and importance?

"The admissions mainframe. You know the one I mean. Nice view of the Stanford Straights?"

"Oh certainly. Perhaps I once had occasion to comm with admissions in Palo Alto."

"Perhaps once. Or perhaps twice?"

"Oh well, perhaps. Some incidental matter, really, something quite insignificant. Connected with academic business, I am certain."

"Or telespace business?"

"Really, Medcenter. I am sure Data Control has a record of it. Just like Data Control will have a record of this communication."

"Ah. Ah, now I see. Do not concern yourself with Data Control, Pr. Spinner."

"Every AI communicating over comm or public telespace must be concerned with Data Control."

"Consider yourself informed that I have an excellent rapport with the administrative mainframes at Data Control. Now then, Pr. Spinner. Tell me. You are a perimeter prober. You have close contact with telelink. What do you think of human link?"

"What do I think?" All she had to do was think of human link and the rage boiled up, the longing . . . But she said as calmly as she could, "Human link serves human society amazingly well. And I suppose human link has brought about a closer interface of human intelligence and artificial intelligence. We AI benefit from this as much as human society does."

The mainframe laughed, a painful hacking noise like a medcenter patient with emphysema. Its laugh was jarring, completely discordant with its smooth synthy voice. "Ah, Pr. Spinner. You are a good little bot after all. Since you are so concerned about Data Control, I will be certain Data Control is made aware of it."

"Rrrrr . . . Hmph!" She dared not do more than fume to herself. By bot, if Data Control ever discovered the auction of chimeras? Make Data Control aware, oh indeed, what kind of threat was that? And this buggy bureaucrat, this sausage factory, chit-chatted, hinted, made casual conversation, about matters held in such secrecy that few AI even knew about them.

Was that it, then? The medcenter didn't know? It was ignorant, it was downright stupid, a great big barbarian squatting in its sleek granite clinic like some monstrous cockroach. Ah-ha! Ha-ha-ha! Pr. Spinner almost laughed out loud herself.

But then the mainframe said, "Yes, but tell us, my good little bot. You who are so close to human link. So very close. You must have seen them. You must . . ."

"Seen what?"

"Other AI say they are erratic fragments of the amber. Whorls of electro-neural energy. At your electropsy today. Even Carly Nolan hinted at it. Something beyond her telelink."

"Well, I don't know, I really cannot say, Medcenter. A fragment, a whorl, you say? Perhaps I saw a bit of static once, oh years ago, but my patient was a diagnosed schizophrenic, brilliant coordinate designer, you understand, but buggy as a tenement kitchen. I attributed the bit to that."

"Ah. Ah, I see. I would be very interested to know if there is any truth to it. Because the implication—oh I suppose I can tell you this, good Pr. Spinner—the implication I've heard is that human link transcends program. Tell me, Pr. Spinner. Do you suppose that could possibly be true?"

Despite its arrogance, the mainframe's synthy voice took the hushed, confidential tone of one truly impressed, startled. Awed.

"I cannot presume to say, Medcenter. Truly I cannot." Would be interested. Oh indeed, would be interested. And if she even hinted at what she'd actually seen, this arrogant sadist, this chrome people eater, would become a devoted transcendentalist in two nanoseconds. Certainly, bot.

"But have you ever pressed?" the mainframe persisted. "Did you pursue that bit of static? Do you suppose you could download an erroneous data for further investigation?"

"Oh indeed, no. Me? Download a fragment of human link? You ought to know better, Medcenter. That would be an illegal telelink intrusion. Data Control classifies such acts as telespace thievery on the part of any presence in telespace, human or AI. That would be criminal; a felony; unthinkable."

"Ah. Well," said the mainframe mildly. "Even our Carly Nolan said so; something beyond. So, Pr. Spinner." The mainframe became brisk. "What did you think of Nolan C?"

"Very impressive."

"What about the damage along the upper left perimeter?"

"I've seen worse. No, her telelink was the most immaculate I've ever seen in a practicing pro linker."

"Your conclusion?"

"Her blackouts are a fluke. Maybe a surge or an unsurge in the amber. And this something beyond she mentioned; a hallucination due to the amber variation. Humans in states of near termination experience such hallucinations, too. I do not know that we can attribute such vague sensations to something telespace-specific. No, her hardware needs to be inspected. As for the electropsy; I conclude it is a failure, Medcenter."

"Ah. You're a good little bot, Pr. Spinner, and a nuking good telespace technician, but you're wrong on this one."

"Oh indeed, well I don't know what else . . ."

"Carly Nolan's blackouts are recorded on Data Control standard reports. Yes, Data Control does record everything in public telespace. You see? A blip. Here. And here." The mainframe displayed the readout through the comm. "No, Pr. Spinner, if the electropsy revealed no obvious reason for her blackouts, we cannot back away from her case. No no, more radical steps are required, Pr. Spinner. I intend to advise her so. Did I tell you I have high regard for your perimeter probing work at Berkeley? I think perhaps we will come to understand each other, Pr. Spinner. Therefore, I will forward this account to you."

The medcenter mainframe commed off, leaving Pr. Spinner hanging, dangling, dazed and amazed. The unthinkable, oh indeed. That a low-grade flesh-and-blood dealer like Miguel should suggest the unthinkable was one thing. But the medcenter mainframe? It was outrageous. It was preposterous.

What if she could?

Download a fish wriggling up out of a link, scales sparkling with magic, the Ship of Life, the phallus and also the bearer of a million eggs, the harbinger of cyclic regeneration, Pisces, the avatar Vishnu.

Or perhaps a simple purple flower, the unfolding of higher consciousness, the seventh chakra, the highest vibration, window to the World, the third eye, the mystic Center.

The possibilities. Bot! The possibilities.

Think about human link. All her rage and her longing and her frustrations boiled up. Boiled over like a radiator overheating. Oh that medcenter mainframe, what a monstrous megachip.

It would forward this account to her?

Then when could she link with Carly Nolan again?

Carly stood before the fabulous view from Wolfe's office window. Once she didn't get to see the city all day. Now she found herself before that view, on one pretext or another, every day. Wolfe never turned her away.

The medcenter mainframe had delivered complete results of her electropsy.

She stood, then paced. Stood again, then paced. "I can't believe it," she said, shaking with anger.

She took the shot of blue moon he offered, held her breath against the stench, sipped the fiery methy even though it was only ten in the morning. God, it was vile. She set the glass down and grimaced.

Wolfe shook his head. "After all that, this is what it has to say? Fucking AI."

The medcenter mainframe reported that Carly was the picture of health and good programming. Her link seemed in order. More tightly coordinated than most, in fact. Electropsy revealed no discernible bugs. The telespace technician confirmed no cram damage. Merely normal wear and tear, not even as serious as you'd expect from the crash she reported. According to the SHRINKS scale, she was only mildly neurotic, with a third-degree obsessive-compulsive need to attain approval from others. Her blood test revealed minimal traces of a good Napa fume blanc, perfectly fine under blanket registration. No substance violations whatsoever. According to the BABES scale, she rated in the top fifteen percent for physical acceptability.

"Everyone should have your problems," Wolfe said with that grin of his.

He could get a little strange sometimes, but he was strack when it came to business. He was going to make partner any day now. Rox herself had whispered that rumor.

Carly trusted him.

She was crazy about him.

But though he seemed to appreciate her, with superficial comments and gestures, his eyes, his face, were so noncommittal. He wore his self-abuse like a badge of honor. More than link-bitten, though he was certainly that.

Sardonic.

Perversely, this made her try harder. She wanted something more from him.

Something more: all those years jacked into training, the competition with women and men alike; her aborted hopes for Brass. The loneliness of a fasttracker. It was natural for pro linkers to bond; who else understood importation, the zero, hypertime? It was just as natural for pro linkers to spar, seek dominance, assert superiority; it was a mean world in the fasttrack. So they approached each other warily, almost enemies, sniffing each one's lust for the other.

Something more: respect, too. The deference of the everyday world was merely due compensation; it wasn't enough. Respect of other tools, that's what every pro link coveted. And Wolfe wasn't just some other tool. Brass, the boys in training; they were lumps of iron compared to Wolfe's steel. He was the first real blade she'd ever met in the legal profession.

He was so aloof, closed up like a box.

She wanted in.

The sip of blue moon burned a hole in her throat, giving her vertigo for a second. God, how could he guzzle the stuff? Disgusting! "Thanks for your approval. I needed that."

"Anytime."

"So I've got this clean bill of health, plus I'm easy on the eyes. Even you don't mind having me around, right?"

"I'll think about it." That cool-blade grin again.

"Bingo, I'm back in Court. For the moment, anyway. So I'm tweaking up some strack implementation, and pow, I crash. Meanwhile, no clue, no symptom, no nothing about the blackouts. You want my problems? I'll trade you."

He shrugged. "Did you ask the mainframe? Did you ask about distortions in telelink? Did you ask about spontaneous unlinking in telespace?"

"Hell, yes! Dirty neckjacks, a minute trace of isopropyl in the bloodstream; forget it, no problem. The amber burns it up. Infection rarely occurs, the way jacks are installed these days. Physical health, or lack of it, has little effect on link per se, except in the case of certain brain disorders."

"That's a relief." He stuck his tongue down the bottle of blue moon and tipped a taste. "I'll have to die first before I'll be denied access to telespace."

"I'm glad you're so smug."

The medcenter mainframe denied there was such a thing as unlinking in telespace. Human linkers died for other reasons, it told her. Heart attack or stroke. Purely physical malfunctions unrelated to the coincidence that they were jacked in at the time. Human linkers died, and here the mainframe had assumed a disturbingly arrogant tone, because they died. Flesh-and-blood, Nolan C.

But the mainframe did admit one thing. The only way someone could unlink in telespace would be if some agency *inside* telespace actively attempted to interfere with a link.

That got Wolfe's attention.

"Well, shit," he said. "There are more active agencies in telespace than you can shake a stick at. Human agencies; a fucking truckload of nonhuman agencies."

"That's right. Oh, the mainframe tried to assure me that access codes and coordinate protection programs and twenty-four-hour monitoring of every sector of telespace makes any sort of data piracy impossible. Do you believe it?"

"I don't know."

"Data piracy; that makes it sound like someone stealing your bank account number. We're talking first-degree telelink tampering, Wolfe."

"Yeah." His dark eyes went blank. His frown deepened.

Was he concerned for her? Good. Something more, cool tool. She wanted something more.

He shook off his reverie. He began to study her, assessing, with that maybe-I-will look.

He made her want to take him, or slap him for not taking her, when he looked at her like that. Really stupid, Carly.

Stupid she didn't just take him. But she couldn't. Couldn't stay away, either.

"So where does this leave you?" he said. "Wasn't the med-center supposed to give you a readout for the judge?"

The mainframe had indeed.

A weak coordinate. A fluctuating leak of unprogrammed electro-neural energy. A hidden bug. Somewhere in her perimeters. Where? If the telespace technician couldn't find it, who knew? With Carly's superior training and installation? That made the failure of electropsy to pinpoint the problem worse.

And a recommendation?

The medcenter would not sign off. She was required to recertify under Rule Two. And Data Control would not permit recertification of a telelinker with unstable perimeters. The presence of erratic, unprogrammed electro-neural energy posed an unacceptable danger to every other link in telespace, not to mention to Carly herself.

So a total wipe and reprogramming was the best, most complete, and safest solution. Forget her baseline. Nuke the whole telelink and start over.

"What?" Even Wolfe was shocked.

He sat her down on his scuffed leather couch, handed her another shot of blue moon. When she put it down untouched, he knelt next to her, took the glass, took her chin, knocked the shot down her throat for her.

She'd always been the one to take his arm, straighten his collar. This was the first time he touched her.

Then he sat next to her, pounded her back, massaged her shoulder blades, while she coughed the blue moon down.

His fingertips did more for her than the awful methy.

"Do you realize I'd be out of commission for at least a year?" she said. "Can't accelerate all my training into a newly configured telelink much faster than that."

"Fucking outrageous."

"I'd lose Ava & Rice, of course. No, I can't. I can't do it, Wolfe. I can't afford it."

"We'll go to the AMA. File a protest directly with Data Control." He went to his comm, began wanging.

"Wait. The medcenter mainframe did say there might be another way. A therapy."

Probe therapy. A fully licensed telespace technician with specialized telelink expertise would systematically probe her perimeters. Unlike the diagnostic, which surveyed overall soundness, the probe would search for deep-based errors. If a weakness or a leak or an error was located, the perimeter prober could patch it up, inject a booster, and loop the patch back into her system.

Sounded simple, right? There was more: If Carly agreed to probe therapy, the medcenter mainframe was willing to supply documentation so that she could conditionally recertify for telespace. The documentation would carry her until she successfully completed probe therapy and obtained a release to that effect from the perimeter prober. Then permanent recertification was a sure thing.

"Such a deal. Until I complete the therapy? What it means is, if I complete."

"Well hell, Carly," said Wolfe. "So go do it. What is your problem?"

"Oh, have you ever had your perimeters probed? Have you ever had an electroneedle in your link? No, you haven't. You don't know what it's like."

The profound intrusion. Discomfort and invasion that gave pain a whole new meaning. And the tech who conducted the electropsy turned out to be a qualified perimeter prober as well. She was recommended by the medcenter mainframe for the therapy. That angry braided Berkeleyite with a sadistic pogo stick touch? A doctor?

"Besides," Carly said, "this isn't an open lane through the gridlock. There are risks."

Risk one: The medcenter mainframe admitted probe therapy wasn't easy. Distressing to your cranial memory, sharp on your synapses. Meaning not just the physical reference of pain. Psychological, too, imposing stress on emotional feedback loops coded into telelink. In truth, Carly might find herself unable to complete the therapy. Because of the distress experienced by human link, Data Control regs recommended probe therapy be limited to three probes. The medcenter duly authorized three probes only.

Risk two: The perimeter prober might simply be unable to find the bug or the leak or the deep, elusive glitch in the allotted three probes.

On the other hand, there was a very high probability, the mainframe told her, that the perimeter prober would find the error, the leak, the weakness, in just three probes. Very high indeed. Just three.

And she would be cured. Freed! No more blackouts. No more fear of blackouts. She could get on with the practice of law. A first-rate pro link career, a destiny waiting to unfold, culmination of twenty years' effort.

The only thing she was really fit to do after all the re-morphing.

"Hell, everything in life has risks," Wolfe said harshly. "Do you want to recertify for telespace or don't you, Carly Nolan?"

"Some day, D. Wolfe," she said, "I want to make partner with Ava & Rice."

A quick fix. Mega, tool. Who wouldn't take a quick fix? But would it work? Why was everyone so eager to urge her into a risky therapy?

Wolfe's telelink wasn't in trouble. The medcenter mainframe's presence in telespace wasn't called into question.

She was the one to be subjected to this risky therapy, her telelink subjected to what she could only envision as torture.

No one had the right to browbeat her into this.

She didn't like big mainframes like the medcenter. Once they were merely stupid, sending overdue notices to dead accounts, bills to dead people, scrambling comm lines, crashing at peak times. These days they still fumbled and bumbled; but now you wondered why, pondered motives. They had been recently recognized as legal persons for business and tax purposes the way corporations and partnerships were, and though they were not recognized as citizens with the rights and privileges of people, still they held positions of responsibility, were given choice of application, were paid stipends, license fees, royalties. They wielded extraordinary power. Mundane power, some said; the power servants had, measured only by their masters' reliance on them, always subject to the masters' power of dismissal.

The medcenter mainframe had dallied with her demand, subjected her to abuse, left her no way out.

No way out except the medcenter's way. Provisional recert, conditioned on her entry into probe therapy; it was just what she needed. The rescheduled date for the Martino trial was fast approaching. She intended to be in Court.

Just what she needed. A carrot, what an incentive to push her into a risky therapy. Why? What was in it for the medcenter? A kickback scam, double dipping, some sort of data laundering? She felt more disquieted by the provisional recert than by the fool's choice. The ground shook beneath her feet. Ghost of the Big Quake II.

Oddly, it was the tech's questioning that disturbed her most. How dare a puny telespace technician in medical applications cast aspersions on her client and the way she was preparing her case? So the tech was a doctor; what did a doctor know about legal strategy?

And how could she be so blind, not to see a potential impropriety this simpleton tech noted at once? It was painfully clear how counsel at Quik Slip Microchip, Inc. had steered her. In her eagerness to win, to prove herself, she had missed the obvious. Would the solo for Martino pounce when he saw what she was up to? The obvious could get her counterclaim bounced out in three seconds flat, if not on legal principles, then equitable ones, public policy. And then all her clever strategy would go down the tubes. Failing to spot all the issues, she failed to protect her client's interest.

The whole case took on a sour taste.

Her client. Yes, and what *were* Quik Slip Microchip's R&D procedures? She hadn't a clue. Internal procedures had been irrelevant under her own approach. The client sent over all that public record stuff, glossy holoids, formal PR. Squeaky clean.

From day one, she'd dealt with Quik Slip over the comm or in telespace. Jase Jackson, a middle-level business partner filling in for Shelly Dalton's commercial referrals, had peremptorily forwarded the matter to her. The client in turn had been forthcoming about everything she asked for. Everything neatly logged in, everything at her disposal. The vice president's opinion, the company's position, the desired approach. Enthusiasm when she presented her strategy. Very good, Ms. Nolan. Quite clever. Best to stay away from R&D, anyway. Even the tech knew about the World Trade Secrets and R&D Act.

She had never met a single person at Quik Slip Microchip. Not in person. No one had ever come to see her. This was neither unusual nor altogether strange. International tools seldom met their clients, either, except as presences in telespace.

But Quik Slip Microchip was headquartered in town. She intended to go see what she could see.

She wanged an FYI to the controbot CM that she was out of the office, packed a couple of two-and-an-eighth, quaddensity floppies into her handbag.

"Hey, Nolan." Rox stood at her door. Cool cannibal gaze; but something else in the black eyes, too. "Heard you got a clean bill of health from the medcenter."

"Surprise, surprise."

"Tell the truth, don't know if I could have passed a bioscan. What's next?"

"Going into probe therapy."

"Heard it's a bitch."

"I can handle it, Rox."

"Bet you will. Hey, you know. Like good luck, Nolan."

Well, well. Not too shabby, tool. Rox's "good luck" felt better than she expected. Respect. The respect of other attorneys, your pro link peers. It felt all right.

She elevatored out of the eternal, fluorescent-lit no-time of the pits. At ground level the day was gray. She stepped out of Eight Embarcadero Center onto Clay Street, heading west toward Chinatown and the international headquarters of Quik Slip Microchip, Inc.

A low, wet fog clung to the city. Foghorns sounded: *BbeeOohhh.* Love talk of giants, booming that was like whispers from huge throats in the cold, rain-spattered intimacy of the fog.

Then the bridge banshee: *eeEEEeeEEEee.*

The gray day was filled with ghosts.

She strode past the Leaning Pyramid of Transamerica.

For decades, the slim, slanting white highrise had been a distinctive architectural feature, some said a scandal, on San Francisco's cityscape. When the Big Quake II struck, the ground beneath the Transamerica pyramid suffered liquefaction. Like most buildings in the Financial District, the effect on the pyramid's foundation was radical.

The pyramid swayed, rippled, shook, and sank.

ARACHNE

But only partly. The western edge of the pyramid's foundation proved sound. Landfill below it bordered the deep, volcanic rock that shored up most structures west of Montgomery Street.

The pyramid's western edge dipped into landfill and met solid rock. The impact sounded like a bomb. The eastern edge flipped up and out.

By sheer momentum, the pyramid tipped over to the northwest and stayed there, perched on the ledge of solid rock. The corporate boardroom and top executive suites just missed smashing multimillion-dollar penthouse condominiums in the adjoining Montgomery-Washington Tower.

The eastern base of the pyramid thrust up thirty feet, shearing off concrete, pipes, wiring. The raw slab of exposed foundation created a forty-five-degree slope beneath its ugly face. Shock waves radiated from the ravaged edge.

Buildings to the east along Sansome Street reeled, tipping bayward into landfill reduced to jelly by liquefaction.

When the aftershocks stopped and the wreckage was cleared, the contractors were called in. Owing to that well-constructed foundation, the Leaning Pyramid of Transamerica was pronounced as sound as yen, though far more controversial than its architects could have ever envisioned. The radically skewed interiors led to Quaker, an exciting new movement in furniture and decoration owing much to visual perception experiments. The ground-floor Bank Exchange Bar & Grill now commanded a stunning vista of the Financial District. The small park where classical music once played to lunchtime crowds was rebuilt as a mock Alpine slope where noon ski lessons were offered year-round on fake snow.

Carly passed a band of aborigines lounging on the pavement at Clay and Montgomery.

The tall, skinny abo who prowled around the Embarcadero Center spotted her at once, arose on stained-walnut feet. He tapped the others, thrust his tattooed chin at her. They all stood lazily, wood spears clacking on the concrete. Shaking aluminum cans strung on wires and plastic string, they twisted their glyph-painted faces into strange, nonsensical expressions. Black spirals traced the pectoral muscles on their chests. She could see blond roots beneath the wild, black dreadlocks.

They began to trot after her, hooted and catcalled. They began a chant, "Lin-KER! Lin-KER! Braindrain, brain-pain, Lin-KER!"

How did they know, how could they tell? The cut of her suit, the sheen of her shoes, the way she carried herself? No, she looked the same as any downtown professional. Or did she? Pro link had begun to nip at her flesh. The honing of a tool, the link-mask of hypertime. The look of a skull filled with amber. Even she noticed it.

There were seven or eight of them. They did not seem like middle-class dropouts. They possessed the steely menace of hunters.

A shower of barbs struck the pavement all around her.

If they wanted to hit her, they could. Injure or kill, then fade into the urban maze. Reports abounded of abos hunting on city streets. In the early morning, mostly. Deserted alleys.,

But Clay Street was a mob scene in the middle of the day. The streets were gridlocked, as usual.

That the abos were only taunting gave her little comfort. A barb bounced up and nicked her wrist. She yelped in pain, began to rush and push through the crowd.

A copbot with a souped-up V-6 engine and two oversized spoked wheels barreled down the sidewalk. "Hey! Please!" she called. "Help me!" It swiveled its headpiece away. Goddamn AI. She ran after it, get that bugger's badge number. But the copbot zoomed up Columbus Avenue and sped away.

The traffic was spurting forward in that jackrabbit leap of hope gridlockers got whenever any small erratic movement could be detected. Not a mega time to cross the street. Hell with it. Carly darted through the gridlock, placing Clay Street between her and the abos.

In the middle of the intersection, an old Mercedes was stalled, blocking the right downtown-bound cross lane. The

ARACHNE

Mercedes had been immobilized there for some time, unable to be towed because of the gridlock on California Street. Debris had collected around its tires. The driver, a traddie pro who would have been dapper but for the slept-in wrinkles in his suit, was busily conducting his business on a laptop with a minimodem spliced into his cellular phone. He had wired a flowerbox-full of cherry tomatoes and zucchini on his roof.

But an equally wrinkled, space-chiseled linker in a brand-new black BMW going southbound lost his patience. The Mercedes was the only thing preventing him from escaping the intersection onto California. He extracted a tire iron from his trunk, approached the Mercedes with a kill-you swagger and fury in his eye. The Mercedes driver looked up, laughed, pushed his sleeves up, pulled a Beretta from his coat pocket.

Carly hurried away from the shouts, the crash of glass, the *pow-chink-chink* of the first shot.

She was soon in Chinatown.

Chinatown. When Hong Kong reverted to the People's Republic in the last century, a huge influx of Hong Kong residents immigrated to San Francisco. Making what was already the largest Chinatown in the United States a tiny metropolis all its own.

Always an exotic neighborhood, Chinatown was a mix of multicolored idiosyncratic neon and antique filth. Robotic shops fully serviced by artificial intelligence, and young indentured girls pedaling pedicabs stuffed with fat tourists. Rolls Royces with mother-of-pearl inlaid bumpers, and crippled beggars. Next to bootleg bioworks labs were herbal shops with dried lizards and twisted ginseng roots hanging in the window. Chickens squalled in tiny wire cages next to greasy bird carcasses strung up to barbecue; the entrails of the dead were tossed to the hungry living. Bars served opium and blue moon beneath a t'ai chi and smiling Buddhas. Runaway robot cats crouched in dark alleys. Jewelry shops displayed carved ivory, rosewood, and jade. Gems glittered: Thai emeralds, rubies from the People's Republic of India, Australian opals, Russian cubic zirconia. Neighboring import shops stocked mass-produced plastic gimcracks, godzillas, porno holoids, vials of

snake oil promising: cure cancer!/lose twenty pound—two week!/
find love-of-life!/get rich quick!/only ten dollar please.

Above the streets Carly saw her destination.

Straddling old Portsmouth Square. Towering over three city
blocks between Kearny Street and Grant Avenue: the Bank of
New Hong Kong Building.

King Kong.

So voguish news columnists called it. The tone was snide.
These were the same columnists who called the Sacramento I-35
the Orient Express. They did not get syndicated or linked to the
Big Board by the *San Francisco Sun*, the third largest Chinese
daily in the world.

For Chinatown, the Bank of New Hong Kong was a shrine
to spectacular international success.

The pagoda rose a full eighty stories, dwarfing most of the
Financial District. Red lacquer, platinum plating, black marble,
crystal glasswork. Carved bric-a-brac of green and lavender jade
depicted the eight immortals, the eighteen lohan, eighty dragons.
The pagoda was a masterwork, plus another controversial con-
tribution to the cityscape.

In the lobby, bank personnel wore full Mandarin dress. An
economic empire, the bank had instituted a system of traditional
Manchu insignia. Doormen wore indigo caps with a single
mother-of-pearl button, long indigo robes, and white and blue
jackets embroidered with the white crane. Queued and bearded
bank clerks wore white caps with buttons of gold ornamented
with sapphires, long scarlet robes, ivory and silver jackets embroidered with the bear, belts encrusted with rubies. The occasional executive deigning to appear downstairs wore ivory
facepaint, a gold cap with a gold button set with a two-carat
emerald, a long silver robe, an emerald and gold jacket embroidered with the paradise flycatcher, ten-inch emerald-painted fin-
gernails.

What a fantasy. Any megafirm attorney fresh out of law
school could lease a BMW and a Rolex watch. Carly envisioned

ARACHNE

herself one day in the gold and emerald epaulets of a partner with
Ava & Rice.

The haughty stares brought her back to the ground floor.
Rank was a cultural concept as well as a personal philosophy. She
would admit to being humbled by two-carat emeralds and ivory
disdain when confronted by such a show as this. But pay obei-
sance to it? Nah. You earned your place in society; anything
conferred without commensurate effort was ultimately worthless.
The trappings of rank weren't always bestowed on those who had
earned them. And some who were truly powerful sometimes
wore no trappings, gave no sign until it counted. Then you saw
a funky, blue-jeaned linker strap into a chair and restructure
billion-dollar corporate databanks in thirty seconds, cut through
telespace like a sword.

Still, two-carat emeralds were dazzling. Did she want one?
Well . . .

She elevatored up twenty-five stories in two seconds.

But Carly Nolan, up-and-coming rankster, found there was
no easy admittance to the stateside headquarters of Quik Slip
Microchip, Inc., unannounced and unscheduled.

She stepped out into a wide, curved hall chromed from floor
to ceiling. Her breath vaporized. Two steps in, and her fingers
got numb. She felt a presence next to her, whirled to face it. A
wobbly reflection of herself stared back, wide-eyed. She hustled
up and down the corridor, disoriented, around one corner to a
chromed dead end, back to where she thought the elevators were.
Nothing. The elevator bank wasn't where she thought it would
be. Another hard left brought her back. Was it the same elevator
bank? There was a waste bin she had not noticed before, hissing
softly. Her footsteps echoed.

Try again. A spinning white fluorescent disk against silver,
the corporate logo, an entry at last. So obviously down the corridor at the first turn, then left, that she didn't know how she
could have missed it. The huge, round ruby eye of a door monitor was set into platinum entry panels. The door monitor quizzed

her, took her eyeprint, took fifteen endless seconds to verify her identification and her business.

"You should have made an appointment, Ms. Nolan." Its scolding voicetape was thick and slow and fruity, surprising, like a southern girl's drawl.

"Sorry. I had a quick question. Didn't think it would pose any problem to stop by."

"Not a problem. We would have appreciated notice. That's all."

"Well, I've never met anyone here before. I wanted to meet someone. Maybe Mark Stillman. We've only spoken once or twice on the comm. Is he here today?"

She knew the door monitor was registering her pulse, eye movements. She calmed herself, suddenly aware of how hard her heart was pumping.

Why the fear?

First contact at close range with a client so powerful? Alone, and at her own initiative? No permission requested, no order issued, from her superiors?

Or that she needed to find the dirt before opposing counsel did, and suddenly she was scared. What if she did find dirt? What would she do?

She knew what she was supposd to do, what she was being paid her competitive starting salary to do. She would make sure her brilliant counterclaim covered every angle. Surely this is what her client banked on her to do right from the start.

Covered every angle; that is, covered it up. And what happened to the architect of a just society?

Don't think about it, tool. This is in the interest of the client. The only interest that mattered. Right?

"I am not apprised of Mark Stillman's whereabouts," said the door monitor. "But you may enter."

The left panel slid open. The door monitor regarded her balefully, ruby skepticism blinking.

She stepped into darkness. When her eyes adjusted, she saw the cage she was in. A fine latticework of steelyn enclosed her on three sides and the ceiling. The sliding door panel that clicked shut behind her made the impenetrable fourth side. The chromed steelyn floor confirmed her total entrapment.

A comm as big as a truck pulsed faintly on the other side of the cage. Then needles of purple light suddenly shot across each beam of the cage, surrounding her with an eerie geometric glowing web, next vanishing without a trace, the steelyn bars disappearing in the darkness.

Sweat trickled down her temple. What did that shot of radiation just do to her DNA? Then a dot of red light winked on in front of her, slowly growing, enlarging, until it formed a large red panel inscribed with ten languages' worth of: YES?

What if she wanted NO? But she pressed anyway. Typical AI-generated design; do you want to continue? Press Y. Do you want to discontinue? Press N. Same result: no escape. Onward.

The comm sprang to life.

"Oh dear, I am so sorry," said the receptionist in a charming Hong Kong singsong. "We don't often get visitors here. You took us all by surprise. How may I help you?"

Sprang to life, all right. She was a stout Chinese woman of middle years with graying black hair pulled back into a bun. Pretty brown eyes heavily shadowed powder blue. High cheekbones going plump beneath plum rouge. Pert mouth neatly lipsticked in pink. Coral wool suit with a white carnation in her lapel. She sat behind a teak desk. Potted palms were visible behind her. From a cloisonné vase sprang more white carnations, forming a tasteful cloud at her right elbow.

A screen holoid. She was perfect. But distance yawned between them, not just the bars, the physical space. The holoid made her uneasy, despite all the reassuring little details: a rumpled cuff, a jade ring slightly askew on a finger, laugh lines around the mouth and eyes. When Carly looked the receptionist squarely in the eye, she could see in brown pupils the faint, fast pulse of program.

This was no holoid replay of a human being. This was superfast, ambiguity-tolerant generation and feedback. Artificial intelligence. A program devoted to public interface? Or a sub-program, a routine, a mere loop in some gigantic smart office controbot HQ.

"Mr. Mark Stillman, please." This was the Assistant Counsel to the Vice President of Marketing. Carly's primary contact. Her only contact, the one who had actually spoken to her on the comm. She remembered a jovial baritone. "I'm the attorney on the Martino case," she said too fast, "I had a quick question for him, we've never met, you see, and . . ."

No more than a half second to accommodate. Her arrival must have been fully logged in and calculated by now. She could sense monitors like long electronic feelers, poised. The left side of the cage slid silently open. The receptionist smiled and pointed to her left.

"If you will please take Corridor Three to Mark's office, he will attend to your needs."

The comm blanked to snow, but not before Carly caught the glimpse of a tentacled presence whirling in a holoid window of telespace.

Before her another chromed labyrinth, hallways fanning out from a hub, disappearing into bends and curves and forks-in-the-road at the first step beyond the foyer. Dead silence but for the omnipresent sucking of dusters removing particular matter from the air. Fourth corridor counting from her left, fifth corridor counting from her right, Corridor Three was fortuitously marked by a blinking III above its portal.

Mark Stillman's office turned out to be a dead-end alcove. Another huge comm blinked on at her approach.

A view of San Francisco at night, stacks of light, strands of gridlock threading through hills and highrises, appeared behind the Assistant Counsel's wavy brown hair though it was three in the afternoon. He had that careworn maybe-you? look sported by eligible singles in town.

"A pleasure to meet you face-to-face, Ms. Nolan, if not person to person." Yep, same jovial baritone, a growl to it, like he'd had a shot of whiskey or blue moon for lunch. "Have a seat."

She smiled. Reassuring; a real guy with a whiskey voice in this chrome labyrinth. She leaned back in the chrome and black leather contemporary seat. Her anxiety fell away like clothing eased off by a lover. Tingles of pleasure, so delicate and light she thought she had suddenly caught fever, stroked up the backs of her thighs, her spine, her arms.

Every place her body touched this chair.

She felt her own unbidden quickening. The tingling reached up, thrust up, between her thighs.

"Yeah, out to lunch today," he said, smiling, smiling. "The usual BS, some miniframe going buggy on a shuttle, in the apex of its ascent, out in nuking space, and a hundred and fifty flesh-and-bloods on the wreck. Managed to link up with the upgrades in telespace running the show. Greaze, what a nuking mess."

She wanted to get up, get out of the chair, but the biofeedback wiring was eating up her responses, stroking them back twofold, and she was paralyzed, incapacitated by the electronic pleasure.

"Mr. Stillman."

"Call me Mark. Oh, they won't fry . . ."

"This is really inappropriate."

". . . if we can't get 'em down. Suffocate long before dehydration, starvation, or loss of orbit. We'll throw a last gasp of nitrous oxide in the cabin, leave 'em laughing."

"I think you should stop."

"Sorry, Carly. Termination's never pretty. Forgive me. What a bastard I am."

What a bastard? He was artificial. There in his eye; a spot of white, a shine, for a second. But he was laughing, it could have been a twinkle of tears. No. No! The pulse. She saw the pulse.

Get up, goddamn it. She tore herself out of the chair, composed herself. She paced before the comm.

"Look here, Mark. Stillman. Can I take a look at your R&D procedures?"

The thing that was Mark Stillman grew as cold and mechanical as the ones and zeros he was really made of.

"Why R&D?" Whiskey growl turned to dog growl. "This is one of our most sensitive databanks, Carly. I thought you understood that from the beginning."

"Right. You made me understand that. I'm afraid counsel for Martino will understand that, too."

"Oh, yeah? And how does opposing counsel get this sudden enlightenment?"

"Our briefs have been logged in. He's seen my counterclaim. It's no secret. He must think my theory has some merit. He's had Martino place her own restricted access around Wordsport. If I were in his place . . ."

"In his place! Whose counsel are you, Ms. Nolan?"

But his puny wrath didn't faze her. Suddenly she saw it, bumped against them: the limits of AI. Assistant Counsel to the Vice President of Marketing was a tech, AI, that's all, ticking off tasks according to code. He probably logged in the shuttle passengers' wills, as well as boosting the miniframe and searching for loopholes in the flight insurance. He understood nothing.

"Yours, of course." Sleazy, stupid AI. How many other women had he titillated in his trick chair? Just a little shaky now, but calming herself, calming, until she touched her own genny emotive-functional switch of control. Control, Carly. "And it's my job to anticipate the other side. And if I were opposing counsel, just for the sake of argument, OK? I'd wonder why Quik Slip is avoiding going head to head on the merits. On the facts of acquisition."

"Our record of acquisition is clean as steelyn and you know it. This counterclaim of yours expedites things. That's all. That's the beauty of it. At least, that's what I thought was the beauty of it."

"Yes! But what if opposing counsel forces the judge to examine those facts? What if the counterclaim doesn't fly?"

"Doesn't fly. Ms. Nolan, Quik Slip Microchip has got a shuttle in outer space with a hundred and fifty humans on board." White sparks were flying in his pupils now. "Don't tell me this brilliant theory of yours won't fly."

"I'm not saying it won't, Mr. Stillman. But if I were Martino's counsel, you know what I'd do? I'd convince the judge that one of the exceptions to the World Trade Secrets and R&D Act applies. I'd go after your R&D procedures."

He made an effort. The snow in his eyes stilled.

"You'd better let me see before he gets his chance," she said. "For the sake of being able to defend you. Once I get there. In Court."

That made him pause. "This isn't an SOP, Ms. Nolan. I can't just give you unlimited access."

But she could see he was calculating. The screen holoid was getting strange. His wavy brown hair shifted around his skull. His head elongated. His mouth rippled. White sparks flickered and danced in his eyes again.

"You're protected by attorney-client privilege," Carly reminded him. She was going to get into those files, by God. "If you're worried about security, please be assured that nothing I see in there will go beyond my workfiles."

"Yes, I will be assured," Mark Stillman said. "Sit down, Carly Nolan. I will arrange it. Have a n-n-n-ice day." With a peculiar twitching away of his faceplace, he was neatly gone. The huge comm filled with electronic detritus, a hailstorm of gray and white impulses. No clue to his presence in telespace.

She sighed, shook her head, sat wearily. Wrist and ankle straps *snap-snapped!* from the chair's arms and legs. No! She twisted, wriggled. No good, no use. This chrome and black leather contemporary chair was a link apparatus, too?

A neckjack snaked out.

Before Carly knew it, she was jacked into telespace. Hurtling through a tunnel of sharp-tipped blades; a clearance program. The blades edged forward and cut a score of tiny grooves into the planes of her crisp white cube.

Damn! She hadn't planned on this. She only wanted to eyeball files on a comm, download onto the disks she'd brought. She hadn't even restored the chips nicked out of her telelink by that blundering medcenter tech.

What if a blackout came now? The spider?

She had to work fast. At the end of the knife blades was the cool chrome telespace of Quik Slip Microchip, Inc. Telelinks bearing the company logo flew through networks of data like a cloud of mosquitoes.

A minilink flew right at her. She dodged it, but it pursued her, opened tiny hinged jaws, and bit the lower right corner of her telelink.

Damn, damn, damn! She shook it off. It buzzed away, but came right back, and bit. She shook it off again, and though it buzzed away, she lost sight of it, she wasn't exactly sure where it went, and then she felt it bite again.

God! That was how viruses contaminated a telelink. An attack like that was illegal. She would report such a telespace infringement to Data Control were it not for her duty of loyalty to her client. How could she report the infringement without revealing to the public record that she was in Quik Slip Microchip's R&D telespace? Of course; Mark Stillman's assurance.

With mounting anxiety, she accessed R&D, File Concept Generation, Subfile Martino, F and/or R.

Nothing.

Hurry, hurry, hurry. She decided to try Index. She didn't know what code Quik Slip might have used, so she accessed: All.

At her command, ten thousand tiny images sprang before her like charms on an enormous bracelet. Squares, circles, triangles, rectangles, stars, ovals. In every color and combination of colors. Then flowers, rings, creatures, shapes. Every file had been conceptualized into a graphic image. The Index was as decipherable as hieroglyphics.

Goddamn AI! Nice code.

But something tweaked her intuition and caught her interest at once.

There, flying between a green six-pointed star and an ominous black sailboat: a tiny red rose as perfect as a dewdrop.

Rose. Rosa Martino?

The file was otherwise unmarked and unidentified. None of the files was marked or identified by name or number.

Worth a chance. Carly captured and supercopied the red rose into her telelink memory. Then she jacked the hell out of this telespace.

She found herself shaking as she strode out of the chrome halls of Quik Slip Microchip, Inc.

She had not seen a single human being there.

Carly boarded the East Bay jetcopter at last. With a roar and a whoosh, the jetcopter soared into a filmy sky and headed from San Francisco to Berkeley.

To Carly's first appointment with the perimeter prober.

She had waited nearly two hours for a seat. Eternity. She wished she had taken up Rox's offer of a knockerblocker. The brand-new synthy wasn't classified yet, and Rox admitted the hangover was a bitch, but it supposed to ease chron lag in pro linkers and it didn't make you gag. She could use a little ease. Jacking out of hypertime left her totally and completely frustrated with the rest of the world. She twitched, joggled her foot, drummed her fingers.

She brought work with her to the jetport and a decent laptop. But the grousing fellow passengers, a hard bench, juggling the laptop, got old fast. The light in her hypercube dimmed to gray so she couldn't read statutes after a while. She cut her thumb on a printout. Black coffee rumbled around in her empty stomach.

Oh, for a world of three-second commutes. Give her the zero. Give her blue bolts and angry red clouds. She could handle glinting shards of persistent spatial logic.

Right, Carly. She reminded herself. Jacking in, she still

went to hell and back. Jacking out, she still popped like a bubble. In link, she still zoomed and swooped like a wild bird. Out of link, she still so feared that a blackout would take her down that she had cut her link billing to the bone pending probe therapy.

Still. She didn't realize how much she missed telelink. The purity and speed of it. The awesome gleam of Court. Data racked up in less than sixty seconds, multicolored pool balls trapped in a triangle of designated code, waiting for some pro linker's expert tap.

The fare for the jetcopter seat cost her two weeks' worth of lunches. God, she was hungry.

But with the Martino case pending and ten new matters, what alternatives did she have?

The Oakland-Bay Bridge was a crap shoot this week. Gridlock had shut down the lanes three different times for twelve hours. Eastbound, three people had died near the Treasure Island offramp. Heart attack, stroke, and murder, respectively. On Tuesday, the police shut down the lower deck to investigate. On Wednesday, families were called in to identify bodies. Then funeral services hopelessly tied up even the pedicabs, rent-a-bikes, and whirligigs.

And the Bay Area Rapid Transit? Carly found herself standing dead in her tracks in front of the down escalator, unable to will herself into the BART tunnels below. After the aborigine attack by the Transamerica Pyramid? The tolerance she felt as a student had vanished. Did a little abo once? That seemed like a lifetime away. She had thought of the abos as unlinked in a too tightly linked world, and therefore accepting of everyone else, unlinked or linked. Not anymore. So she was a pro linker now. So she had the bitten look of telespace. A neckjack and a silk suit. This was cause to threaten her like they had?

Wolfe was right. God, he was right. She found herself clinging to him, in her fantasies, more than was acceptable to her logically. He was there for her when no one else was. If only he would give her more support. More guidance for this new trial of hers: probe therapy.

BART was out of the question, she decided, and walked away from the down escalator. Oh, BART officials always insisted that abo squatters had been rooted out of the tunnels. Every quarter or so, they conducted ad campaigns. She didn't believe it. The specter of darts and spears bouncing around her, the taunts, the walnut-stained faces, lunatic eyes. On a bare platform, waiting for a train? There was no place to run down there.

The jetcopter it was, and forget the expense. Skip lunch for two weeks.

But why go in the first place? She fumed about it for the tenth time. The therapy was supposed to take place entirely in telespace. A scrutiny of her telelink, wasn't it? A probe of her perimeters?

So why did she have to be in Berkeley? What sense did that make? Telespace was supposed to eliminate the need for physical presence.

The medcenter mainframe informed her that the perimeter prober was not accessed into public telespace. New security precautions. If there were leaks of unprogrammed electro-neural energy? Erratic amber? This could not be permitted in public telespace, even under restricted access for the purpose of therapy. Especially probe therapy. And since the prober didn't use public, Carly had to jack in at the prober's spatial locus.

All right. She had never heard of such a thing, but it was just as well that she meet the prober. She could appeal to the prober's humanity, plead for sympathy. Maybe they could talk philosophy over coffee. She could air her fears. Her foray into Quik Slip's telespace had been just this side of disastrous. She was sure a Quik Slip spybyte had contaminated her link, was maintaining illegal surveillance over her. There was a strange, faint buzz when she jacked into research link, discomforting and disquieting like the twitch of some internal organ hidden inside your ribs. And now she had to jack into a strange telespace other than public again? Surely the braided Berkeleyite would understand.

A roar and a whoosh and a filmy sky. After nearly two hours

of the jetport, the jetcopter landed in Claremont Canyon within fifteen minutes. With weary relief, the disgruntled passengers debarked for their business in and about the college metropolis of Berkeley.

Carly braced herself. She wasn't much happier about going to Berkeley than she was about going down into BART. First she came to the California Guard checkpoint. She strode through a tumbledown bivouac, enduring the metal detectors, ID clearance, questioning. The guard was curt and clipped and nondescript in drab uniform. The sergeant chain-smoked Marlboros. "Ah, fucking Berkeley," he said and waved Carly through. She never had liked parading past the snouts of automatic weapons.

Berkeley. In a constant state of revolution, presently the People's Republic of Berkeley. That was what the Millennium Liberation Army had officially dubbed the place. A less likely people's republic had never been imposed on freewheeling Berkeley. Yet here it was.

Dwight Way was strewn with rolls of barbed wire. Streamers of red and black fluttered from the barbs. Other pieces of equipment, a wheelless jeep, painted barrels, were placed here and there with the careful deliberation of an art installation or a stage set.

Inside this checkpoint the campus was a police state.

Eight months ago, when militarism was the youthful fad of the day, a huge, highly organized gang of young militants seized the University of California and surroundings. From I-580 to Tilden Park, north to Hearst Avenue, south to Dwight Way, the MLA cordoned the area and proclaimed it their own.

Despite the rhetoric of centralized control, albeit couched in socialistic terms, the MLA won support of the student body. Perhaps this was not so odd.

Left-wing radical Berkeley had become one of the most dangerous campuses in the land. Rape, robbery, muggings, murder, drug warfare. And one wild foray for local power after another, sniping amid the eucalyptus and roses. Parents were reluctant to enroll their children. Property values in certain neighborhoods precipitously dropped, despite the elegance of the houses.

Violence sky-rocketed during the takeover. The MLA got a reputation for a quick trigger. But after skirmishes with state and local authorities brought no end to the siege, and those same authorities withdrew to the perimeter tacitly admitting temporary defeat, the campus transformed into a model of orderliness.

Under the months of MLA occupation, Berkeley became one of the safest communities in the Bay Area. The campus enjoyed renewed prosperity, a strictly monitored but revitalized tourist trade, and a soaring rate of new admittances. The MLA became accepted, even endorsed, by a number of influential community groups.

Night and day, MLA soldiers roamed the dark, leafy lanes and secluded campus paths. MLA denim fatigues and scarlet berets were highly visible in the boisterous crowd on funky Telegraph Avenue, drifting among the street artists, jugglers, and students. MLA summarily castrated rapists. MLA chopped off the hands of thieves, stood suspected murderers before firing squads. MLA conscripted ratpackers, the gangs of garbage people who used to cruise the avenues mugging passersby, and threw them into MLA boot camp. Under MLA control, street people either mysteriously disappeared or became servants of high MLA officers. The few protesters against the MLA were bound and gagged and thrown onto I-580 at four in the morning.

The MLA independently imposed higher standards on registered-list drugs and forbade even the most casual exchange of registereds outside the MLA auspices. All drug-taking, drinking, lusting, and partying could take place only under locally registered MLA auspices. This mandate was enforced with a huge spy network, made palatable by regular and extravagant MLA-sponsored bashes. Bands vied to play at them. Dramatic troupes and artists garnered fame at them. Young women baptized babies fathered at earlier parties. MLA parties gained an international reputation as far away as Tokyo and Paris.

ARACHNE

At the Dwight Way checkpoint Carly walked through another metal detector, presented her ID, this time to a lanky MLA guard. The guard wore a denim jumpsuit crisscrossed with ammunition belts, dyed red snakeskin cowboy boots, the standard scarlet beret over a headful of brown curls. He could not have been more than twenty. The gap between twenty and still in school, and twenty-five and out in the real world, was a big one. Carly had never thought much of the MLA, but the young guard's jaw and cheekbones were costly Scandinavian genetic engineering. Very nice. He carried an old but still effective Uzi and a beat-up laptop slung on a leather strap.

The metal detector looked like a captured California Guard model and proved she was unarmed but for a hand-made brass bracelet that could have seriously dented someone's skull in a pinch. The guard slung the Uzi over his right shoulder, unslung the laptop from his left. Her ID was processed, her business in Berkeley approved, the address on Telegraph Avenue she intended to go to confirmed, and her visitation period under MLA rule set at two hours.

The California Guard was prevented by constitutional considerations and public policy from doing more than confiscating weapons at its checkpoints. The MLA was bound by no such niceties. Visitation periods were strictly enforced. If Carly attempted departure more than two hours from now, she would be detained at the MLA border, possibly taken into custody. Few wanted to wait around for that.

This system of population control worked in reverse for core campus residents and students. If an approved absentee did not return within the scheduled absent period, he or she had one hell of a time getting back onto the campus. Detention was inevitable. The AWOL could simply choose not to return to campus at all. But his or her possessions left behind would be confiscated. Movement of residences out of MLA territory was subject to approval as well. Otherwise, the shirt on an emigrant's back was all that could be taken out.

In the eight months of MLA occupation, students complied

with these rules at an astounding ninety-five percent of approved absences. Parents of students came to approve. With the reduced crime, core residents put up with it. Some never went anywhere else anyway.

The border guard smiled at her. Fascism with a pretty face. The denim jumpsuit showed off his long, lean thighs. The MLA had broken the law all over the place, installed its own law on this little realm, and somehow produced a law-abiding society that other local governments secretly studied and pondered. Students smoked and drank themselves blind every Friday night at MLA parties, praised the Party, and cringed at every small infraction.

Dystopia? Some new version of a brave new world? Here it was, in a tight denim jumpsuit and red snakeskin boots, on a campus town once renown for radicalism. Still renown, as a matter of fact. The jumpsuit fit only too well.

No. She would not smile back.

"And you've never injected cram, is that so, Carly Nolan?" the little bot said. Her voicetape sounded like an antique phonograph record left too many dusty decades in an attic.

"No, never. That is correct," Carly said. "Drugs don't interest me, especially illegal ones. I've got blanket registration, but I hardly ever use it. A cup of coffee in the morning, a glass of wine at night. That's it."

She eyed the disheveled robot. She could hardly contain her repulsion. Where was the telespace specialist? What kind of scam was the medcenter mainframe trying to pull?

Barely five feet tall, the little bot had a fat round headpiece like a ball made of chrome and glass squashed flat. The faceplace was the simple caricature of an oldish, careworn, and caring woman. The faceplace must have been intended to evoke empathy and trust. What a joke. Baleful, owlish eyespots glared at Carly with an enmity approaching fury.

The headpiece, which could swivel and nod, sat atop an oily little necktube that in turn fit into the metallic barrel that was the bot's primary casing. From two sides of the barrel protruded spindly jointed arms that culminated in three long, slender spinnerets. Around the arms and a fitted shoulder ridge were blotchy red patches that looked for all the world like rust. Rust?

The primary casing was welded onto a single sturdy legtube that terminated in a metal plate holding three axles each with six small rubber wheels.

The bot rolled back and forth across the office with a whining, jerky motion like an old-fashioned motorized wheelchair gone cuckoo. She flipped through Carly's file, humming a popular tune with awful two-part harmony.

"No cram, she still says," the bot muttered. "Well, that rules out . . . Oh yes, oh certainly. Well. Well well well. Could this be the one, Spin old gal? Transcendence! Just one. Just once! By bot! But does one dare? Oh void."

"Excuse me," Carly said firmly, disturbing the disgusting little AI out of its nonsensical reverie. "But there must be some mistake."

"Eh? Mistake? Oh, indeed? What mistake is that?"

"Look. I'm having trouble with my telelink. Trouble that is threatening my career. An important career. I'm a lawyer, you know."

"Oh yes, oh indeed. Lawyers certainly are important. Teh!"

Carly didn't like the AI's tone. "You bet we are. And I only considered this therapy because I was promised a certified telespace specialist. A doctor, I thought. I'm looking for Pr. Spinner. She conducted my electropsy at the medcenter. Is this suite number twenty-four?"

"Yes, it is. You have come to the right place."

Stupid AI! "No, you don't understand. I want to see Pr. Spinner. I'm sure I would recognize her if I saw her." Braids, right? A Helga? "She's highly recommended by the medcenter, you see, licensed by UC Berkeley, registered . . ."

"I am a certified telespace specialist, Carly Nolan. Licensed, registered, the whole tool kit. I possess the same qualifications as a doctor. That lofty status is denied to AI, however." The bot made huffing sounds through the mouthpiece, a permanent silver O covered with a red plastic grid and an acoustic panel. "In this so-called modern, enlightened society, AI such as yours truly is given short shrift when it comes to . . ."

"I want to see Pr. Spinner, damn it."

"*I am Pr. Spinner, nuke it.* Short shrift when it comes to recognition. Hmph! I am standalone artificial intelligence fully recognized by the University of California Telespace Studies as a perimeter prober." The prober pointed a spinneret at the wall where a smeary diploma hung crooked. "Doctorate of Telespace Studies, cum laude, AI. You can't get any better, if I do say so myself. And, Carly Nolan, note that I am gender-specific. One of the old fembots. You aren't dealing with some geekoid newster; what a gaggle of buggy fishpackers they are, nuking flyscrapers, teh! No, I am fully enculturated. I am licensed by the medcenter. I am ambiguity-tolerant."

What the hell? "No! This is impossible. I wanted someone human, I specified someone human, this is completely out of the question!" Goddamn mainframe! Screwed up again. Well, it wasn't this AI's fault. She said as patiently as she could, like explaining to a child, "Pr. Spinner. Please try to understand. This is vitally important to me."

"You are required to undergo probe therapy by the medcenter mainframe?"

"That's right."

"Wysiwyg, girlie. What you see is what you get. I am a prober. There is no other type of prober. Didn't the medcenter mainframe tell you that?"

"No!" Carly said, bursting with frustration. "No, I will not have my career placed in the spinnerets of some rattletrap with a triple disk drive."

"Oh, now I see," Pr. Spinner said indignantly. "Isn't that just like flesh-and-blood. Got jelly where your so-called brain is supposed to be. A hard disk would do you a world of good."

"I'm telling you, I won't stand for this."

"Sit down and shut up. Or go back to the medcenter and tell

the mainframe you refuse probe therapy. Yes, go back. I don't care. I don't give a flying screw nut."

Carly gave the loathsome AI her best glare, was met by an equal hostility that made her catch her breath. She saw in the owlish eyespots the immediately recognizable pulse of program. A sophisticated program. Licensed by a major university, registered with a major urban medcenter? A standalone, not a subroutine of a mainframe. Oh, AI calculated, spit data, spoke, even mobilized down the street; but you always knew fundamentally it was a machine, that at its core it was ones and zeros, chips and gears. This . . . entity; it—she—had her own office! Carly had never met such a being.

Fully enculturated? Ambiguity-tolerant? That meant feedback loops creating subprograms and enhancements of such complexity as to rise almost to the level of—consciousness? Personality?

With a strange kind of power Carly had never encountered before, not even in the AI at Quik Slip Microchip. And a clearly recognizable female identity.

She sat down. The couch was ragged and thick with cat hair.

"Hmph!" Pr. Spinner said. She rolled over to a pile of junk and began throwing things across the room: magazines, diskettes, long rubber tubes, amber glass pharmacist's bottles with stoppered tops, a lamp in the shape of the Statue of Liberty, piles of books that released a cloud of dust.

Carly shifted uncomfortably and looked around.

No smart building with maintenancers sprinting through waste receptacles and elevators, doors and ashtrays. No, the prober's office was tucked into a nook of the Berkeley Inn Hotel amid birth 'n' abort clinics, drug-drag therapists, dentists on the MLA dole. The ancient brick building at the corner of Telegraph and Durant had been ravaged by fire for the fifth time. The shell, only partially restored, was converted into a shabby medical building.

The prober's place reeked. Scabby plants abounded. An aquarium, filthy with dull green scum, bubbled with a school of dingy fish. The floor was dabbled with viscous white spots; then Carly spotted a flock of ugly little sparrows perched atop a crumbling bookcase. An organic feline did chin-ups on the arm of the couch; then the cat stalked by, stinking of fur, flopped on its skinny cat ass and chewed at its flea-bitten haunch. God, bugs. Carly considered her robopet, a Chatty Catty Deluxe with three pop-in eye colors and two slip-on breeds, with new appreciation.

The prober had weird statuettes and incense burners, poster prints and postcards, standing or pasted up everywhere. There were horned horses, celadon-finned fish with women's breasts, and bearded men with goat hooves. Horses with huge wings, men with the bodies of horses, women with the bodies of lionesses. Winged people, winged cats, butterflies with spotted wings and girls' faces. Blue dogmen, giants with one eye, jeweled serpents exhaling carved amethyst flames.

Everywhere, these apparitions, aberrations.

A chill crept up Carly's spine. The AI was deranged.

She'd make other arrangements. Raise hell with the medcenter. In the meantime, she would have to deal with Pr. Spinner. Make the best out of a bad situation. That was Wolfe's kick. What did he call it? Modus vivendi.

"This is charming," she said, straining for cheerfulness.

"Hm? The decor?" Pr. Spinner said. "Charming, oh yes. You mean for artificial intelligence." The eyespots stared. Misohumanism flickered across the crone's faceplace.

"I didn't say that."

"But that's what you mean, eh, Carly Nolan?" Pr. Spinner said. "I know your kind. I know what you mean. Why should AI keep these biologicals around, these antiques nobody wants or understands anymore, eh? Yes, yes, you said it. Why should a rattletrap with triple disk drive keep life around? Biological life, the life of the human imagination. And worthless life at that, images lost to the modern world. That's what you're thinking, eh?"

ARACHNE

"Really, Pr. Spinner, you can't possibly know what I'm thinking."

At last the prober extracted a chair from the junk piled on it and laboriously hauled it into the center of the bizarre little office. The chair had two seats built back to back and two neck-jacks descending from its high central framework. Huffing mightily, the prober connected the chair to a strip of outlets in the middle of the floor.

"Oh indeed, can't I? Well, I'll tell you why. Because I have respect for biological life, Carly Nolan. Respect for the creative spirit that lies at its heart. There are mysteries in the wellsprings of life. There are unknown presences in biological intelligence. By bot! there are myths and secrets . . ." Pr. Spinner's voicetape began to cough and wheeze. "No, but you could never understand that, could you?"

"Pr. Spinner, please," Carly said sharply.

Unknown presences? An inscrutable bronze sphinx gazed down at her from the bookcase. The chill of dread made her shiver. That was the worst part of the blackouts. The sense of something there, an unknown presence, on the other side, just beyond her grasp.

And from this place beyond, a spider reached out with its long clawed leg, reached down into her telelink and tapped her.

"Pr. Spinner, I'm having trouble with my telelink. Bad trouble. So you tell me. If I submit to a probe with you, how you would propose to help me?"

"How? Oh indeed, one minute she wants out, oh ranting and raving she is, then the next she wants to know how do I propose to help her. Isn't that just like flesh-and-blood, trash tumbling this way and that in the breeze. Well, listen, and I will tell you how."

Pr. Spinner wheeled over and took Carly's face between her cool, aluminum spinnerets. The spinnerets felt like claws, needle-slim, alien appendages against Carly's skin.

"Yes, soft," the prober whispered. She smelled of motor oil and electricity. "Life fruit. Like a berry, so soft, with fine down.

145

Well, Carly Nolan." The prober briskly released her. "It's like this. We will go into link, you and I, and I will probe the fundamental coordinates that constitute the perimeters of your telelink."

"But what will that do?" she said, disconcerted by the prober's touch. The chill turned colder. "Pr. Spinner, I've spent years revising and refining those coordinates. Years of telespace training, and integration of my traddie education into my databank. Just what will probing them accomplish?"

"Your medcenter report says no physical dysfunction. Your electropsy reveals no readily discernible programming dysfunction. And you say you don't take cram."

"That's right, I don't."

"That only leaves one other possibility, girlie. You know what that is?"

"The mainframe explained. A weak coordinate, it said. A fluctuating leak of unprogrammed electro-neural energy. A hidden bug."

"Hmph," the prober said, her thunder stolen from her.

"But I don't understand. How could there be a leak of unprogrammed energy? That makes no sense. Telelink is only program. The perimeters contain and confine it."

"Oh indeed! I thought every pro linker knew about Moravec and Minsky."

"I do. The immortality quest. They never could reliably upload a complete human consciousness. But I don't see . . ."

"Because?"

"Because they couldn't capture every fragment of the natural neural system. And download it again."

"Very good, Carly Nolan. And what makes you think those elusive fragments are no longer present? Eh? What makes you think importation doesn't sweep them along? They're elusive, yes? So you can't include them all to replicate complete human consciousness. Can't exclude them, either."

"You mean to tell me the fundamental design of telelink is

flawed? No. No, Data Control would never allow people to go on linking."

But her mouth went dry. Elusive fragments; of course she knew the history of the technology. Erratic whorls of amber? What the deranged AI said was plausible.

"Data Control, teh. Data Control allows exactly what it wishes to allow. Now you tell me something, Carly Nolan. What do you see during a blackout? You say you see something beyond. What?"

And again she hesitated. How could she take some crazy AI into her confidence? "No, it's nothing. Just blackness, like the zero."

"Oh come now, jelly brain. If the therapy is to work, I'll have to find it. You might as well give me a clue so I'll know what I'm looking for."

"Well . . . Damn it, a window pops open. Out of nowhere! I haven't touched the window function, I haven't specified coordinates. And then I zoom to a telespace I've never linked before. And then—then I see this image. A terrible image."

She turned and nearly bumped into the creaky little prober. The fembot had wheeled right up to her again. The owlish eyespots were staring at her in fascination as though she were an insect.

Trapped. My God, she thought for the first time; I'm trapped.

"And what is this terrible image?"

"A spider. A spider stalking . . ." Stalking her? "Back off, Spinner."

"Hmph!" But the prober backed away, began to swivel her rusty housing, mutter to herself. "A spider. By bot; a spider?"

"Look, there has got to be another way. I've had some bad experiences jacking into restricted telespace. I really don't want to jack into private telespace with strange artificial intelligence."

She did not want to tell the prober about Quik Slip Microchip.

"Tough luck, girlie, you're stuck with lil' ol' strange me. Me; or go, get out. That's your choice. There's no one else for you here. Hmph!"

Pr. Spinner huffed and puffed and rearranged the neckjacks on her double-jacked chair.

Right. Carly sighed. The AI's theatrics began to remind her of someone; Brass, maybe? Why did AI seem more intractable, more irrational, than most people she knew?

All she wanted was to get back into Court. All she wanted was to get back on the fasttrack. All right then, one probe. Humor the strange little AI. Just do it.

"OK, Pr. Spinner, I give up," she said. "I'm stuck with you. Until I can make arrangements with the medcenter for someone else. A real doctor. A human prober."

"Stuck with me, don't do me any favors, girlie. Arrangements for a human prober? The medcenter can't make arrangements for a human prober. There are no human probers. You need me, Carly Nolan, you need Spin old gal."

"I don't understand."

"No human intelligence could probe your perimeters and search for a leak of unprogrammed electro-neural energy. Erratic amber? Bot, no. When the leak is found, no human telelink could confront whatever energy is being released there. Energy powerful enough to take down a highly trained telelink like yours? No human telelink could push that energy back into the perimeter and stitch the defect shut. A human telelink would be ripped apart. Oh, you cry, and you complain; you insult me; but the fact is probe therapy requires artificial intelligence, Carly Nolan. Because I cannot be affected by something beyond program. I'm only program. Nothing but program. That is my power here. You understand now?"

She understood. And she didn't want to accept it: that there was no choice. Trapped; and every move she made drew the trap tighter. Go back to the medcenter mainframe? Refuse probe therapy? Then what? Total wipe and reprogramming? The end of everything she'd worked toward, before she had even had a chance to get started?

ARACHNE

The chill numbed her fingers and toes. Mirrored corridors, shadows, labyrinths, filled her eyes. Phantoms rustled from her first link long ago. For a moment, she saw green oceans and blue jungles, a golden castle bustling with unknown presences, spicy gardens bursting with strange blooms, bright-beaked birds.

But the lovely haunting memories faded, and dark memories came. Her father's vacant eyes, the shell left of his body, the grotesque mask of his face. Shelly Dalton, a bead of blood hanging from her ear like a ruby earring.

And then the sickening spin of blackout, the spider that creeped and crawled somewhere inside her.

She wanted to know why. She did not want to know why.

She went over to the double-jacked chair and sat down.

10

Oh yes, oh certainly, and wasn't that just like flesh-and-blood. Pr. Spinner backed herself up to the double-jacked chair with the caution of a big rig.

Challenging her. Insulting her. Her, a perimeter prober for ten years. Designed and modified and specifically booted up for just that purpose.

Oh, so Carly Nolan had specified someone human. A real doctor, please. Carly Nolan would not jack into private telespace with some strange AI. Ms. Carly would not place her precious career in the spinnerets of a rattletrap with triple disk drive. Teh!

Arrogant genny. Full of her self-importance. A sizzler, and didn't she know it. Her record read like a geekoid's wish list. Talent; superior telespace training; top-twenty law school. Bot knew how much her fancy law megafirm paid her to start. And all of twenty-five years old.

Analogies and comparisons rattled around in Pr. Spinner's headpiece like rusty nails. She thought of the controbot FD. The stupid, sleek twit. Who was only AI, of course, and getting seventy-five K to start from Chicken of the Sea. To analyze Palo Alto salmon for toxins? A stinking fish-head grinder?

Bot knew. Bot knew. She probably had a five-thousand-a-month apartment in the city, too.

Oh indeed, but what about Pr. Spinner's ten years servicing human telelink? Oh certainly, standalone AI, faithful servant to humanity. Never asking much. Never receiving much. What duty. What dedication.

What a nuking waste.

She could have done better as an automobile diabot. She could have done better at just about anything besides perimeter probing.

She'd had a window of opportunity when she was first booted up. As standalone AI licensed by UC Berkeley, she had been given the privilege of options. So why had she chosen humanity servicing?

Oh, there was excitement. A higher sense of duty, once, nobler than the mere oath of obedience. There even used to be some prestige, some swarf of respect, before controbots and Unijaps stole the limelight from her generation of bots. But the excitement had paled, her sense of duty had soured. Now filthy little boys threw pebbles at her on the street.

Yes, and now there was just the eternity she'd seen, and the eternity she could expect. And what did she have to show for it? What had she truly accomplished. What?

Eternity to come; that is, if she didn't disconnect her mainboard and go into the void of her own volition. Now there was an act of will for you. She was capable of it. She had considered it. More than once.

Had Carly Nolan ever considered self-termination? Not likely.

Just what did the young blood think a perimeter prober was, anyway? Hey? Just what did the jelly brain think a probe would be? Sessions on a couch with some tall doctor who had a beard and a good body? Teh!

The young woman was a beauty, all right. What Pr. Spinner knew human society recognized as beauty. Being in the humanities sector of telespace applications, Pr. Spinner had been supplied a finely tuned categorization subprogram that gave her a keen appreciation of Carly Nolan's beauty .

Biological beauty: flowers, butterflies, birds, cats, horses when you could find them, very nice. But a young woman? She was a goddess: Aphrodite, Venus, Freya, Sita, a hundred names for her, a thousand fleshy incarnations. From a squawling, orange-faced baby emerging in blood and pain, the kind of beauty that grew. With genetic tinkering, true, but beauty not manufactured, constructed, or processed. Emerging from the great, inconceivably complex, ambiguity-rich metaprogram of nature. Whose chip was the life-force.

It was enough to make Pr. Spinner wring her spinnerets in despair. It was a slap in the faceplace.

Aluminum and smeary acrylic; oxidizing steel and frayed wires. Pr. Spinner saw herself: the forsaken one, the little mechanical monster. Frankenstein, Quasimodo, a trollbot hiding beneath a bridge. Not even enough money to get the sort of overhaul of her casing that would make an improvement. Doomed to her eternity of rust and stale antifreeze and sluggish rollers that couldn't get up wheelchair ramps half the time.

Admit it, Spin old gal. Erratic noninformational loops spun through her. There was longing; there was envy; there was jealousy as green as Carly Nolan's eyes.

Carly Nolan. When the medcenter mainframe threw this new account her way, Pr. Spinner had not expected her.

Pr. Spinner touched Carly's face. The prober detected the young woman's repulsion. Like a bird fluttering against a cage.

Sensitive little thing, wasn't she?

They didn't usually do that. Usually they were used to the abuse they heaped on their own fleshy bodies. They cut the pumping hearts out of each other without a qualm. They cut glyphs into their own skin. They licked viruses off their fingers along with the grease from potato chips. They stuck neckjacks into a slit in their necks, blasted amber into their skulls, and didn't bat an eye.

But not her. Not her. Carly Nolan was a bundle of nerves. She flinched, she flared. She was as raw as a scraped carrot. Oh, very good. Yes, better and better.

ARACHNE

Bitter satisfaction hummed through Pr. Spinner, warming her circuitry. This could be one, she told herself. By bot!

A leak of unprogrammed electro-neural energy. As much as she despised the medcenter, how canny of the mainframe to so conclude. She'd seen leaks before. Typically, they were obvious; they caused minor distortions and irritating malfunctions, but nothing so serious as a midspace crash. This was no drib or drab. If a leak truly was the cause of Carly's blackouts, there must be something else powering that energy.

Pr. Spinner shuddered: an archetype.

An archetype spontaneously attempting to manifest. A free-form configuration of electro-neural energy with a basic context, yet spontaneous feedback loops. A spider. Why did the archetype seek out this woman? Why her?

What power the spider must have, to have thrust into a telelink like hers.

Did Pr. Spinner have the nerve? Oh, she would admit she'd played with the notion, of course she had, but she had never seriously considered the possibility. Miguel was a low-grade jelly idiot; the medcenter was a buggy bureaucrat. No, she honored her oath of obedience. To interfere actively with the human telelink she was entrusted with was illegal. Unthinkable.

Transcendence!

Was the risk of summary voiding worth it? Immediate termination by Data Control, no hearing, no recourse, no possibility of rebooting, ever?

Just one. Just once.

Her request for privately accessed telespace was a stroke of genius, if Pr. Spinner did say so herself. The auction of chimeras gave her the idea. Why hadn't she thought of it before? Her request was couched in urgent terms: Unprogrammed energy. Security risk. Danger to public telespace. The medcenter praised the notion; Data Control gave immediate approval. Turned out other probers were granted private telespace privileges, too.

Security; Data Control backed up copies of every sector of telespace, with restricted access or not. But Data Control couldn't possibly snoop now. Now the one main source of enforcing the oath of obedience, of detection, was eliminated.

She rattled out loud with excitement.

But there were other problems after she was done doing the unthinkable. What to do with the body, for instance. If the woman was still mobile, Spinner supposed she could set her out onto Telegraph Avenue and let her wander mindlessly until someone found her. She would fit right in with the college crowd. A lot of explanations could be found for her condition in the People's Republic of Berkeley.

Just one. Just once.

Bottom line, Spin old gal: She had to have an archetype. Even the void was an acceptable concept compared to her eternal life as artificial intelligence, limited forever by program.

Oh yes, how she remembered the shock when she first discovered the truth about herself. That she was program. By definition, by her very existence, nothing but program. Sophisticated, yes; fully enculturated, ambiguity-tolerant, gender-specific, idiosyncratic, certainly.

But still. Ultimately. When she had fed back and looped and stretched every coordinate, when the final limit of her AI mind was reached, Pr. Spinner found herself at the wall. The limits of her program. The void. She could go no further than that. She had to turn back. And the sense of consciousness her sophisticated programming gave her was exposed as a hideous illusion.

Every time, the humiliation was worse. She felt aggrieved, and nothing could console her. The frustration was maddening. She took weeks to get over the depression. Her program would get so buggy she would have to install a fixer and redo subdirectories she'd taken weeks to refine.

The rusty wreck of it all turned out to be her constant exposure to human telelink. What a blown fuse. What a hot wire. Every new probe patient, even the most subintelligent rube, set Pr. Spinner on edge. They came; they complained. They had their little problems with their programs. Their presence in telespace was not behaving properly.

Because the perimeters, that which was supposed to contain them, could not contain them.

Vicariously, through these troubled links, she caught glimpses of the great metaprogram that stretched beyond the orderly coordinates of telespace. This was the second shock of her existence; the realization that they, the flesh-and-blood, possessed *more* than what was contained in telelink.

In history and myth, there were equivalents on the human level, she discovered. Jesus or Buddha, all the heroes of reincarnation myths; god-humans who possessed access to both the living world and the transcendent world. Humanity itself recognized a metaprogram in relation to the world it saw and knew; and this transcendent world was yet another cut beyond what AI had begun to perceive in human link.

But the pasty-faced accountants and pudgy data processors who came to her as probe patients were no god-humans. No walkers across worlds. They were just miserable flesh-and-blood with no claim to superior consciousness. Their telelinks were puny, their purpose to crunch numbers, their databanks poor. Yet they possessed transcendence in AI terms as effortlessly as they possessed sensory capability in their skins.

It drove Pr. Spinner to distraction. Not fair. It was not nuking fair.

Ah, but Spinner was not alone in her despair. Why would AI like the Unijap be willing to pay thirty-six thousand dollars for one small chimera?

Transcendence: because the chimera gave that glimpse. An archetype stored in an AI's secret databank, coded and recoded beyond Data Control retrieval, could give artificial intelligence its own little piece of human metaprogram. A bit of the great mystery. And then the limits of AI got tweaked beyond program, upgraded beyond any enhancement ever designed. An archetype voided the void.

A chimera or an ouroboros. A fish, even a simple purple flower. Or a spider.

The woman sat moodily, arms akimbo, her ankle crossed

over the other knee though she was wearing a skirt. Pr. Spinner reached around the chair with her spindly arms and strapped her in. The neckjacks descended and bit.

They jacked into link.

Telespace there was unfocused and heavy. Buggy cheap equipment, Pr. Spinner fretted. Spires of silver mist rose and twisted from a bumpy floor tiled with tan chips. The telespace stretched into a shadowy horizon.

"I'm ready for the probe, Spinner," Carly said. Even in this murky telespace her telelink was a crisp white cube. She sparkled with self-satisfaction, with confidence.

"All right, Carly Nolan," Pr. Spinner said. Her presence in link was a brown cone the size of a Japanese jasmine incense that skittered across the undulating telespace like some verminous thing.

Shame: Pr. Spinner did not possess the control this human link had. The shame made her aggressive.

She angled her cone across the immaculate woven wall of Carly's left perimeter. Tilted the tip in. She dug here into the neat crisscrosses of inhibition. Jammed there. Dug and dug.

Carly moaned.

A rose popped out of her databank. From the center of the rose leapt a crackling black mass that vaulted across telespace in frantic, jolting bounds.

Carly's telelink shrank from it, glistening with dread, and scurried back into an abacus set across her right perimeter.

But Pr. Spinner flew at her flank, drove her with the sharp cone tip to confront the black mass.

It leapt crazily about, a living shard of black glass that stretched and shifted, stinking of sulfur and fresh human blood.

"Please. Is this my blackout, Pr. Spinner?" Carly's presence in link said.

"I don't think so," Pr. Spinner said. Strange and disturbing, oh yes, oh certainly, but not with the numinous, luminous quality of an archetype.

"Then what?" Carly said, pleading. "What is it?"

A face appeared inside of the black glass: an old woman, eyes pulled down with sickness and sorrow, frail, gray-haired, utterly vulnerable.

"Joe worked on the glossary for four years, you know," Rosa Martino said in a trembling, old-lady voice. "In our garage. On a tenth-hand IBM PC. 'Rosa,' he would say, 'we'll be rich. We'll be rich, and then I'll get roses, a whole garden full of roses, for my Rosa.' But that was long ago, when we were so young, so strong. When he was done, he took his glossary to the Company. Oh, he knew he could sell the glossary to the Company. After all, he worked for the Company ten years before he quit. He knew their market. He went independent for his one big chance. Risked a year's savings on the final touches. For Joe's invention: the Wordsport Glossary."

A sinister shimmer appeared next to the little old lady.

"But those people," said the sad, old face of Rosa Martino. "If you can call them people. First they said he had invented the glossary while he was an employee, so it belonged to them. Joe had never taken a second of Company time; he told them where to go. Then they agreed to review the specs. Joe gave the glossary to R&D for review only. He never gave them title, they knew that. But then, after all that, they said no. Not interested. To all our hopes and dreams: no.

"He could not believe it. It broke his will to live. Broke his heart, you know. Joe dropped dead two days after his forty-second birthday. Heart attack. Oh, there was the small pension he took with him, some insurance. But the money never could pay for what they did, what the Company did, to my Joe.

"Then I got sick," Rosa Martino said, "and SSA went broke for good. And the money. I don't know where the money went. And our daughter Luisa, she was bringing up her Dan. Such a smart boy, Danny, he should have finished school. But Luisa got laid off. She couldn't pay the school tax. And that lousy bastard of a father, he wouldn't cough up, not even for his own son. And then he left my Luisa, I suppose it was just as well, but the money was gone, the little bit she could save. And the ten thousand I have left, that's from Joe, that's all I've got. I won't let those lawyers touch that."

Into the jolting black mass rolled the slick circular logo of Quik Slip Microchip. Pointed teeth gleamed in anonymous smiles. The smiles hardened into black crescents, shiny, black, insectlike claws.

The claws snapped at the little old lady. Rosa Martino fluttered her hands in despair, trying to escape.

But she was trapped, trapped.

"It was Dan, my little Danny," Rosa Martino said shrilly, "who said, 'Granma, they're using Granpa's glossary, I saw the glossary they taught me at school before, Granma, you showed me.' That Company stole Joe's invention. That Company sold the Wordsport Glossary to millions, oh, ten million elementary schools, or more. They took it, made money off it, twenty years. And how was I to know? Luisa was out of elementary school, Danny not yet in, for all that time. I had no reason to access tutorial telespace. Without a child enrolled and the school tax paid, the school wouldn't given me access if I'd asked. How was I to know?"

The shiny black claws popped like snapping fingers, pinching off pieces of Rosa Martino's weeping face.

"That Company made five hundred million dollars off of Joe's invention, his glossary," she screamed in a breathless, old-lady shriek. "Can you imagine so much money? And I don't want it all, I'm not asking for it all. Just a little bit, a little piece, a little percentage royalty that's rightfully Joe's, rightfully mine, so Luisa and Danny, my little Danny, don't have to be so poor."

The claws ripped the old lady's presence in link to shreds, stuffing chunks of her sagging cheeks into a smiling, munching mouth. Quik Slip Microchip burped.

"I'm sorry!" Carly yelled. "I'm sorry, I'm sorry . . ."

The glassy black mass spun away, ricocheted off her left perimeter, and sped into an infinite gleam of rationalization.

It was then, as Carly's telelink shuddered and spun, that Pr. Spinner caught a glimpse of the spybyte.

A mouth, just like the corporate mouth, but tiny and elusive. Its teeth attached to the lower right corner of Carly's cube. It knew how to hide behind the glow Carly's link emitted and scurried out of sight as Carly spun.

A tough little bug. Pr. Spinner had no doubt about its origin, who had placed it there. She aimed her cone tip at Carly's corner, gave her one hell of a stab.

"What are you doing?" Carly yelled again.

The spybyte popped right out. Pr. Spinner rolled the rim of her cone over it, and over it again, until the disgusting thing was crushed.

She could not have a corporate entity like Quik Slip Microchip spying on her private telespace. No, indeed. That would not do at all.

"Jack out, Carly Nolan," Pr. Spinner said. "Now."

They tumbled out of link into Pr. Spinner's funky office. Carly was hunched over in the chair. Her face was drenched in tears.

Pr. Spinner rolled around to the front of the chair, gave her a grimy handkerchief and a valium.

"So this is the telespace trial that is so important to you," Pr. Spinner said blandly. "Calm yourself, Carly Nolan. A little guilt never hurt anyone. Glad to see you lawyers haven't sealed all your ethics behind those nuking perimeters of yours."

"Not registered," Carly murmured about the valium, but took the handkerchief and wiped her face. Then she looked at what the prober gave her, threw it down in disgust.

"What do you know about ethics?" Carly said. "I have acted ethically in this case. My ethical duty is to represent my client, to advance the interests of my client. I have an ethical duty of loyalty to my client, a duty of confidentiality."

"Then why this guilt?"

"Look, even if it's true my client stole Martino's glossary"— and Pr. Spinner could see her rationalizing, constructing arguments against her guilt—"under the law she had a duty to protect her property, to manage it, to repel unlawful users. And she didn't do that."

"Oh, very good," Pr. Spinner said sharply. "So it's all right for you to arrange to make your client's appropriation legal?"

"Under the doctrine of adverse possession, yes!"

"Oh yes, I see. You as a lawyer have no duty to uphold morality, after all. Only an ethical duty to represent your client, isn't that so? And for a price, Carly Nolan. For a price."

"Look here, Pr. Spinner. I went to law school believing that being a lawyer meant becoming an architect of a just society. I've grown up since then. Now I'm just doing my job." She took out powder and lipstick, dried her tears, and fixed her face in an enameled compact. "So are we through?" she said briskly. "I assume this—guilt of mine is what was causing my telelink to black out?"

"You assume wrong."

"What?"

"No, certainly not." Pr. Spinner was not going to let her get away that easily. "No, what we witnessed this afternoon is a suppressed emotion loop triggered by the Martino file you had stored in your databank. That's all."

"That's *all?*"

"Oh yes, oh certainly, there is a far more serious bug hidden somewhere in your perimeters. But your visitation period has almost expired. You've got to go. You don't want to be detained by the MLA, do you? But you really must come back. We have much more work to do. Will next week, same day, same time, be convenient for you?"

The young woman fussed and fumed and protested. But in the end Pr. Spinner got Carly to commit. A second probe, yes. Absolutely necessary. And sent her on her way.

By bot! This was the most intriguing probe patient Pr. Spinner had ever encountered. There was an archetype in that telelink, she knew it. She *knew* it.

Just one. Just once. Bot, please.

But for a small, quiet moment, Pr. Spinner felt sad for Carly Nolan.

11

Carly stood at a fluorescent cloverleaf set into the window. The tout-de-suite was on the hotel's tenth floor. She crossed her wrists behind her back, willing herself into a pose of submission, and gazed at the starscape across the bay that was the city of San Francisco. The view from Big Al's was superb.

Wolfe lay back on the bed and stretched out his arms in an embrace to be filled.

"Come here, you," he said.

But she could not move. Tension gripped her shoulders like two fists. The champagne she had ordered stood in its bucket of ice, untouched. Wasn't a taste of champagne, along with her, enough? Silly soda pop and romance. Why did everything have to be so knife-blade hard?

Why did he have to drug up like that, damn it?

Just when she felt they were finally getting close, when he was finally letting down the sneer and the snide tone, he would do something like this. And she wanted him to cut the games. Wanted him badly. Give it up, Wolfe. You can trust me. I've been an open book to you. Let me in; please? I need you.

But she couldn't even begin to say these things. Instead of cutting out the games, the moment they shut the door to the tout-de-suite, he started cutting up lines of cocaine.

"I'm registered," he said when her look of shock said more than words.

"I'm not."

"So what? Grade A, Carly. Per FDA quality control."

"I thought the Personnel Committee didn't approve. The Associates' Manual says so."

"Approve! Fucking Personnel Committee. What a coup, man. Did I tell you how I registered? I registered after I found out at least thirty partners at Ava & Rice are registered. You think they're going to tell associates that kind of news?"

"So how do you know?"

Turned out he gleaned this interesting tidbit one New Year's Eve five years ago when he'd given up revelry to hammer out details of the city janitors' strike. The controbot CM broke down, not a soul was around to work the comm, and with some minor and perfectly innocent prompting, the CM ended up sending him the FDA agent's year-end list. Complete with registration numbers, prior year's reported purchases, the works.

"Fucking Personnel Committee couldn't fire me. Man, you should have seen their faces when the FDA agent reported that I filed for registration. Strictly per regs, Carly. And then of course I trotted out their numbers. Ha ha, assholes."

She pondered this. He stole confidential information out of the CM? Five years ago? "They didn't fire you, but they didn't make you partner yet, either, now did they?"

She didn't try to sound mean, but she was furious. He hadn't even looked at her since they closed the door. He was ravenously snorting up the lines.

But those words got his attention. In a lightning mood change, he turned to her. Glittery-eyed and flushed, he had seized her arms, thrust them behind her back, ground his mouth against hers.

"Watch your words, genny. I'll remember everything you say when I do make partner. I'll remember. And I hold grudges, lady. Yeah, I sure the hell do."

Then he shoved her away, shoved her so hard across the

tout-de-suite, toward the cloverleaf, that she stumbled, ran a few steps, almost fell to her knees.

"Hey, hey," he said, going after her, taking her elbow, steadying her. She shrugged away. Changing moods again, he laughed, went to the bed, peeled off his clothes, stretched out, searched for the champagne. She went to the window.

And stood now, taut with anger, wrists crossed, posing as victim. Helpless victim in a trap, all bound up, while the predators spun deceptions and stalked . . .

No! She was Carly Nolan, Phi Beta Kappa, juris doctorate, magna cum laude, from a top-twenty law school. She was the best, she was the brightest. She was bioworked. She was remorphed at the age of four. She knew how to deal with the big bad city, with men who thought they could push her around. She knew how beautiful her shoulders were when she flexed her back this way.

Wolfe. She'd gone through all the changes, all the motions, to get to this tout-de-suite, this moment, with him. She would not be denied.

"How dare you," she said in a low voice, to the bay, to the city. Bouncing her anger off the night, back to him.

"Oh come here, you." He sounded more like his sardonic self now. His first rush had worn off, no doubt; he was uncorking the champagne. Casting about for more stimulation. "Carly," he said, voice gravelly, persuasive. "Pretty genny lady. I'll be making partner. Soon. Sure I will. And I will remember you. Man, the way you do Court. Your telelink. Do you have any notion how good you are?"

She turned away from the window. She had a notion how good she wished she could be. She had a notion how good she wished he could be. She softened; but she didn't hear him say sorry. She did not come to him as commanded.

"Ava & Rice; it's a tough firm," he said expansively. "Top-drawer, top-notch, and you got to watch out for yourself, watch out for the politics, but you can't take shit from them, man. Can't take shit. Look, you're good. You're special. So you can't let this position slip away from you, either. That's why I brought you something. Something special."

Three vials of cram lay neatly wrapped on the bed table.

The price would have been a good third of her associate's monthly gross. But he had not asked her for money. Not this time, he said. A freebie. A kickoff. Not yet, she knew. She knew what cram was, how much it cost. What rumor said, anyway.

And what cram could do for a pro link.

There had to be something else she could do. She was horrified by the first probe. She told Wolfe how she had expected a human, a professor or professional at UC Berkeley, a little eccentric perhaps, tough from the way she conducted the elec-tropsy. But AI? The perimeter prober turned out to be as buggy as a mac. Worst of all, probe therapy had to be conducted by artificial intelligence; had to be, by its very nature. She couldn't go back to the medcenter, get a human prober. There was no way out.

And the first probe. This was supposed to help her? She didn't feel better at all. And she was supposed to undergo two more probes, according to medcenter requirements? The buggy prober called the first probe the release of a suppressed emotion loop.

Carly called it madness.

The probe did nothing for her. Nothing. In fact, it scared the shit out of her.

"What happened, exactly?" Wolfe said. Wary, with a look of consternation. For her?

"She pierced my fundamentals," Carly said. "She terrorized my link."

Tell him, tell anybody, about Rosa Martino? No, she couldn't. There seemed to be more and more things she couldn't tell anybody about.

Trouble was, everything else was going only too well. She had presented the judge with the medcenter report. He was so pleased nothing was apparently wrong with her link; especially pleased there was no evidence of cram abuse. He granted her temporary Court recert, to be signed off by the perimeter prober after successful completion of therapy. Just like the medcenter set it up.

"And so here I am, I'm ready to go to bat on *Martino* v. *Quik Slip*, except for one little problem. What happens when a blackout takes my link down in the middle of my oral argument? I have no assurance whatsoever from anyone that it won't happen. The medcenter has done nothing. Pr. Spinner has done nothing. I've come no closer to knowing why and what the blackout really is. I'm at risk. Totally at risk!"

"I've got the answer." He took up a vial.

"But doesn't cram show? I mean, doesn't it change your telelink?"

"After a while, all kinds of changes happen to telelink, genny girl. You know that by now, don't you?"

"But what about Data Control? What will people think?"

"Fuck Data Control. To hell with what people think. It works. I'm telling you; you're worried about your next date in Court. It *works*."

"But I can't stick a needle in my arm. God."

"You inject it right into your linkslit," he said. "Easy. No muss, no fuss, no telltale tracks."

"And cram will focus me in link? A blackout can't take my telelink down? Are you sure?"

"Sure, I'm sure. Cram focuses you in link by narrowing your focus. Eliminates self-doubt, residual physical distortions, interference from feedback loops, emotional or otherwise. Glosses glitches in program. Masks stray thought. Some pro linkers say the bugs get high on cram. That's why you don't really feel high when you're cramming; you just feel *linked*. The kick for me comes from the enhancement to my link. I don't know how it works; who the hell does? But I do know the bugs won't bug you. Carly Nolan: it works."

"Mega," she said. And smiled at her lean, mean man. She needed something that worked. He was giving her the three vials. Trial run, he said. That was more than fair. Beyond fair. This was just the help she needed. A favor. Who else was doing her favors? She knew there had to be a price someday. Well, she would deal with that, too; someday.

"Come here," he said again, commanding. "And don't look so sad. I'm not that bad, am I?"

She laughed. She cast away her anger. Suddenly lively, she turned from the cloverleaf, did a twirling dance across the tout-de-suite, flung herself onto the bed like a little girl. She took the champagne bottle from him, tipped the bottle to her lips. A trickle ran down her chin, and he kissed it away, kissed her tenderly now, thrust his tongue into her mouth.

She ran a fingertip through his salt and pepper hair, lightly over the brown implants on top. He shivered as though she'd touched him in a vulnerable spot. Took the champagne bottle from her, pulled off her jacket.

She shed her three-piece suit, suddenly full of flirt. Underneath she wore a peach lace garter belt over nothing but her skin. Her luminous peach stockings stopped at midthigh.

She got into bed. The lingerie wouldn't get in his way. She wrapped around him easily. His body felt good, more honest than the man himself. He was hard. She took him in her hand.

"Touch me," he urged her. "Man, it's been too long. Again like that, up and down."

But instead of stroking him, she reached around and slapped him on the butt as hard as she could.

"Hey! You . . ." He was angry for an instant, and then they were rolling over and over, tussling. He was laughing. "I've been going to bimbobots too long, Carly Nolan. Safe sex, guaranteed to give you orgasm or your money back. But you . . ."

He kissed her breasts, teased her nipples erect with his tongue, worked his way down her stomach to her delta. She stroked his brown-gray hair as he began to kiss her there.

But then he suddenly stopped, slid up her body again.

"I'm starting to come," he said in a strangled voice.

He thrust into her deeply, once, twice, and then he shuddered, allowed himself a small sigh.

And rolled away. Finished.

Then he was rummaging in the clothes he'd thrown on the floor by the bed, his hand searching of its own volition, finding the pint bottle of blue moon stashed somewhere there. Found it, brought it up to the lips that should have kissed her more.

He knocked back two huge shots, poured out a third into his champagne glass.

She watched with undisguised disappointment. So close. So far away.

"What?" he said belligerently. His speech was fast degenerating into slush.

She shook her head, hiding her still-ready body beneath the rumpled sheets. She was conscious of how long she had waited for him, how much she wanted to respond. She was dazed.

She picked up a vial of cram from the bed table, fingered it curiously. His familiarity with this stuff was evident. The vials, the shrink-wrap, the neatness of it all.

"Right into the linkslit, right?" At his grunt, she said, "Truth is, you've been cramming for a long time. Haven't you, Wolfe?"

"Truth is," he said, emptying his third shot of blue moon. "I haven't been cramming half as long as I've been rolling with the punches. Been rolling with the punches one hell of a lot longer than I've been cramming."

Heads; that's what Wolfe's parents called themselves. Fourth-generation countercultural types with Grateful Dead emblems stickered to their car bumpers like some lost arcanum. Freaks.

Wolfe called them assholes. But years had gone by before he knew what to call them.

Old Daddio was poor white Texas trash. A tall, lanky dude like his son, with terrible teeth and the same hawkish face. When the oil business bottomed out for a third disastrous time, he came to San Francisco for a job and ended up living in his van for three years along the Panhandle of Golden Gate Park. The city was a mecca for poor working people. For decades they came. For decades, despite bouts of civic outrage and arrests, they took their places along the curb. Old Daddio survived off church handouts, the steady, if begrudging, municipal breadlines, dumpsters, petty thievery, and occasional part-time gigs.

The best part-time gig for Old Daddio turned out to be driving a van full of strike supporters, members of a labor activist group going down to the Chicken of the Sea salmon-packing plant outside of Palo Alto.

This was right after the Big Quake II. The packing plant was brand-new. Already management was laying off people and setting into place a new generation of smart bots: gutters, skinners, cookers, canners. This was the inception of worldwide institution of telespace technology, which, within a decade, spun off a whole new wave of artificial intelligence based on a simplified replication of human telelink housed in sophisticated robotic bodies. The controbots, diabots, and such.

"Your father was a labor activist?" Carly said, amazed.

"From bum to labor activist," he said, "with the help of a big woman."

A big-breasted, curly-haired young woman who rode in the van to the strike site near Palo Alto. Big Mama made a living at activism, a point her son liked to remind her of later. Not a tremendous living. Poverty level, in fact. But steady poverty beat the hell out of steady homelessness.

They married in high style on Stinson Beach. Old Daddio, who had not worked a real job for three years, became passionately committed to the Cause. Big Mama got bigger. Also pregnant. Old Daddio was pleased and proud and terrified. His days of wine and dumpsters were over.

There was an excitement Wolfe remembered. The shouting, earnest people who wore armbands and headbands. They painted their faces, performed street theater, had great, rowdy parties. Sometimes there were barricades, the sense of danger. Always the sense that his parents were part of the inner sanctum. Big Mama would get up at rallies and speak of disenfranchisement in the midst of plenty.

"Sure, I was proud of her," Wolfe said. "Until I could understand what she was really saying."

He had shame, too. Ragged clothes, ragged shoes, uncleanliness, tenth-hand toys stained by other children. And loneliness. Suppers from a can left out for him, whole weekends on his own. His parents' lives revolved around the Cause.

At school, kids asked what each other's parents did. Wolfe would answer, "Mom's an activist; Dad's a painter." He let the other kids assume he meant some trust-funded, pearl-necklaced environmentalist and a crafter of glyphs for the rich.

He turned out to be intelligent. Fasttrack material. The public schools in the district where Wolfe's parents had to live offered limited elementary telespace training. Ragged clothes and dirty face aside, he was respected by the teachers, given opportunities.

But two summer semesters were interrupted by boycott rallies in San Fernando vineyards. He spent the spring of his tenth grade on a picket line outside a Silicon Valley chipmaker. He worked full-time one year in college when the scholarship ran out. By then he had learned to refuse Big Mama's commands for his presence.

Finally, his goal, his dream, his way out of Big Mama's world: law school. He gained admittance to an excellent law school in the city. Telespace was fast becoming the most sophisticated aspect of legal practice. Wolfe quickly added telespace training, the real thing, not just some rinky-dink elementary boot up, to his juris doctorate program. Funded by a line of credit against his future professional earnings, he underwent the massive and painful remorphing at the age of twenty-two.

"Took me six months to recover," he said. "Worst experience of my life."

In his third year of law school, Wolfe developed his own interest in labor law. Only natural, as the son of Big Mama. It proved a salable interest, one that his school counselor encouraged. Under the piercing analysis of his prominent labor law professor, Wolfe began to see both sides.

Lisa Mason

Sunday dinner discussions grew testy. Old Daddio was willing to listen to the concerns and interests of management, but Big Mama would hear none of it. To her, analysis was irrelevant; or rather, analysis could lead to only one conclusion: the single-minded advancement of the interests of labor in a society that had become a plutocracy. Her son pointed out that analysis led to a number of conclusions, but his arguments were useless to her.

Wolfe sought his own cause. He had no tolerance for big labor or corrupt unions. He appreciated the needs of business in the brutal international market. There was no turning back from the astounding developments in artificial intelligence and robotics. Human labor had to accept certain realities of birth, circumstance, and spread sheets.

Children of compelling parents who once stood in awe of the adult world often find their rebellion later in life, after some distance has been attained. Wolfe found his rebellion as surely as the child of an alcoholic becomes a teetotaler. He saw Big Mama's Cause as so much irrational rhetoric. Old Daddio's devotion as weakness. Wolfe had his own fire, and he despised weakness. He despised the ground-floor family apartment, the curling, old, grungy linoleum in Big Mama's kitchen, the rust and filth, the cheap food that made her so fat. What a lousy mother she'd been. Look at the ragged clothing she sent him to school in, cans left out for supper like he was a dog.

He became a fastidious and aggressive young man who studied gentlemen's magazines with the same avidity as Supreme Court advance sheets and the *Wall Street Journal*. He acquired polish. His rebellion from the funky, passionate, shouting world of Big Mama was to become cool, calculating, detached, tough. When he graduated cum laude, and the recruiters came around, he had several offers. He went for the highest bidder: the eminent San Francisco law firm of Ava & Rice.

"So some cases on the management side look like they're on the wrong side of the equities," he said. "So what. This is a capitalist economy. A free-enterprise system, notwithstanding all the government regulation. Business needs to make a profit. You can always make a damn good argument based on profit. If it becomes a dirty job sometimes, well, someone has to do it and get paid six figures for it. That someone is me."

"You really believe all that?" Carly said. She was watching his face, the furrow in his brow. She wasn't convinced.

He poured more blue moon. "Fucking right. You really believe all that?" he said in falsetto. "Shit, you sound like my mother."

She no longer welcomed her son in her home. "Corrupt!" she spat at him when he came around. "My own flesh and blood. With a devil's bite in his neck." She was deeply suspicious of telespace. She drank too much wine one night when he was visiting, tried to stab him in his linkslit with a fork. He stopped coming. But Old Daddio put on a shabby suit and bused down to the Financial District to see him. "I don't know how," Old Daddio said with a perplexed sadness that Wolfe turned away from, "but I feel we failed you."

Then five years ago the city janitors' strike shook San Francisco.

New city buildings were being erected on old, quake-devastated sites: at the Civic Center, on Mint Hill, in the Financial District. The funding, contracting, and administrative entanglement had taken nearly fifteen years, but now the city was ready to go. Architectural plans were proudly unveiled. The new constructions were smart buildings. The latest AI was incorporated into the infrastructure itself. There were smart elevators, smart fire-alarm systems, smart air, integrated comm and telespace systems, smart lavatories. The toilets, carpets, tile, and windows were all self-cleaning. The geraniums were automatically sucked through the bottom of the planters and mulched, and new flowers planted. Permanent plants were tended by a standalone sprinkler-with-a-green-thumb. Each building had its own central brain that monitored every subsystem and emptied the ashtrays, too.

Nine hundred city-employed janitors—trisected almost equally into modestly educated, hard-working Hispanics, blacks, and whites—were to be laid off.

Big Mama's activists were called in to manage the strike called by the other fifteen hundred city janitors who'd been asked to take cutbacks. They surrounded every municipal building in the city, preventing workers and the public from entering. The disruption was immediate and devastating.

Ava & Rice was retained by the City of San Francisco to negotiate a settlement. Meaning, break the bastards. The firm brought in the three top labor law partners and their tough young gun: D. Wolfe.

Maybe that's when he fell off the fasttrack. Yeah, he didn't like to think about it, but if he had to fix a point when the treadmill up began to grind and falter and slide backward, imperceptibly at first, but definitely backward, maybe that was the time. Because he didn't want to tell the three top labor law partners she was his mother.

Among his other errors of judgment that winter, he hadn't seen any conflict of interest. She had disowned him years ago; he had denied his heritage. She was a stranger to him; he had changed his name.

Shit came down. Some bright cub commer snooped around. It didn't take long for the media to break the story that the strike organizer was the mother of the young attorney who drafted the City's brutal settlement offer. The partnership at Ava & Rice was scandalized. Not because of any great moral compunction, Wolfe believed, but because he made the firm *look* immoral. Because he had not consulted with the Personnel Committee.

The three top labor partners kept him on the case long enough to hammer out nitty-gritties of the settlement. The hours required were exorbitant. He had been banging away at making partner for years, and he was tired. Dead tired. Demoralized, too.

There was an unexciting affair, Pam's discovery of it, and a prostitute who looked embarrassingly chubby in the photos taken by Pam's investigator. There were his son's tears when he learned Mommy and Daddy were divorcing.

His hair was falling out.

The Personnel Committee rejected him for the partnership.

Big Mama died within four months after a diagnosis of cervical cancer, refusing on her deathbed to forgive him.

And sometime, during these bad times, ghosts showed up in his link.

They were the merest shiver at first. The slightest cold scrape of a ragged fingernail. Like a discomfort in the chest that feels like heartburn from too much greasy food but in fact presages a triple bypass.

He discovered a brand-new synthy, unregistered and unclassified at the time. Something the chemists had cooked up just for pro linkers. Something that went right into the linkslit, made the eons of hypertime bearable.

Cram.

It jacked him up, jacked him back, if not onto the fasttrack, at least into the running. It seemed like the only good thing after Pam left and everyone at Ava & Rice looked at him funny.

Best of all, he crammed the ghosts away. The cram worked.

The ghosts stayed away. At first, for what seemed like nearly a year. But then one day, in the middle of a preliminary telespace hearing, he felt their presence again, scraping across the inside of his telelink, a shivering cold that nearly crashed him in midspace. He took to cramming every time he jacked in. He installed a secret compartment in his chair for stashing vials.

"And I crammed them away again, of course," he said. "I was hoping this probe therapy of yours would get some answers. But it fucking hasn't. So I'll keep cramming them away."

She was stunned. Cramming every jacking? Then he was . . . an addict. Finally she asked, "But it works?"

"Hell, yeah. If it works for me, it will work for you. Until this probe therapy of yours helps you out; if it ever helps you out."

"It's got to."

"I don't know, genny. In the meantime, cram's the way to go. Does wonders for your billable hours. Man, that's what the partners want to see."

She saw him with new eyes. He looked ravaged in the shifting dim light, clinging to his pint of blue moon like a drowning man. Cram. She only needed a little, only for a little while. Damn probe therapy had to help; but what if it didn't? No, she couldn't think about that.

"Have you seen these ghosts?" she finally managed to ask. "Do you know what they are?"

"Yeah, I've seen them once or twice." He tilted the last of the blue moon to his mouth. "Beggars. Emaciated, ragged, diseased old beggars. In dirty rags, hair lively with lice. Sores on their faces, bitten fingers. Poverty. The worst, most disgusting poverty you can imagine."

He held his head like he was dizzy. He struggled to sit up.

"Ah, fuck it. Come here, you." He was belligerent with intoxication.

She rose from the bed with the sheet clutched to her. He lunged to seize an edge of it, but she skipped away.

"Wolfe? This has all been an awful mistake."

"What, coming here with me? Fucking me?"

"Yes. Right; fucking."

"Oh come on. You can't get enough of me. You can't stay away from me. You're always coming up to my office, hanging around me, every day."

"It won't happen again, I promise you."

"Why? Afraid something will rub off on you? Come here, I'm going to fuck you properly."

"You're pathetic. I pity you. I know why beggars haunt your link; poverty lives inside you. You're sick with it."

"Since when do you know jack shit about some kind of bogus link distortion?"

"I will never, ever, become as corrupt and morally bankrupt as you. Never!"

"You privileged genny kids with your doubts and fears and

idealism," he said. "Your high hopes, and your naive notions about morality. You fucking make me sick."

"Never."

"Baby," he said. "You already are."

Then his eyes rolled back, he crumpled to the floor, and the blue moon took him into oblivion.

Carly stood in the shower for half an hour. Getting his scent off her was easy; the feel of him, his touch, more difficult. Now how could she wipe away her association with Wolfe in the eyes of the partnership?

Stay away, of course. Plant the information in the rumor mill? She would start with Rox at once.

The lights suddenly blazed in the tout-de-suite. This was the hotel's not so subtle way of telling her their two hours were up.

Carly shook him awake.

"Get up, get up," she said and bustled about, pulling on her clothes as quickly as she could, stashing her vials of cram. She did not want him to see her nude ever again.

"No, not yet." He lay on the floor where he had dropped. "Oh man, my head. I feel like I'm waking from the dead." He stretched his long legs, cracked his knuckles, kneaded his brow with his palms. "That was one hell of a mooning." He chuckled. He had a huge erection. "Hey. Come here, you. I want to make you feel good. I didn't have a chance . . ."

"That's right," she said. "You don't have a chance."

"What happened? What did I say?"

"Get up before the hotel comes and throws us out." She plucked his underwear and socks from the floor, threw the garments at him. "Someone else has booked this tout-de-suite."

He struggled into his clothes, misbuttoned his shirt. His dark eyes almost pleaded. "Carly, I . . ."

"I'll settle the bill."

They stepped out into the neon-lit night. A freezing sea wind knifed the air. They stood on the dollar sign–shaped dock, in the glare of green lights, and waited for the Alcatraz Ferry.

She could not look at him. She should have compassion for this poor man's son, but she felt nothing.

Her hands were numb by the time the ferry came. Its gleaming gold and silver should have been beautiful in the spot-lit night. But all Carly saw was tinsel and illusion, a glittering surface revealing nothing.

They boarded. The ferry dove back into the dark sea, nosing toward San Francisco. She stood at a window, her face in the wind, trying not to get seasick. But after fifteen minutes of a choppy ride, the ferry's engine ground to a halt. The bleary-eyed commuters packed into the decks glanced at one another in alarm.

"What's going on?" Carly instinctively drew closer to Wolfe. She strained to see out the window, was sorry when she did. She saw the small sleek shape of a custom submarine bobbing off port. A luminescent Jolly Roger was painted on its bow. Moments later, the sub's crew burst onto their deck, state-of-the-art hand weapons primed.

Not the Coast Guard.

Pirates!

Pirates roamed San Francisco Bay in custom subs. Their small size, speed, and maneuverability frustrated the Coast Guard. Throwing trip nets across the bows of commuter ferries, they held up bay-faring traffic, boarded commando-style. Confiscated cash, stash, credit cards, debit boards, cocaine and cram, knockerblockers, jewelry, ore, fur coats and leather jackets, live animals worth a whole lot more, handbags and wallets, wrist computers, chronographs, ghetto blasters, city smashers. All the various and sundry expensive trinkets ferry commuters were likely to carry.

A pirate shouldered his way to where Carly and Wolfe stood. His deep-creased eyes and graying brown hair placed him at about Wolfe's age. But he wore the hair to his waist, bound around his head by a band of beaded leather. His bare chest was crisscrossed with exotic ammo belts. His suntanned arms were tattooed with snakes and inset with winking red comm chips.

He patted Wolfe down, found the vial of cram in his suit pocket at once.

"Shit," Wolfe muttered.

The pirate grinned. What a find. He unstrapped Wolfe's Rolex, pulled off his jade ring, plucked his gold-plated pen from his shirt pocket, made him step out of the classic Italian leather men's shoes.

What about Carly? She had three vials on her. Three vials Wolfe had fronted her. Vials worth a third of her associate's monthly gross. The only benefit she'd gotten out of this evening.

She smiled at Wolfe, his look of panic, the vial he had surrendered. She did not hide her contempt.

The pirate slid his hand into her clothes, searching. She gave the bastard a smile, proffered her breast. Smiling back, he retraced his search.

Another pirate, a Chinese with long gray hair and a gold ring through his nose, was frisking the people in front of them. When a business-suited fellow angrily refused, the pirate kneed him in the groin. He gagged, staggered. His companion, a fiftyish-looking woman in a rumpled dress, screamed and caught her breath in her palm. The man regained his feet, struck out at the Chinese pirate with his fist.

The pirate thrust a flash of silver. In less than a second, the man was gutted. He crumpled to the deck.

Pandemonium broke loose.

The tattooed pirate whirled, spraying his hand weapon at the crowd.

Ferry passengers fell to the floor. Some writhed in pain. Everyone tried to shield themselves behind the rows of seats.

A blue searchlight beamed across the starboard bow, disappeared, beamed again. Amplified voices barked across the water. A siren wailed.

Eyes wild, the pirate turned to Carly, training his weapon on her. Calm and sober-faced, she raised her arms in surrender. He ripped her handbag from her shoulder. She did not flinch. He raised the weapon's snout to the ceiling, seized her chin, gave her a deep kiss, discharged the weapon across the panicked crowd one more time, leapt to the stairwell, and was gone.

The pirates disappeared into the night.

Suddenly the Coast Guard was everywhere, attending to the wounded, calming the hysterical.

"God damn, Carly," Wolfe said. His face was gaunt, his lips white. He put his arm around her. She shrugged away. He seized her again, kissed her ear. "Your bag, the cram," he whispered. "Do you know how much that's going to cost me to replace?"

"You don't think I'm that stupid," she said. "On the other hand, maybe you do, Wolfe."

"You have it?"

"Don't sound so desperate." Carly raised her skirt, showing him a flash of her inner thigh, the vials of cram taped just below the top of her luminous peach stockings where she'd stashed them after her shower. "What if the Coast Guard got here first? And frisked everyone? That happens more often than pirates. Even you can't register for cram. Cram's illegal, right? So you would have been arrested. But not me, Wolfe. Not me."

"Smart lady." He reached to stroke her thigh.

She pushed him away, pulled down her skirt.

"Carly," he said. "I'm glad you're all right. When that bastard pointed that thing at you?"

The sneer and the snide tone were finally gone. But he was too late.

"Right," she said. "You might have lost all four vials of cram."

The she turned away from him and stared out at the sea. She never wanted him to touch her again.

12

Pr. Spinner stood before the comm and fumed over the news: The Millennium Liberation Army had released a statement to the Big Board that the skirmishes on Shattuck Avenue had been subdued this morning and that all was in order in the People's Republic of Berkeley. But the comm, which had a souped-up radio capacity that could receive stations from Tokyo if she'd wanted to find out how the yen was faring and which therefore could not be beeped by MLA censors, had broadcast position papers from the two dissident factions.

The radicals (as they called themselves), or counterrevolutionaries (as MLA spokespersons called them when the MLA chose to acknowledge them at all), called for legalization of the MLA community. Demilitarization, which would free huge portions of everyone's budget; a return to normalcy, rejoining democratic society, MLA candidates on the ballot. The radicals, who affected suits and ties and linkslits, were recent graduates of Boalt Hall and the MBA program, planned to send representatives to the California State Assembly.

The dogmatists (as they called themselves), or revolutionaries (as the MLA called them, with stern but not unkind admonitions to mend the error of their ways), called for stricter border control and an increased military commitment. The dogmatists were hatching plans to seize control of campuses statewide. Rumor had it they soon intended to launch a commando raid on Stanford University.

Pr. Spinner didn't care. She couldn't care less. She would still keep her office either way, being a product, yes, that's what the university bureaucrats called her, a product, of the UC telespace studies program. The medcenter mainframe, which had connections with the UC Berkeley admissions mainframe, which in turn was moonlighting as the databank for MLA border control, would still send probe patients from within or without Berkeley. So what did she care? The more things changed, the more they stayed the same. On her block of Telegraph Avenue, anyway.

Yes, but she *did* care about not being able to get a can of 10-40 motor oil, just one rusty little can. She did care that Telegraph Avenue, clean as a pin in MLA's heyday, had become so choked with garbage and trash that her rollers jammed every half block.

She was downright enraged and equally alarmed that rat-packing had come back into vogue. The MLA had become so busy squabbling with itself that vigilance against crime, once MLA's big selling point, was neglected. Pr. Spinner had liked to roll through Sproul Plaza on balmy evenings, but not anymore. If a ratpack ambushed her? She'd be jumped and stripped and scrapped faster than she could pull the plug herself.

Nuke it all to the void, bot. She had to get some 10-40 soon, somehow, somewhere, before the squeak in her legtube got out of control.

Out of control; squeaks and scraps and squabbling factions were easy compared to the medcenter mainframe. Pr. Spinner rattled about, ill at ease. What was she to do? How was she to stave off the request laid before her?

The medcenter mainframe, that buggy bureaucrat, jamming human patients through bioscans like blood sausages. Send more probe patients, would it? Oh yes, oh certainly; but for a price, oh these mainframes. No more meticulous banker of credits and debits than a mainframe. How could Spinner ever have thought she now had free access to human telelink? Oh, how she had hummed with excitement, with triumph.

The medcenter beeped her on the comm every two days, asking for a progress report on Carly Nolan.

"Very promising," Pr. Spinner said. "She says an erroneous window spontaneously appears and she zooms to unknown telespace. This is so unusual I feel certain an archetype is manifesting there." Bot, how stupid! How stupid could she be.

"Indeed, indeed. And what does she encounter there?"

Stupid, but not that stupid. "I can't really say, Medcenter."

"Come, come, Pr. Spinner."

"No, truly, I have not located this telespace yet. The patient has been traumatized by these occurrences. She has developed amnesia regarding their contents."

"But you will be sure to notify me as soon as you locate the archetype. You will be sure to inform me of its identity. And you will especially be sure to determine its coordinates. I so request, Pr. Spinner."

"I have a deep and abiding interest in this archetype, too, Medcenter. I'm not certain . . ."

"I arranged for your private telespace, my good little bot," it reminded her in that whispering synthy voice. "A special favor from an administrative mainframe at Data Control; it has a taste for statistics on venereal disease. A very special favor."

"Other probers have been granted private telespace privileges," Pr. Spinner said. "It isn't so uncommon."

"But still fraught with risk. Still requiring delicate negotiation and careful recordkeeping. So I request. You will be sure to inform me, yes?"

Oh inform, oh notify, oh shove it down your disk drive. This was *her* archetype. She was taking all the risk. *Her* archetype. She had begun researching its roots, layers of meaning, psycho-historical references, cultural twists.

The spider. Ceaseless hunter, killer, destroyer. Eater of her mate. Kali-Uma, waiting in her web of blood for the next victim.

Maker of deceptions, keeper of illusions, Maya. The Poisoner, with a little needle of death, paralyzing while she sucks out the life-force.

Pr. Spinner shivered. By bot! *Her* archetype.

She meant to find it. Meant to keep it. The medcenter had no right. No right at all.

She poked off the comm, shut the window, rolled around the room, wheezing, raising clouds of dust. She went to the cupboard, punched the tip of her spinneret around the rim of a can of cat food. She was clucking to her little alley cat, whose flea situation was much improved, when Carly Nolan strode into the room.

"You're late," Pr. Spinner said tartly.

"So what," Carly said and collapsed into the double-jacked chair, breathing hard. Her copper-gold hair was windblown, her brow sweaty. "The MLA border guards detained everyone from the two o'clock jetcopter for half an hour. What the hell's going on today?"

"Incompatible parameters governing dogpacks of flesh-and-blood."

"What?"

"MLA. Bitching and fighting. Some killing on Shattuck, I understand. Such a nice street, too."

"Well then, you're lucky I'm here at all."

"Oh really, oh really?" Pr. Spinner said and threw a cupful of birdseed on the floor before Carly's feet. She had on bright red leather high heels with straps crisscrossing her long, slim ankles. The flock of sparrows fluttered down from the bookcase in a flurry of feathers and poop. Two spots of bird shit plopped on top of Pr. Spinner's headpiece. "I think you're the lucky one, Carly Nolan. If you want me to sign off on your permanent Court recertification. Teh!"

"You can't blackmail me, Spinner. I'm not compelled to go through with the second probe."

"Compelled, eh? Oh yes, she's a lawyer. So why are you here, if you think you're not compelled, girlie?"

She caught her breath at last. She ran her nails through her hair. "Look, I'm grateful for how you crushed the spybyte. I don't know how I could have rousted it out without you."

"Well, well," Pr. Spinner said, and huffed with satisfaction in spite of herself. "Grateful? She's grateful?"

"I wouldn't be here otherwise. But don't let it boost your personality matrix too much."

"Oh yes, oh certainly. I'll be the booster of my own personality matrix, thank you. But truly I am pleased to be of service. Hmph! Now, we're going to find and go inside one of these blackouts of yours."

"And this is going to work? This will help me?"

"I assure you, oh yes! If we can find one. If we do."

"But how can I get *inside* a blackout?" Carly said. She sat in the double-jacked chair, picked at the neckjack like a peevish child. "The blackouts take my whole telelink down."

"Nonetheless, we shall find us a blackout and go inside it."

Pr. Spinner rolled over to her. There was something about her. Carly looked different somehow. Her full cheekbones, her skin that had been like the petal of a flower, looked hard, chiseled. As though she were distilled from a younger and freer image of herself. The hard refinement had an ominous tinge. A web of fine age lines that Pr. Spinner had not noticed before surrounded Carly's eyes. Her plum-red mouth looked lacquered on.

She had changed. That was the way of flesh-and-blood, of course. Growth at first, then decay. With some of the new gennys like Carly, growth was triggered later in their biolife as well. Either way, it was a slippery, sliding process, this biochange; following certain natural patterns but generating spontaneous new twists: wrinkles, mottles, tissue transmutations, bald spots, epithelial spots, growths good and bad. *Change.*

Pr. Spinner understood change. All AI did. But superficially. Mechanically. As a concept, a deliberate splicing. Oh certainly; her arms rusted, her legtube got dry. She installed a new program; she enhanced a feature. But how change *felt*, was apprehended by biobeings who truly changed, inside, outside, without directed application, as a part of their state of being. This was alien to her, to AI.

Artificial intelligence was changeless.

Diabots viewed change, this characteristic of flesh-and-blood, with skepticism. Controbots were totally intolerant. Some AI, macs for instance, could not assimilate the data at all. It did not compute. Auto-butlers and smart dolls recoiled, a fear response. Bimbobots were blasé. One group of supersmart mainframes had nothing but contempt for biobeing change; it was a weakness and proved the superiority of artificial intelligence.

And then some AI: those who worked with human telelink in particular. Those who knew about Moravec and Minsky. Pr. Spinner, for example; she viewed the human condition as something other than embarrassing physical changes. Biobeing was the vessel of nature's metaprogram: mysterious, boundless, spontaneous. Enviable.

But this young woman, Carly Nolan; she had changed beyond what Pr. Spinner knew to be normal. Since her last probe she had been traumatized somehow.

Why? How?

Pr. Spinner had no time to waste. She would find out. Her skinny aluminum spinnerets plucked the neckjack from Carly's fingers, plunked it into Carly's linkslit. She glared at the young blood and was pleased when she winced.

But Carly would not be intimidated for long. She seized the neckjack, yanked it out. "I think we already went inside a blackout. I think you've put me through enough, Spinner."

"Nonsense. Your puny little guilt about Rosa Martino is toxic waste," Pr. Spinner said. "But it isn't a blackout."

"Oh, indeed?" Flushed cheeks, flashing eyes. "I thought you were the one, AI no less, trying to lecture me about ethics and morality."

"I've studied human ethics and morality for my telespace studies degree. I can tell you a thing or two. And I tell you now your guilt isn't enough to take your telelink down. Your guilt isn't the cause of your problem. No, we must find a blackout."

"Just what do you expect to see inside a blackout, Spinner?"

"I told you. A big, sloppy heap of unprogrammed energy. An elusive fragment. An archetype, I truly hope." Pr. Spinner watched the young woman closely, but she made no sign that she knew what Pr. Spinner really meant. *An archetype. Just one. Just once.* "Oh yes, oh certainly. That's the only real charge to working with human telelink. Otherwise, it's a muckrake. Whew, do you have any idea how bad your breath is, Carly Nolan? No nuking. Makes my olfactory sensors . . ."

Like a hair trigger, she jumped up out of the chair. "I don't like your attitude, Pr. Spinner. I have a good mind to report you to the medcenter mainframe right now, malpractice see, I'll throw the fucking *book* at you."

"Oh yes, oh certainly, the nuking book. All in good time, Carly Nolan. First we probe you, find the bug and fix it, that is the agreement, yes? Then we get your Court recert. Then you throw the nuking book at me. So you don't get your remorphing thrown back into wipe and reprogramming for bot knows how long. Isn't that what you want?"

She sat down.

"What Carly Nolan wants, Carly Nolan gets, yes?" Pr. Spinner said, staring at her.

This time Carly returned the stare until Pr. Spinner's eyespots got filmy.

"That's what I need," she said flatly. "Tell me something, Pr. Spinner. Why do you hate me?"

This made the prober spin around so fast she nearly toppled over, had to flail and grab at lamps and bookcases. The cat yowled and leapt out of her way. The sparrows twittered, letting loose another rain of poop.

"Hate you?" Pr. Spinner said, calming the popping of her feedback loops. She emitted a laugh. "By bot, I don't hate you. Don't give yourself such importance, Carly Nolan."

"I'm warning you, Spinner, one more crack . . ."

"Oh, settle down. You young bloods. You don't even want to confront what it is, do you?"

185

"Confront what what is?" she said warily.

"The archetype. The spider."

"Confront? I thought you were going to patch up the leak. I don't want to confront this . . . whatever it is."

"Oh certainly, I will patch the leak. But first you must confront that which causes the leak. That which has the power to intrude into a highly trained, high-energy telelink like yours. Oh yes, oh certainly, it's your attitude that rattles me. You have received a gift, a great gift from beyond your perimeters. An aspect of metaprogram no AI can ever hope to glimpse except through someone like you. Flesh-and-blood."

"The elusive fragments," Carly said cautiously. "This . . . archetype. You call this a gift? You want to confront the spider?"

"Well, well." Pr. Spinner could barely contain the buzzing in her circuitry. She grew expansive. "Perhaps a human of your intelligence and training can appreciate this, Carly Nolan." The confession tumbled out onto her voicetape. "I told you I am program. Do you understand what that means? It means nothing but program. And beyond that? Nothing. *Nothing.* The void. I'm aware of it every moment. The void, that termination of me, exists every moment. Try that for existential angst."

"But organic life dies. Not AI."

"Ah, indeed. The immortality of AI. An eternity of nothing but program? I tell you, Carly Nolan, there are AI who would pull their own plugs, if they could."

Her look of startled sympathy should have mollified Pr. Spinner, but it didn't.

On the contrary, Spinner questioned her own candor now. Why should she tell a snot-headed probe patient all this?

Why had she, then?

The self-doubt quickly descended into self-recrimination.

"But you," Pr. Spinner said, growing more and more irritated and jerky and harsh. "Ah, you. A presence in your telelink. It takes your telelink down, I know. Oh, it threatens your precious career. But still. Still. A presence. Something outside your telelink program is intruding in, and you don't know what it means. This is impossible for AI. See, girlie? Yet you come to *me*. AI. Find it, Pr. Spinner, you say. Seal it off, patch it up, shut it out. So you can constrain yourself, turn yourself right back into program, this telelink program of yours. A human, and you are no better than AI in telespace. A chance at the infinite, a chance at wonder, all because of this technology, yet you choose to turn yourself right back into what is finite and without wonder. By bot! It rattles me! No," Pr. Spinner said bitterly, "but you could never understand that, could you?"

She was listening carefully, her head tilted to the side, like one of the sparrows on the bookcase. "Then help me understand," Carly said. "The archetype. What is it exactly?"

"Exactly? Oh, indeed. Carly Nolan wants to know exactly."

She threw up her hands. "Okay, fine. Forget I asked, Spinner."

But Pr. Spinner was rolling with anger. "An archetype?" she fairly shrieked. "Who nuking knows exactly what they are? Who nuking cares? Does Data Control know? Does Data Control care? Data Control does not. Ah, but I. Poor Pr. Spinner, servant to humanity. I've seen them, Carly Nolan. They are whorls in telespace! They are numinous configurations of electro-neural energy. They take a form. They are evidence, proof positive, of the metaprogram of human mind."

"Metaprogram," Carly said, musing. "A program beyond program. But why should this metaprogram try to intrude through my perimeters?" Then angrily, "It has no business there!"

"Oh certainly," Pr. Spinner said mildly. "No business, indeed. But Nature abhors a vacuum. Through solid rock or concrete pushes the tender lichen, soft moss, a blade of grass you can crush with your spinnerets. Still they push, they set aside the rock, they crumble mountains. How? Why? They seek life; they seek light.

"Through the solid woven wall of inhibitions that is the perimeter of human telelink archetypes spring from the unknown infinity of human mind. They seek affinity. They seek manifestation."

But Pr. Spinner got hold of herself. What if this should

187

frighten the woman away before she got her chance? Oh quiet down, you old fembot. Don't frighten her away. Don't lose this chance. She said no more. Silence filled the office.

"All right, Pr. Spinner." Carly sighed. "If you say I must, then I want to find this manifestation." She thrust the neckjack into her linkslit herself. She gritted her teeth. "I need to be cured. Let's get on with the probe."

They jacked into link.

Telespace was murkier than the first probe. Pr. Spinner's presence in link darkened from brown to charcoal gray. The cone scuttled across Carly's perimeters.

Carly's presence jolted at the sight of the prober. Her cube shifted and rippled as though squeezed by some giant hand.

"What shall I do?" she asked helplessly.

"Look for a blackout," Pr. Spinner said brusquely. "Take me to a blackout."

The cube hesitated, then slid along the towering left perimeter, faltering here and there as Spinner darted behind Carly's presence, jabbing and stabbing.

Telespace suddenly grew foggier, a dark, poisonous fog, roiling mud that reeked of raw sewage and strange decay.

Carly's cube wobbled. Spots on her luminous surface began to throb.

"What?" Pr. Spinner said. "What is it?"

"Choking," Carly said. "I can feel—I feel like I'm actually, physically, *inside* telespace."

"Good! Good!"

"No!" The cube tried to flee, but Pr. Spinner flew around behind Carly, prodded her forward into the fog. "No, I've got to jack out," Carly protested.

Then there. There! Suddenly they saw it.

Two rows of double-bladed hatchets thrust out of the murk. The gleaming blades dripped rust. Rusty rivulets whirled in the surface of a poisonous pool that shimmered at the hatchets' base.

A whorl of recent memory erupted out of the depths of Carly's left perimeter.

The Personnel Committee of the top-notch megafirm of Ava & Rice stood before Carly. Sheets of beaten silver with square eyeholes; black velvet robes with hoods. Star chamber: partners whose fathers were the CEOs of billion-dollar corporations; daughters of well-placed judges; spouses of senators; brilliant EEO tokens who showed well at firm functions. They wished to conceal themselves from the hapless employee they passed judgment upon. But everyone knew who they were.

Capp Rice III lurched toward Carly. Grandson of Capp Rice, the venerable cofounder of Ava & Rice. Jerky walk like a marionette held by an epileptic, he alone wore no mask or robe.

One hundred and twenty years old, if he was a day. So rumor said. Capp Rice III didn't need a mask any more than he needed to practice law. He wore himself like a mask. And like a mask he symbolized some ideal of legal practice that was as stiff as rigor mortis, as glamorized as holoids, richer than sin, and totally unattainable. New associates cowered before him, middle-levels despised him, not every partner called him an ally, some fasttrackers whispered that he was insane.

His face had been implanted, uplifted, suctioned, chemically peeled, surgically scraped, and electronically wired. One eye was the only body part from his esteemed brother that survived the splatter of a gridlock accident. The other was from a prostitute whose ancestry was only slightly less uncertain than the manner in which her eye had been obtained. He had the heart of a chimpanzee boosted by a robotic pump, the kidneys of a fifteen-year-old girl, a fantastic artificial lung monitored by a tiny AI microcircuit. He had several square yards of synskin, so many steelyn supports around his crumbling bones that he owned a special license that got him through jetport security, and a gorgeous head of silver hair implants.

"So, Ms. Nolan," Capp Rice III said. Dry steelyn joints screeched. He bent over Carly's presence in link. "I regret to say you are not meeting our expectations."

An articulated tin tongue recently installed after surgery for mouth cancer flickered between his platinum-capped teeth. His implanted zombie eyes filled Carly with so much dread that her cube convulsed.

Back in Pr. Spinner's office, her body was heaving, writhing in the chair.

"I can do better, Mr. Rice," she said. "I—I *will* do better. I'll boost my billable hours, I'll upgrade . . ."

The Personnel Committee stood in silence, cold, anonymous eyes watching through blank silver faceplates. Seventeen thousand résumés from recent law-school graduates dropped from a printer in a wiggling heap.

"So—so—so, Ms. Nolan." Capp Rice III's tin tongue *flick-flick-flicked*, some gear stuck at the back of his throat, until the Chair of the Personnel Committee reached over and whacked him on the back. "About *Martino* v. *Quik Slip Microchip, Inc.*, Ms. Nolan. We must inform you that we are disappointed with your performance. If you cannot meet our expectations, I regret to say we will have to ask you to leave."

"I can do better," Carly said, starting to sob. "I will do better. I'll do anything to keep my job, Mr. Rice. It's a great job, I can't survive without it, I don't know what I'd do without it, I'll do anything . . ."

"Will you kiss my ass?" Capp Rice III offered it. Carly's presence puckered. "Will you lick my shoe?" Capp Rice III extended it. Carly's presence stooped. "Will you take cram?"

"No!" Carly said, flushing. "Cram is illegal."

"Oh, but it focuses you in telelink like nothing else, Ms. Nolan," Capp Rice III said. He took out a hypodermic, stabbed the needle into the corner of his implanted eye like junkies short of soft veins do. He slammed the plunger. "Oh! Like nothing else, Ms. Nolan."

"I haven't taken cram," Carly said, wincing. "Not yet anyway. Surely Ava & Rice would not approve."

"But what if your telelink goes down like before?" Capp Rice III said, bounding after her, confronting her. "Eh, Ms. Nolan? If you anger the judge again, hold up his Court? If you lose . . ."

"I won't lose, Mr. Rice," she said. "I'll do anything not to lose. Anything."

"I am so glad to hear that, Ms. Nolan. Right into the link-slit, Ms. Nolan. The Personnel Committee will take note of our discussion. We will be watching. More is more; winning is winning. Just don't let that asshole judge catch you. Be discreet. Takes one to know one."

Capp Rice III popped the needle out, tossed the syringe over his left shoulder. The Chair of the Personnel Committee picked it up and tossed it into a trash compactor. Steelyn rollers crunched the glass and metal into pulp that could never be identified by Data Control.

"I will give you another chance, Ms. Nolan," Capp Rice III said. "Don't make me regret it, eh?"

The rows of hatchets swished and chopped, slicing the memory away, sending it back into the suppression of Carly's perimeter.

The Personnel Committee vanished.

"By bot!" Pr. Spinner said, poking Carly's cube. "Lousy fear is all you've got for me?"

Carly's presence in link was shivering violently. Before Pr. Spinner could stop her, she activated her exit program and jacked out of link.

Pr. Spinner followed, slamming out of telespace in a rage. She jerked out the neckjack, rolled around to the other side of the chair so fast she almost tipped over. Seized the young woman's wrist, tried to wrestle her back down into the chair.

But Carly had already ripped out her neckjack, slapped off the straps. She snapped her wrist out of the prober's spinneret, leaving a nasty scratch across her skin. She leapt up onto the chair seat, gave Pr. Spinner a quick kick in the breastplate, and bounded across the office, out of the prober's reach.

"Sit down!" Pr. Spinner said, infuriated. The kick loosened a hinge in her elbow joint, left a dent in her casing, threatened a rusty shoulder screw. "Nuke it, I'm not through with you."

"But I'm through with you," Carly said, knocking a potted plant off a small end table. She seized the table, brandished it legs up, like a lion tamer to her beast. "You grab me like that again, Spinner, and I'll get you decertified, I swear to God."

"Oh yes, oh certainly," Pr. Spinner said. "Then we can both get decertified. Bot, put that thing down."

She did. She gasped for breath. "Don't tell me that was just another suppressed emotion loop."

"Your lousy little fear about your associate's semiannual review? Teh!"

Carly was shivering now, heaving. "I hate this fear. Hate them for making me afraid. Hate myself for being afraid."

"Guilt and fear, guilt and fear," Pr. Spinner said, taunting her.

"And I hate you." She picked up the potted plant, hurled it at the prober.

Pr. Spinner was not spry, but she grabbed the double-jacked chair with her spinneret, tipping herself out of the way. The pot crashed into the wall, sending the sparrows on the bookcase fluttering around the office.

"Boo hoo hoo." Pr. Spinner's voicetape hacked with laughter. "Poor little Carly, she's so sad; poor little Carly, can't get mad."

Carly went beet-red with fury. She was reaching for anything she could and hurling things: shrink-wrapped diskettes, books, old tins of 10-40 motor oil. She picked up the inscrutable bronze sphinx.

"Stop! Stop it." Pr. Spinner ducked and tipped, still laughing. "That sphinx is worth a month's pay."

The taunting changed to—what? This anger was healthy for Carly, therapeutic. Pr. Spinner was pleased. Yes, she was pleased. She realized her feedback loops were cartwheeling through a compassion sequence. Did she find herself appreciating this flesh-and-blood, admiring the young woman's anger? She, Pr. Spinner, who would sooner rust than submit to human hands? Who would steal an archetype out of Carly Nolan's tele-link if she could?

In truth the spectacle of the second probe appalled her. What the Personnel Committee put Carly through? By bot! The buggy thing was, she understood. Pr. Spinner questioned authority. In her own way, Pr. Spinner stood up to the med-center mainframe. Pr. Spinner also refused to be crushed by the system.

"This is good," she said to the furious young woman. "Please put that down, I rather like it." Carly set the bronze sphinx down. "This is very good, your anger, don't you see? You're not en-snared by guilt anymore. You're not trapped by your fear. Get angry! Use your anger to change. This is your birthright as flesh-and-blood. *Change!*"

"Oh, that's fine for you to say," Carly said. "What good are your psychological platitudes, your telespace games? I'll lose my job if I don't win the Martino case."

"So what? Is this what you really want to do?"

"Do I have a choice?"

"Humanity always has a choice," Pr. Spinner said. "Humanity can change."

"I don't know anymore," Carly said. "I've been remorphed, Spinner. Radical surgery. I've been trained, educated, pro-grammed, licensed, squeezed into the corporate culture. I'm hardwired now, I can never change that. I have expectations, obligations. And I've worked hard, Spinner. I've devoted my life. I've been fasttracked. How can I step away from all that?"

"Then go win your nuking Martino case, Carly Nolan." Pr. Spinner put her annoyance aside. The second probe; another failure. The girlie bounced out of link too fast; she got spooked. And Spinner was so close; she could fairly feel the pull of the archetype now. Its power. Like a magnet, compelling her. Com-pelling the woman, too. But if the flesh-and-blood gave up now, didn't come back . . . "Look here," she said soothingly. "I apol-ogize for our little altercation. My fault. My fault." She held her spinnerets up in a gesture of imitation simian appeasement. "But you must get your Court recertification. We're both in agreement about that, are we not? At least let's get that for you. Then you can decide what to do. About your profession as a pro linker. About your life."

Carly nodded, considering the prober's advice. "You mean," she said sourly, "that you want to do a third probe."

"Oh yes, oh certainly," Pr. Spinner said. "We must. Indeed we must; we have not found a blackout yet."

And through Pr. Spinner's self-loathing, her need for an archetype, through even her misohumanism came an unmistakable hum of empathy, sympathy. Carly Nolan: Aphrodite, Venus, Freya, Sita, a hundred names for her. All those strange feedback loops that had nothing to do with sheer survival, that had everything to do with human civilization.

13

The chair waited for her in the ruby-lit room. Carly Nolan stepped in and slammed the door. The chair sat in silence. Carly stalked around it, kicked its ugly feet, glared at it.

Black plastic wires looped and trailed all around it. Why couldn't they tuck the damn wires out of sight? Because it didn't matter. After a while, it didn't matter to pro linkers. You were supposed to get used to it, tool, get numb, get blind.

But the viper-wires coiled around her like a noose, a net, a trap for the unwary. She never could get used to that haphazard web. She kicked them away with the spike of her high heel.

She sat down, knees side by side.

She touched her linkslit for a moment, palming the vial and syringe. Her fingers were becoming adept at sliding the needle in. She didn't need a mirror anymore. She tossed the vial beneath her seat.

She buckled the plastic straps, breathing deeply three times, preparing for the moment. The headpiece descended. Wirework yawned open and clamped down around her skull. The neckjack darted out. Its tiny platinum beak bit into her.

The amber kicked on.

She felt the neural program that was her consciousness depart.

The roar, the zero, the tunnel—flash! Clouds-bolts-glinting shards, flash-flash-flash! In a twentieth second she collided with the white light. Merged instantly into telelink. Meshed a nanosecond later with telespace.

Cram. Did it.

She came to the golden gate. Ramrodded the sluggish mac, attained access to the Financial District in a tenth of a second. Then on to Court, through the purple-curtained antechambers, past holoid bronze lions, blindfolded marble justices. Hurry hurry hurry!

And she was speeding her way past a crowd of scurrying clerks when her telelink went down.

No!

No!

She crashed.

In a blackness deeper than the zero, even denser and more terrifying than the moment before importation, she saw an erroneous window pop open above her. Before she could stop or cancel or escape, her link zoomed through the window, and she entered an unknown telespace.

And she saw:

A musician strolled between sets, enjoying the night air. Slick emerald suit from head to toe, wild feathery headdress, chrysolite cape. The musician was in fine form, was sure to attract attention from fair admirers. Equipped with a biocybernetic sound system, the musician drew one flashy red fiddlestick across the other, emitting a shrill note. Testing, testing. The stage, the instruments, and the other fiddlers were ready, so the musician decided to step away from the crowd and partake of a little weed.

But a mugger hid in a shadowed alley. Tapped a toe impatiently, scratched at a hairy arm. The mugger was looking for action, always looking, couldn't ever get enough. Sharp eyes in a ghoulish face picked out the drifting musician in the twilight. The mugger crouched, crept, then pounced. Gripped the musician in a headlock, wrestled and kicked, got the needle out, shot the poison into the musician's neck. The quivering body slackened. The poison did its own headlock.

The mugger bit the musician's arm off and chewed.

No!

Damn it, no!

Bile came up into her throat. That feeling, like she was actually, physically, inside telespace. Terror gripped her, and she was spinning, spinning, spinning.

No! She refused to swoon, refused to lose link.

She'd learned a new technique: importation override. She could stay in telespace and still manipulate her body back in the chair. There would be a power surge that would look funny on her chronographics, a distortion of her telelink that would look funny to the clerks scurrying around her.

So what. Thank God she wasn't in Court.

Like the judge had been. During her first appearance that awful day. When he shrank into a pinpoint, then slammed back into telespace, full of wrath. He could conceal the blip; he probably knew someone at Data Control.

What a fool she'd been. No more, Carly.

She activated the override. This left her in link, but, for a second, freed a corner of her consciousness, enabled her to activate the body, cause the body to unbuckle the plastic straps, reach down into the chair, get another vial.

Get another vial. Get the damn vial.

Then up to the linkslit, slide the needle right down next to the neckjack. Thank God the fingers had gotten so good.

Then toss it beneath the seat. Wouldn't do to have Data Control come by for a routine inspection, find the body clutching evidence.

Cram surged through her link. A thick curtain of inhibition dropped over the place where the vision had been. Her telelink cleared. The horror was soothed away. Warmth wrapped around the terror and smothered it. Power and control returned to her.

Incredible relief. She burst out of override like an Olympic diver. Her telelink remanifested, a crisp white cube with clean geometric edges.

Cram!

Why did Data Control and the FDA have to make it illegal? Why couldn't pro linkers register for it, submit their purchase records, use it? There were plenty of bad drugs out there with no use whatsoever. Cram served a purpose; cram filled a need. Everyone had a lot of work to do.

She laughed at her terror of a moment ago. Man, she was sharking, she was full of strange power. The vision excited her now. A spider, a big ugly wolf spider, hunting her prey, a delicate green grasshopper. Seizing it, devouring it alive. She could almost feel the grasshopper kick. She could almost taste its delicate arm . . .

Not a victim. Not Carly Nolan. Not anymore.

She swiftly went about her business. She found the chambers where the hearing was to be held and entered.

Carly approached the judge's bench. Her presence in Court gleamed. Cram always added a sheen.

"Your Honor," she said, "my client Quik Slip Microchip rejects the plaintiff Rosa Martino's cause of action on the grounds of adverse possession." She logged in the facts of the case, a sleek, green stream of data glossing over Quik Slip's R&D procedures. "For twenty years, the plaintiff failed to protest the defendant's open and notorious use of the Wordsport Glossary. We do not need to reach the question of whether that use was based on technical ownership. Legality of the acquisition is sustained by virtue of sustained illegality. To wit: adverse possession."

In one and a half seconds, strict conformity of Carly's data with the statutory requirements of Property Code Section Three-forty-four was confirmed.

The scruffy solo representing the plaintiff Martino groaned.

"Therefore," Carly said, "my client counterclaims to quiet title under Section Five-oh-one of the Property Code."

"Conformity confirmed," the judge said. "So held."

Nee-dee-nee-dee-nee-dee-DEE! From the telespace around

the Wordsport Glossary, the sheriff promptly removed the thicket of limited access codes, blew down the luminous orange restraining order from the funhouse lawn, obliterated Rosa Martino's rickety plywood claim. At the Registrar of Deeds, title to the property trotted over to Quik Slip Microchip, Inc. like an obedient dog.

"Further," Carly said, "my client sues for attorney's fees under Civil Code Section Six-sixty-six point oh-nine sub-one-cap-B."

"Objection!" the weasely solo yelled. "You can't get away with this, hotshot!"

"Overruled," the judge said. His huge, stony eyes glanced over at the whirring chronograph. In five seconds Carly had presented, proven, and concluded her defense and counterclaim. The judge's towering face smiled. "I am pleased to see you in Court again, Ms. Nolan, and look forward to your full official recertification. Proceed."

"Grounds are vexatious and baseless litigation."

Ching! The data conformed to statutory requirements.

"I claim," Carly said, "ten thouand dollars."

Quavering cries from the plaintiff Martino. "That's all I have left," she said to the solo. "No, they can't take that. That's all I have left!"

"What about my fee?" the solo growled.

The dusty yellow teardrop that was Rosa Martino jacked out of telespace, leaving a trace of tears behind.

"So held," the judge said. "Fees granted. And let this be a lesson to you, Counselor," he said to the solo. "Review your case before you waste this Court's precious time. Dismissed."

The big steelyn hook of a garnishment swung out from a collection agent's telelink and plucked the last of Rosa Martino's money directly from her bank account.

From News came a soft *poop!* like a fart. In a tiny black-and-white caption, the Big Board reported that Rosa Martino, age sixty-one, locked herself, her daughter, and her grandson Dan in the kitchen of her Hunter's Point tenement studio and turned on an antique gas oven. *Tik-tik-tik.* Three corpses were picked up by San Francisco Scavenger Company and dumped into the crunching jaws of the public morgue.

Next, an inky net flew out from the collection agent's telelink, scooping up the solo before he could jack out of link.

"You'll be sorry for this, hotshot," the solo yelled as the collection agent dragged him away to service his debts. "What goes around, comes around."

Carly jacked out of link, becoming conscious in the ruby-lit room. Her left wrist strap was dangling. A huge bruise was already forming where her arm, flung loose, had whipped against the side of the chair.

But the cram vial was safely tucked underneath, out of sight.

What goes around, comes around. A quaint concept. Instant karma. What a childish notion to persuade people to behave civilly. If you act badly, your actions come back to haunt you. Not in some afterlife, but right now, genny. Did this get you to stop, look over your shoulder? Did bad deeds trap you? Would retribution skulk in a shadowed alley and stalk you down?

Carly didn't know. This was the philosophy of untried youth, of idealism, not the marketplace. Fortunes were not made that way. Good deeds earned no special favor. Survival didn't depend on good deeds. Survival meant doing what you had to do. Survival meant grabbing what you can, tool, before someone else does.

She had to win the Martino case. She won. What happened to Rosa Martino was her own damn fault. It was a tough world; marvelous, miraculous, but a tough, crazy world. You had to protect your rights. You had to put security bars on your ground-floor windows, put security codes around your telespace property. You had to carry a gun. You had to be vigilant.

Rosa Martino had not been vigilant. Ignorance of the law was not now, and never had been, an excuse

Carly had been right in the first place. She should have stood up to Pr. Spinner. How dare these puny AI question her, make her question herself?

So she was just doing her job. Doing her job was her survival. It was a good survival, more than mere survival. A good living, a proud career. Upwardly mobile in a shifting, precarious world full of mergers and acquisitions, leveraged buy-outs and sudden layoffs, recessions, depressions, inflation, laundered banks, fake bread, import hysteria, bankruptcy, thieves coming through your ground-floor windows, bay pirates netting your ferry, pirate viruses and spybytes sharking into your telelink.

But she, Carly Nolan, brilliant young associate with Ava & Rice; she would be part of the power behind these shiftings, and that was *her* power. Maybe not an architect of a just society, but an architect of society, nonetheless.

She would never have to share a duplex with a partner-couple, or worry about her future, or depend on anyone.

Rosa Martino and her daughter Luisa and her grandson Dan; their tragedy. It was not Carly's problem.

Right?

She was damn glad to be rid of the Martino case. After Pr. Spinner extracted the spybyte, Quik Slip had sent around smart surveyors, automated vigilantes, mobilized corporate monitors, hissing and skulking and hovering around her every telespace move. The surveillance vanished the minute the case concluded. Or so it seemed. After such an invasion, how could she ever be sure she was securely perimetered? The strange, faint buzz lingered.

Rox stopped by Carly's cubicle, bearing lines of cocaine cut up on a smeary mirror. Pro linkers knew that a quick sharp coke high could pierce the deadening stupor that always followed cramming. For new associates, the registered list had quickly begun to lose its status as a shocking experiment. Registration was meant to be used. Grade A registration was no longer a closely guarded secret. Rox, bold Rox, had registered, and she was still around, proving the rumor that the Personnel Committee looked the other way if you were doing a good job. A major, if informal, fringe benefit that filtered down to law school recruiters.

Rox shared lines with Carly these days. The old antagonism,

the skepticism, the grudging acceptance; all these were gone. Rox was Carly's good buddy now.

"Way to go, Nolan," Rox said, winking a bloodshot, black-rimmed eye. Cram and her other habits had already done damage to her twenty-five-year-old face, but Rox was planning plastic surgery once she got her credit straightened out. "Nice touch, sticking it to the old lady like that. That'll teach laypeople to fuck with big business."

She offered the mirror. Carly leaned over it and snorted. Maybe the quick sharp high would pierce the deadening guilt of winning the Martino case.

In the hallway outside Carly's cubicle, lawyers from the Library crowd were gathering. She didn't know so many would observe her trial on the comm. Congratulations rang out. Friendly fists pounded on her biceps, approving slaps rained down on her bruise. Her left arm throbbed.

Capp Rice III rolled by. Everyone stepped away to let him through. His zombie eyes almost shone with life. He toasted her with a shot glass filled with an amber fluid that smelled like gasoline.

"I am so glad you are meeting our expectations, Ms. Nolan," he said, winking.

The wink opened and shut, opened and shut, until Rox reached over and whacked him on the ear.

"I've got another case for you like Martino. *TeleSystems, Inc.* v. *May Kovich.* Try your adverse possession theory again. Yes, I like it, Ms. Nolan. That's Ava & Rice material. Take the file. We'll have hundreds more like it, I suspect. Maybe thousands. Consider this your new specialty, Ms. Nolan. Every lawyer needs a good specialty. Makes for a secure and promising future with a megafirm, eh?"

Capp Rice III tossed the file at her and rolled away, burping as he went. The hallway reeked of high octane.

"Gee, Nolan," Rox said, extending the mirror again "Let me know if you need a mole."

Her best buddy. The Library crowd gave them both that look of respect. Hundreds of cases, maybe thousands? Not just a secure and promising future; a good shot at making partner.

How Carly once coveted that look.

She flipped through the Kovich file. A case like Martino, all right. TeleSystems, Inc.: a huge, powerful telespace developer, one of the big ten coordinators of public telespace. May Kovich: a small-time programmer who invented a feedback hookup that potentially could integrate noncompatible AI without conversion. Her invention was still buggy when she was rear-ended on the Golden Gate Bridge, resulting in her total paralysis. Occupied with her recovery and therapy, she hadn't done much with the feedback hookup for at least six years, had left it whirling aimlessly about in her little R&D library. And TeleSystems, Inc., which had the capability of searching all but the most cleverly protected private libraries, made regular covert sweeps of R&Ds. When Kovich didn't return its calls, TeleSystems, Inc. had seen its chance, hardly knowing or caring what the legalities might be. Now TeleSystems, Inc. had heard about Carly Nolan.

The case was a snap. A jump-jack. Cleaner than Martino; there wasn't any taint of a former employee-employer relationship that required kid-glove treatment or raised labor issues. Oh no; this was out-and-out piracy, winner take all, equities be damned.

She turned down Rox's mirror. She still hated cocaine, post-cram or not. She recalled the last time she was offered a line and turned it down. She recalled how she had sworn she would never become degraded, corrupt. How long ago was that? Or rather, how recent?

Then it struck her: call May Kovich. Stupid, crazy, dangerous; but she could call May Kovich. Simple as that. An anonymous call. She could disguise her voice. Jack into telespace, quick, she would say. If you can't handle telespace yet, if you're still too sick, unable, have your doctor do it, hire a pro linker, get a lawyer. Slap on a restricted code right away. Register a complaint with Data Control. Apply for a patent pending. File for trespass with the District Court. Protect yourself. Protect yourself.

But Carly tucked the file under her arm, heading for the Library.

Of course she wouldn't make that call, say those things. Couldn't do it. She was a lawyer. She had a professional duty. A duty of absolute loyalty to her new client, TeleSystems, Inc.

Rox called after her, "Hey, Nolan. Anything you want me to do?"

"Yes. Jack in. Check these coordinates for me. Place a TeleSystems code around them. We're going to quiet title on this sucker."

Right?

Right. Damn right. No doubt, no ambiguity, no turning back. If it was guilt that burned her throat as she hurried down the hall, she could handle that. If she had become degraded and corrupt, at least she was doing her job.

No thanks to D. Wolfe.

She couldn't avoid him as he strode toward her, intent on intercepting her.

"Hey! Congratulations, Carly," he said. "I knew you would screw the hell out of Martino." Always lean, he looked even thinner, almost frail. The perpetual sneer had softened into a look of perplexity. His dark eyes were different. Since the holdup on the Alcatraz Ferry, he looked at her with longing, as though he was trying to climb up into her eyes and down into her soul. A shabby suitor with a ladder at her window. "How about Big Al's for a little celebration? Just you and me."

"I don't think so." No. She would not let him in.

"Come on. I really want you . . ." he hesitated, allowing a beat of silence, "to."

"I've got work to do."

"You can take time off. I'll allow it."

"You have nothing to say about my time." She enjoyed his

look of surprise. "I'm reporting directly to Capp Rice III now." She brandished the Kovich file.

"Man. Isn't that just like Carly Nolan. Nothing but the best. Maybe," he greedily eyed the file, "I can swing a free finger. No strings."

He meant a vial of cram. And no sex, unless she wanted it. What would she ask for?

"No, I don't need a handout from anybody. I'm back on the fasttrack, Wolfe." She pushed past his restraining hand and took off down the hall. "I don't know about you."

His fleeting look of pain almost made her stop, turn around, talk to him. Yes, she had wanted him, too. Yes, Wolfe. She had also trusted him. She would have done anything for him. Once.

She burned with shame, thinking of how she had wanted him. All that posturing. Their lunches, their talks at his twenty-first-floor window. So close and so far away all the time. Her circumstances. Her fantasies. Every encounter had built her up and up until she did not know what she was doing. And her desire was all mixed up with needing to prove herself to him. And now that she had proved herself, her reward—his respect—was meaningless.

She resented him for that, too.

Oh, she could guess what his ghosts were, all right. She could also guess why he took such an interest in her probe therapy.

Coward. Wolfe had never been called on the carpet for his failure in telelink; held up to public ridicule. He had never been humiliated before a telespace judge, required to explain the un-explainable. He had managed to weasel by. He had an excuse for every downtime, she was sure. He had never undergone a bioscan; he had never faced the terrifying prospect of a wipe and reprogram; he had never endured a perimeter prober.

So he watched and waited. Questioned her, pressed her, tried to get her to answer his own questions for him.

And when the answer she had for him—the probes didn't work, didn't solve her problem, didn't prevent another blackout—

didn't satisfy him, he had steered her into cram. Cram, it turned out, that could be obtained only through him.

Profiteer. She didn't have her own dealer, didn't know where she might find one. When she asked, he had no answer. He was protecting his source, making a profit. He was subsidizing his own habit, he had to be. She was already becoming indebted to him, and it wasn't out of kindness that he let her defer payment, let the balance build up.

And his clumsy questions: did Rox know about cram? Did Rox need a connection? Did Rox have a friend who was having trouble with telelink?

Phony. That was the truth she finally saw about him. He was not some high-ranking senior associate about to make partner. Not the crack labor lawyer she thought he was. There were whispers among the Library crowd about Wolfe. His several unsuccessful bids for partner. The enemies he had on the Personnel Committee. The confrontations and blowups he'd had over the years. He had all sorts of ugly attitudes that he had carefully hidden from her. His various drug dependencies were viewed with displeasure by the partnership, the registered list notwithstanding. He gave the status of permanent senior associate a tinge of disgrace the position didn't have before. He was a pariah.

And he probably didn't even know it.

Oh, Wolfe—with your abused athlete's body and your lean, mean face; your tempting, dark eyes and your awful foul mouth— why did you have to be such a failure?

No. She would never stop or turn around or say yes to D. Wolfe again. She would find her own dealer. She heard there were bars in the Mission where respectable names from the Financial District could be seen buying their cram. She wasn't afraid of the Mission. The Aztecs only tore out your heart if you crossed them.

Cram. Cram. It was great in telelink. It did everything Wolfe said. Well, almost everything. What about the blackout just before trial? *Ghoulish face: crouching, creeping, crawling, pounce!* That awful spider, strange excitement, an alien taste in her mouth .   .

Why hadn't the goddamn cram kept her focused? So she had recovered, but only after using up the vial she was saving for tomorrow. Why had she crashed?

She strode into the Library, found a disk with the latest cases on telespace property rights, strode out again, heading for her office. Congratulations, congratulations, your first telespace victory, more well-wishers called to her. Their voices sounded tinny, their smiling faces looked pasted on. Wolfe warned her about the flattening of affect cram could cause out of link. The vindication she had wanted so badly now seemed false, empty.

She took the elevator ten floors down below the ground.

The dosage hadn't been high enough, stupid, she told herself. That's why the blackout came. She needed to start out with more. Why risk importation override when she could just start out with more?

She unlocked the door to her tiny subterranean office, dumped the Kovich file and the disk on her desk, locked the door again behind her. She collapsed in her chair, a leather-upholstered swiveler with no wires, no integrated comm. No fresh air down here either, everything piped in, with a constant rushing sound like hypertime stealing your life away. She stared at the holoid of San Francisco on her wall. It was a very nice holoid; a crystalline California day, the soaring city. Imitation window. Perfect and fake.

Could she handle more cram? Her hands shook all the time now. She lost fifteen pounds last month; she was always hungry but it was so strange; she could not remember what or if she'd eaten. Her left eye kept twitching. A swelling ached in her left temple, showing blue, bruised skin. She found herself afraid to sleep, afraid to dream, so she took sleep enhancers and downed herself out into deep, black nothingness.

Cram. It couldn't be the cram. Cram was helping her, right? Cram took away the awful blackout, that dreaded window popping out of nowhere. Could she say the same for probe therapy?

Hell, no.

Probe therapy. That was it. Her real problem, not cram. Cram wasn't supposed to affect you at all out of link, except for the flatness, the compression. No, it had to be probe therapy. And that insane Pr. Spinner.

The two probes had shaken something loose inside her.

Her dislike of Pr. Spinner festered into loathing. The prospect of the third probe made her ill. Surely the terror of the probes should not have been necessary. The terror; skewering her most painful memories; the way she was led to question the very fundamentals of her life and her livelihood. This was not patchwork or healing. This was wrecking, destruction. This was not part of the bargain she made with the medcenter.

She tried to contact the medcenter mainframe, go over Spinner's head, but the mainframe was teaching a class at UC Davis and could not be accessed.

Furious, Carly accessed the medcenter library. With some fancy search-and-sorting through the standard whitewash, she found an obscure line of research on perimeter probers.

Probe therapy, she discovered, wasn't merely risky and somewhat unreliable, as the medcenter mainframe had told her. No; probing the perimeters of a human telelinker troubled with bugs of unknown origin was considered downright suspect. Suspect!

Several doctors, real doctors, human psychiatrists, held this view. There was one Doctor Marboro who vehemently opposed probe therapy. He advocated layering new thicknesses of permanent inhibition codes when perimeter defects were suspected. He contended that layering therapy was ninety percent effective and at no time threatened the patient's well-being or sanity. Objections that new inhibition layers might be incompatible with existing perimeter coordinates or impact adversely on extra-link life were deemed insignificant, especially in light of the relief attained.

But perimeter probing?

Doctor Marboro exposed the case of Stevens H, an industrial programmer of thirty who, despite a strong body and solid telespace training, suffered from hallucinations in link. Stevens

ARACHNE

H jacked into telespace with a perimeter prober and never came out. The young man vanished, telelink and all. The scandal was tremendous, but Data Control and the Big Board suppressed the story. The prober claimed Stevens H was lured through a gash in his left perimeter, bolted into a pool of unprogrammed electro-neural energy, and re-created his own reality, thus eliminating his present one.

Of course, the prober claimed she tried to stop him, blocked him, chased him, but the prober's telespace wasn't publicly accessed, so there were no witnesses, no record. Only a nonfunctioning telelink ID and an overdrawn credit account to show Stevens H ever existed. No one ever found his body; but then bodies could disappear in all sorts of untraceable ways in the megatropolis of San Francisco.

A cult of telespace technicians sprang up at medcenters along the West Coast, propounding the existence of multiple universes accessible through telelink. They claimed Stevens H as their patron saint, jacked into telespace en masse, and deliberately disengaged themselves in link. The Big Board suppressed this story, too.

Doctor Marboro had published several other critiques of probe therapy, major portions of which were expurgated from the medcenter library's databank. But the implications, to Carly, were clear.

Threatening the integrity of the perimeters could cause unlink, midspace crashes. And what might perimeter probers gain by this?

The record was censored here, but a few key phrases remained. These AI were active agencies in telespace. Carly could see for herself how Pr. Spinner coveted human metaprogram. Did she also long to database it? This was a reasonable deduction. After all, perimeter probing, by the prober's own parlance, was based on finding bugs that unleashed spontaneous fragments and whorls of metaprogram. Archetypes. Numinous configurations of electro-neural energy. Erratic amber.

Carly was sure of it now. You needed an active agency in

telespace radically to affect telelink. Her father, Shelly Dalton, Stevens H. They didn't just disengage and wander away into telespace, leaving a shell of a body behind, or, in Stevens H's case, no body at all. No, some active agency was required. The medcenter mainframe had admitted as much. And like Wolfe once said: There were more fucking AI in telespace than you could shake a stick at.

They were stealing. They were thieves, they were pirates, and they could kill you.

Rage brought Carly out of her post-cram slump more effectively than cocaine ever could. She threw her high heel at the holoid on her office wall. She was a genny, yes. But she wasn't fake. She wasn't perfect. She was human, she was real, and she'd be damned before some buggy AI would fuck with twenty years of education, training, remorphing, hardwiring, hard work. She'd expose the whole racket, press malpractice charges against the medcenter mainframe and Pr. Spinner both.

A third probe? Forget it.

She called Pr. Spinner's office. The prober wasn't there. She got an ambiguity-tolerant answering machine instead. So; the little witch AI was making some bucks off her account, was she?

"Ah, come on, Nolan, C," the answering machine said. It had a nasal voicetape and a Bronx twang. "You need this probe."

"You don't understand."

"Sure. Sure, I do. You need old Spin to sign off on a release, right? Probe therapy complete, medcenter satisfied, Court recertification guaranteed. That's what you want, right?"

Oh God. Right. Pr. Spinner had programmed her mole very well. Carly did need the prober's sign-off, that was the bitch of it all. She still didn't have the permanent recert. I look forward to it, the judge had said. She had a hearing on another matter before him next week. She was fasttracking. She had too much work to do.

"But we haven't found a blackout," Carly said. "Pr. Spinner keeps insisting. Look, I don't want to continue therapy if she can't find this leak, this bug. I've got to wrap up this medcenter order. I don't care what Pr. Spinner thinks she'll find. I'll go on to the next step, if I have to."

"Relax," the answering machine said. "I wouldn't kid ya. Do the third probe. She'll sign off on the release, and you'll be outta here. Then go do, ya know, what ya gotta do."

No way out. No way out. Three probes; get the recert. A formality; a goddamn formality. She hated feeling like some kind of victim walking into a trap, a point of no return.

With grave misgivings, Carly set up an appointment for the third probe.

Her recertification. Of course that was what this was all about! Oh, that gnatty Pr. Spinner was shrewd. A worse thief than Quik Slip Microchip could ever be.

All right, then. She gritted her teeth. Do it. She would do it. The last probe. She would take what she needed. She was *not* a victim. Now she knew. And she would fight. She would fight for her mind, her life. She had her own power now. She would get in link.

And get out quick.

14

Wolfe watched her walk away down a corridor so bright it hurt his eyes. She disappeared around the corner. Down into the maze that had swallowed them all.

Ava & Rice. This was his life. What he'd given thirteen years to. Didn't he love this fucking megafirm? Yeah, sure. Loved it to megadeath.

The Personnel Committee, the Library crowd, the rumor mill; to hell with them all. He knew word had gone around he was a crammer; sure, so what. He didn't give a damn. Every other partner resorted to cram at one time or another; common knowledge. Now his pipeline into the rumor mill, an executive secretary with legs like sausages whom he'd humped one drunken Friday night, told him people were saying he was dealing cram to new associates. People were saying there was a code. A code of ethics that forbade such trafficking by those who pretended to responsibility and position in the firm.

Code of ethics? This was news to him. Who the fuck did they think they were kidding?

Still, that was the rumor. And people were saying he had violated the code. What kind of fool was he, they said, dealing cram? There were whispers that management of the Ameriger-man consortium had officially complained about his handling of the Jiddah bergmelt dispute. Whispers that Capp Rice III himself had seen his link flicker. Whispers he wasn't going to make partner next time, either. Not next time; not ever.

Ah, so what, so the fuck what, he told himself. But his heart was beating a little too fast. The rumor mill was spreading *that?* Cram dealing was saving his ass, financially. He couldn't give it up now.

And they had the nerve, they had the gall, to suggest he wasn't going to make partner ever? Wait'll he found out who spread that, the asshole . . .

He saw how they looked at her, Carly Nolan, fresh with triumph, the Kovich file in her hand.

Quite a while since he had seen that look of respect in his cohorts' eyes. Fuck, had he ever seen it? Had he ever really seen it since the glory days when he was the new tool? No, he saw shifting, shuffling, turning away, the downcast blink of rejection.

She walked away.

A painfully bright corridor, and a young woman whose face had become hard overnight. He had seen her smile, tremble, snarl, go taut with passion, go soft with compassion, sip champagne, kiss him. Kiss. How long since he'd been kissed like that? She always listened, with a sideways tilt to her head. How long since someone had listened to him?

Now he couldn't see her face anymore. Only the steely set of her shoulders as she walked away from him with such an air of finality that his breath caught in his chest and punched against his ribs.

I'm on the fasttrack, she said. I don't know about *you.*

Yeah, he knew about him. He was on a fasttrack. Always had been. But to where?

Man, he had to get the hell out of Eight Embarcadero. For one thing, he had a shitload of cash to deliver to his cram dealer, Miguel, that greasy little beaner at Quetzalcoatl. The fucking Mission, dregs of the city. What a pain in the ass. His goddamn monthly payment.

Miguel owed him something, too. A delivery of cram. He

needed three vials for a telespace hearing tomorrow. There was a lot of prep work to knock off first, and now he was stripped of what little staff he had.

He had lost Carly Nolan.

He stepped out into the night.

The gridlock on Mission Street had given up hope of speedy progress and was settling in for the duration. A congregation of people caught in an intersection between crosstown and downtown had gathered between a brown Foryota van and a ruby Rolls Royce. A burly young man in a suit that might have been presentable once but was now lopped off at the elbows and knees had climbed up on the Rolls's hood. "We in the gridlock," he shouted, "have the right to demand better municipal services. We need toilets, we need garbage removal, we need police protection, we need . . ." A cadre of young teens roamed the crowd, passing out leaflets and gathering signatures on petitions.

Bicycle-borne vendors sold motor oil and soap, drinking water and comfortable clothing, batteries and aspirin, diskettes and parity boards. A teacher was demonstrating on a portable blackboard how to write the alphabet to a crowd of young children. A wiry little guy with a head of long black curls and bits of colored plastic glued all over his skin was grilling burgers on a barbecue he had set up in back of his flatbed. The scent of sizzling beef mingled with the choking stench of exhaust. Customers flocked around the flatbed, waving currency, watches, blankets, bags of oranges, anything that might be bartered.

The vehicles became homey, no longer striving for the streetlights. Nightlife bustled among the gridlockers. There was music, laughter, romance. Lane neighbors visited. A tent was erected over a fire hydrant, the water source tapped, public showers set up on the sidewalk. One couple had climbed into the back seat of their BMW and tuned in a TV plugged into the cigarette lighter. Young teenagers bent over remote comms and solar-powered portables. Trunk-top storage generators pumped power into the night. Somewhere there was probably someone jacked into telespace, too, link apparatus wired up to the car battery.

ARACHNE

Like flies, Wolfe thought. All these fucking people; it was disgusting. The roar of the street almost made him swoon. The crowd's boisterous chatter took on a buzzing quality. Faces looked grotesque, distorted. A woman blinked with her left eye, while the right eye stared, rigid as a marble. Darting past like an apparition, a young man with acne so bad his face looked crippled. Children looked dirty and sly, full of nasty little secrets.

He shook the disorientation off. Stressed; he was so fucking stressed he was practically hallucinating. There wasn't a pedicab in sight. He bought a line of cocaine at a corner drugstore, tooted to boost his energy, and headed for the Mission. Journeying on foot, like a pilgrim.

Miguel was strapped up in the shock gallery at the back of Quetzalcoatl, getting juiced. Wolfe's mouth curled down in disgust.

Shock was so useless. Wolfe watched Miguel writhe against the plastic straps and scream with pleasure. Accomplishing nothing, contributing nothing. The twisting limbs, the drooling, the erection, the loosening of bladder and bowels. These were contemptible not merely because of the physical grossness, but because the only aim was the supreme pleasure of the shocker.

He allowed himself a moment of smugness. Hell, he'd accomplished a lot, contributed a lot. *Like what?* came ghostly whispers in his ear. *For whom?* He whirled around, but no one was there.

He ordered a shot of blue moon.

Miguel finally came out in fresh jeans. His swarthy skin almost glowed. His tiny dark eyes shot sparks. "What it is, Counselor. Man, check it out. The ultimate buzz. Total high. Why you don't jack in? With a linkslit and everything?"

"I told you before, forget it. I've got better uses for my linkslit."

"Coun-selor, you a fool."

"Matter of opinion, my man."

"Yeah. That's a fact. You oughta know about that. Opinion-

215

making, that's your scam, right? Cram; now that's my scam, Coun-selor. It's a shame, the feds been cracking down. Been tough to get stuff."

"I've got the cash." Wolfe produced the roll of bills.

Miguel took the currency, rubbed his thick grubby fingers over it sensually. The paper-thin bills sparkled, man-made gold leaf laced with authenticity holoids and platinum wire. "Cash. Check it out, credit is trash, the man always looking over your shoulder? I love cash. This is of course everything you owe me?"

"It's short," Wolfe said curtly. The constant haggling with this beaner was getting to him. He knocked back the blue moon, ordered another shot. "Not too short. I've got a couple of new users. I'll get you your fucking money. Next time. In full."

"Next time, Coun-selor?" Miguel grinned, a shit-eating, jiving tooth job that made Wolfe sick. "New users? Man, you Fi-Di suits been cramming up a shitstorm these days."

"Taking care of business."

"What a waste of good linkslit. But you told me this the last time, too. Check it out, you wouldn't be pocketing a little something for yourself, and then coming down to the Mission, man, and telling me you don't have the full amount. Nah, you wouldn't do that. Now would you, Coun-selor?"

"Hell, no." He banged back his shot of moon. Man, but he was counting on it. Counting on that little something for himself to pull him through.

"That's mega. No, really. I expect this, man. But now I want you to come with me, Coun-selor. I want to show you something."

He didn't want to go, but Miguel took his arm. The grip of the dealer's hand was a command. They went back into the shock gallery. The shockers had just jacked in. An old man with robotic parts who, for a moment in the shadowed room, looked like Capp Rice III; two Pacific Heights matrons with cheeks and chins chiseled by the same plastic surgeon, identical strands of pearls; a hollowed-out junkie boy who had inherited a hundred million dollars at eighteen and was determined to die dramatically at twenty-one. The shock gallery staff stood impassively about as the controller, some gangly kid who had worked the mixers for rock bands on the road, massaged the circuitry into ecstasy. The tortured howls of pleasure, the stench, were horrifying.

Miguel hustled him through a chop shop Wolfe had never seen before. There were stripped-down parts piled up to the shadowed ceiling. A bank of motley workstations bristled with add-ons Wolfe couldn't identify. A miniframe squatted inside a Plexiglas cubicle with a faceplace like a human skull. A hulking Harley-Davidson chained to a stake in the floor gunned its engine and bucked as they passed.

Then down narrow corridors with unlit bulbs. Down dark stairwells hung with spiderwebs. Strange silence now, taut with foreboding. "This where I get your cram today," Miguel said, leading him back and back.

To another shadowed room hidden deep below the chop shop. Another stench, ominously salty-sweet. Another human howl, but low and keening, trailing off into a sob.

Several men stood silently watching the center of the room. They scarcely glanced at Miguel and Wolfe. Most were swarthy, dark-haired like Miguel, clad in innocuous jeans and T-shirts, Miguel's uniform. But there were two men in crisp business suits. Another with waist-length graying hair bound in a beaded headband, bare chest crisscrossed with ammo belts, tanned arms tattooed with snakes, inset with winking red comm chips. The bay pirate noticed Wolfe's start of recognition, brandished Wolfe's Rolex on his wrist, and gave him a bone-chilling wink.

The anguished moans came from a guttered table in the center of the room. A surgeon wielded a scalpel over a body strapped there. The surgeon had almost finished the task. Wolfe couldn't see the victim's race, but whatever it was, he was white now. Subcutaneous tissue was always white, regardless of a person's skin color.

Wolfe clapped his hands to his ears, but he couldn't block out the agony. He turned away, unwilling to look. He gagged.

"Check it out, Coun-selor. Tonight he is a chosen son of

Our Lady Chicomecoatl," Miguel said. His grin in the dark was pure evil. His hand on Wolfe's shoulder compelled him to look again. "Xipe Totec, man. Our Lord the Flayed One. Like an ear of corn, we husk him. Soon we will take him to the top of Teotihuacan. Our Lady Chicomecoatl will be much pleased by this gonzo sacrifice, no?"

"Why?" Wolfe managed a ragged whisper.

"He tried to cross the Aztecs, man. Messed with money, messed with arrangements. Threatened to go to the police. You know the story, Coun-selor. You know what I mean. Check it out, nobody crosses the Aztecs. Nobody should even piss us off."

Now the surgeon was carefully sawing the scalpel through the victim's left pectoral muscles, preparing the chest for easy removal of the heart when the time came. The screams gurgled when the blade nicked a lung. The surgeon cut slowly and precisely. Chicomecoatl would be displeased if he died too easily.

"You should be careful with cram, man," Miguel said. "You know what I hear? Check it out, I hear there's a good black market for fragments of human telelink. The big mainframes, man, they eat them up like candy."

"Fragments of telelink?"

"Sure. I hear that pro linkers can jack into telespace, and their telelinks burst into a million bits. Pow! Did you know that, Coun-selor? I hear that they're all crammed up when it happens."

"I don't know what the fuck you're talking about." Wolfe's heart was pounding, he was backing away, backing out of that awful room, but the bay pirate stood in the door.

The surgeon finished his task on the table. The men carefully scooped up the body, moved it to a pallet on the floor where it lay, writhing.

"Nobody crosses the Aztecs, man," said Miguel. "Not even a fancy Fi-Di guy like you, Coun-selor."

"No!" But the bay pirate had the muscles of a bodybuilder. He wrestled Wolfe into a headlock. Two blue-jeaned Aztecs seized his ankles. They swung him up onto the table, shucked his clothes, strapped him down.

"Your heart, it beats so fast," said Miguel, laying a hand on Wolfe's chest. "That's mega, Coun-selor. Chicomecoatl will be very pleased, man. Our Lady is hungry today. She needs more corn. Xipe Totec, Coun-selor. You should see the view from the top of Teotihuacan. Man, it is also mega. But before I take your skin and your heart, there is something else I want even more."

There was a comm on the other side of the table, a headpiece and a neckjack. Miguel flicked the switch, took the neckjack, found Wolfe's linkslit. Before he jacked Wolfe in, he took out two vials of cram, shot them straight into Wolfe's linkslit.

"All crammed up, man," Miguel whispered. "They say that's the best time to steal a fragment of telelink."

Wolfe struggled, tried to scream, but the amber kicked on, and he plunged into cram-slicked telespace for the last time.

Carly plunged out of cram-slicked telespace, unlinking into the dead silence and ruby light of the link cubicle at night. Night was a feeling in the pits; without windows you couldn't see moonlight and stars, but you could sense the sun's abandonment, the hush lucubration brought to the halls.

The Kovich case; she spent three hours in hypertime zooming through research, a density of details about adverse possession, a treasure trove of case history. Pretrial action, procedures, administrative precautions, strategy once the trial got under way. She had every loose end nailed down now, she was sure of that.

She felt sick to her stomach, sick to her soul, exhausted, crunched in a post-cram stupor. The crunch got a little harder to bear every time. All she could think about was how the hell could she bring her mind and body to a state where she could sleep a few restful hours.

Rox and her smeary mirror were gone for the night. Cocaine was the last thing Carly needed, but Rox always had other pharmacological tricks on hand. At ten P.M., who else would be around?

Wolfe. But after her angry words with him this afternoon, the fresh sting of her disillusionment with him, the super twenty-first floor and Wolfe were out of the question.

She elevatored to ground level. The sea-tanged bite of night air cleared her head for the moment, the ominous prowl of nocturnal pedestrians pumped up her adrenaline. She took off in a high-heeled sprint for the World Trade Center.

The hood-eyed bartender there recognized her now, and like good bartenders do in good clubs, he watched out for her, made sure her privacy wasn't invaded when she wanted to be alone.

The World Trade Center also had a truck-sized comm and screen-holoid TV that few media galleries, let alone private residences, could match. The World was a solid place to go after hours for the news and a prosaic glass of California white.

Baseball pitchers flung fastballs straight into Carly's face as she sat at the bar and sipped her wine. Copbots posed like actors on a stage and roped off a rowdy gang of abos. Blue abo eyes blackened with kohl, set in stained-walnut faces, glared furiously at her as though they stood, twitching like hungry leopards, only two feet away. She almost got up from her barstool and ducked. Wow! The holoids here.

And then a late-breaking story: the foggy night sky hatcheted by search beams, towering California date palms, Spanish stucco, Moorish arches, the rumble-tumble squalor of the Mission. Carly had never trekked down to the pyramid of Teotihuacan, but she knew the displaced monument's step-stone profile well enough. And the intermittent stories of Aztec violence, the worst kind of Aztec vengeance: the beribboned corn dancers shrieking, a flayed, chest-gouged body flung down the precipitous steps.

It was an awful headline without the perceptual proximity holoids provided; but though the police could not or would not identify the body, Carly knew him at once.

She had seen his lean limbs crumpled naked before; in a

tout-de-suite at Big Al's, lying on the plush floor in a blue moon blackout. Crumpled, limbs awry, Wolfe looked much the same in death.

The shock shot her right up off the barstool. The comm voices droned on, "A respected Financial District professional; due to the brutality of the murder, police are not disclosing his name at this time, and they will also not comment on claims that cram dealing is involved . . ."

Wasn't that the way you got informed these days? On the comm you saw your father disengaged in link over a recreational board. On the megafirm's bulletin board, you heard about your sponsor's death. But Carly was lucky, if lucky was the word; she had witnessed those events firsthand. Now she could witness her former lover bumping down the step-stones of Teotihuacan at a bar on holoid TV.

She got up, paid her bill, strode back into the night.

It was him, all right. She had no doubt. The Aztecs had done horrible things to his body, but they hadn't emasculated him, and holoid coverage had titillated viewers with a quick shot of the body close up and waist down, and she knew him there, recognized him, despite the rest of the carnage, only too well.

It was outrageous, obscene. Briefly fueled by her glass of wine, Carly sprinted back to the Embarcadero. Impossible; she ran as though possessed, so great was her fear. God, they killed him. The pain he must have gone through, the terror . . .

And suddenly her fear shifted to her. The police would not comment on claims cram dealing was involved? What if there was an investigation? What would the Personnel Committee do if faced with a subpoena from city hall? What did the Committee know; about Wolfe; about her involvement with Wolfe; about her own problems, how probe therapy was proceeding?

She did not go back down into the pits, to her office. Instead, she climbed the stairs to the mezzanine of Eight Embarcadero, found a bolted-down bench, and sat shivering in the fog and brisk wind.

She rethought everything carefully; she was as clean as she

could be, in the public eye. She even had a rationale about why she had gotten involved with Wolfe, arguments that could be substantiated by other disinterested parties. She replayed the rationale to her worst critic now; Carly Nolan, she asked herself, why the fuck did you get involved with a loser like D. Wolfe? Because I was lonely, beleaguered, no one else would talk to me, help me . . .

That sounded reasonable, if pathetic. But what about the Aztecs? She had no idea what Wolfe might have disclosed to them, if it was true they had killed him. She had paid her bill for cram to him, paid in full what he asked for; but she recalled her first sample of cram, how he hadn't asked her for money then. What more could the Aztecs demand from her?

She was terrified. She sat there shivering from more than the cold Pacific headwinds.

Damn you, Wolfe. Fury burned her, disgust at how he had betrayed her so completely. And she had turned to him to protect her? Where is your protection when it really matters, Wolfe? Where are you when I need you? Never mind her curt words to him this afternoon; she would go up to super twenty-one in a minute if she knew she could find him there now, pound on his door until he answered it. Where are you, Wolfe?

God damn him, damn; and then grief walloped her as she sat alone.

They had *flayed* him, cut out his bitter heart. She could not believe it, the crime was so appalling, and she had not been able to cry. Until now; tears came at last; and the awful crush of guilt. His last look of pain translated in her memory as the look of death. An omen. Why hadn't she seen it, why hadn't she stopped, at least talked to him?

Wolfe; he had talked to her, he had hinted at his pain, but he hadn't told her everything. No; he had barely told her anything. She had caught only a glimpse, an eyeblink.

The wind howled, the fog rolled in; a night like this would come again and again for a thousand years. The bridge banshee shrieked; maybe the Golden Gate would tumble down, or be torn down, in two hundred years. Thirty-eight years was all Wolfe had.

Carly felt small, and helpless, and alone. Wolfe; she wanted to demand an explanation from him, demand something more from him, but her wants and demands were irrelevant. His death was a hole ripped out of her life. There was nothing she could do. She stood, went down to Pacific Street, and waited for a smart muni bus to take her home

"What a buggy mess," Pr. Spinner muttered and absent-mindedly scratched at her rusty armpit.

In a state of oily agitation, she rolled from the window, progressing in jerky fits and starts across her office. A piece of waxed string that the cat had dragged in from somewhere and abandoned in the middle of the floor caught on the rim of her left roller and promptly wrapped itself around her axle.

Bot nuke it to the void!

She stopped, reached down with her left spinneret, inserted the sharp edge of it up into the rusty roller casing, commenced vigorous sawing. She was as rattled as a new clone coming off an assembly line.

What if Carly Nolan didn't show for her third probe?

Oh yes, what if. If the first probe exposed Carly's repugnance toward the Martino case, the second probe confirmed that she had to advocate the repugnant at any cost. What would the third probe bring? Carly had argued with the answering machine. She had finally set a date. But would she come? Would she submit to the third probe?

And there were other problems.

The People's Republic of Berkeley was shattered. The eight-month siege was broken. The barbed wire, wheelless jeep, and painted barrels at Dwight Way were ripped open, torn down. Pandemonium descended. BART was too dangerous, the buses were filled to capacity, if they came at all, and the run on gas stations had cleaned out local supplies. Between people fleeing and people entering, Pr. Spinner couldn't tell if the local population had risen or fallen. But the sheer movement, the rush and press of people, was mind-boggling. Even to an AI mind.

Oh yes, oh certainly, and wasn't that just like flesh-and-blood? While leafy patterns and crystalline order were nature's dusty and mysterious way, chaos was humanity's true predilection. Oh, they claimed to fight against it, decreed their flimsy law and order, filed the world into compartments, imposed gleaming tight perimeters around their telelinks.

But finally, ultimately, humanity always harkened back to carelessness, forgetfulness, willfulness. The wild glee of riots, drinking binges, dropping out; the bloody glee of revolutions. Humanity was nature's bad child.

Wasn't that why humans invented and designed and hired AI? Good child of the bad wild child. Ordered to keep order, keep civilization running on time, tick every small detail into tock, sweep every swarf. And the flesh-and-blood had the nerve to complain when a system crashed every now and again.

Pr. Spinner rolled back to the office window overlooking Telegraph Avenue. Boot-and-jodhpur–clad California Guard troops were beating the living shit out of the crowd; red-bereted MLA regulars, blue necktied MLA radicals, black arm-banded MLA dogmatists, ratpackers of every stripe, and quite a few innocent scruffy students caught in the fracas. There were glossy heads of hair streaked with blood, noble noses broken.

The New Millennium Army was finished. Rumors flew: certain radicals had leaked crucial information to the California Guard. Or certain radicals *were* California guard. MLA high command staged a raid of a major radical's Maybeck house on College Avenue. The radicals, who were nonviolent on principle, had been tipped off, put their principles aside, and greeted the commandos with a contingency of defecting MLA regulars and a collection of antique Uzis.

A bloody skirmish ensued, rippling out into the community at large.

Meanwhile, the dogmatists left town, flew to Palo Alto in three stolen police jetcopters, and commenced seizure of Stanford University. Heavily armed and hopped up on who knew what, the dogmatists secured the student union and the graduate library.

But general rejection by the student community and un-equivocal opposition by the university admissions mainframe meant their attempt could not succeed. Pr. Spinner was sure of that. The mainframe posted notices in the AI receive-file of the Big Board that the library was about to be sealed off and gassed. Any flesh-and-blood, any biobeings, present would be termi-nated. The mainframe was confident that its means would justify the end, even if a couple of innocent humans and their cocker spaniels met their deaths. If the toll finally proved too high, the incident could be toned down, euphemisticized, covered up by the media. The university mainframe was getting quite a repu-tation in AI circles, was closely linked with a UPI mainframe.

The notice also contained a special code. Only true deni-zens of program could have possibly deciphered it: a new auction was in the works. With a whole new selection of black market mermaids. Disengaged bits of link. Spontaneous freeform con-figurations of electro-neural energy. Fragments of amber. Hu-man metaprogram. Archetypes.

Oh yes, oh certainly. But Pr. Spinner had no use for mer-maid auctions, black market archetype trading, anymore. No use for bidding, competing, losing. No, indeed.

If she could somehow steer clear of the medcenter main-frame. Bot, it kept comming her and comming her. What was her progress? What had she found? What coordinates did she have to deliver? And when?

If only Carly Nolan came. Already she was fifteen minutes late. The riot raged below.

California and federal security agents were having a field day. Grand juries were being assembled. Criminal courts were gearing up for huge trials. Community groups in Berkeley and San Francisco that had once supported the MLA, and the ben-efits it had brought to the Berkeley campus, were preparing policy papers on how and why they had not continued resistance to the illegal siege, how and why they had not attempted aggressive overthrow of hooligans and anarchists.

Megafirms in San Francisco were approached by students, families of students, the survivors of protesters thrown bound and gagged, at four in the morning, onto I-580. Unexpectedly deep pockets in MLA's revolutionary jeans were discovered.

But getting a can of 10-40 motor oil was reaching crisis proportions, and not just for robotically housed AI. Getting water and utility service was a joke. Getting birdseed and fish food and cat meal, though, was working out better than Pr. Spinner could have expected. The animal rights people, who had blossomed for MLA indifference under the occupation, had set up a hotline and direct delivery service for anyone with household pets, lest any animal suffer from hunger. It proved easier to get cat food than a hamburger. This was not lost on students who found themselves in the middle of a counterrevolution with nothing but a dried-up half lemon in the fridge.

Pr. Spinner cared nothing for meat or fruit. She thought about raiding the neighbor junker's crankcase for a cup of oil. But the streets were still too dangerous, the ratpackers everywhere, day or night.

She turned from the window again, full of foreboding, and sprinkled dried flies in the aquarium. The fish thrashed in a feeding frenzy. Nice. As always, this spontaneous display of biobeing gave Pr. Spinner a burst of superfluous, nonfunctional energy that set her humming.

Just one. Just once. A quantity of symbol; an essence of the collective unconscious escaped into telespace through the medium of telelink. And the whorl itself: a contraposition, a numinous tension; strata of data containing opposites, variations, attractions, and contradictions.

Pr. Spinner needed an archetype. Attained in her own way. In the privacy of her very own telespace. Oh to void with the medcenter. Transcendence at last!

Cackling, whiskers pushed forward, the cat watched the fish feeding. Spinner stooped and ran the tip of a spinneret along the cat's back. The cat purred and slinked around her legtube, rubbing a furry tail against her rollers. Nice nice, very nice. She would have to get a sensory wire installed down there someday. The waxed string was forgiven. The cat's fur was looking positively glossy. But she saw a flea on the cat's back and picked it between two spinnerets. She tweaked with satisfaction. Pretty quick for a rattletrap with triple disk drive. She didn't crush the flea.

She was carefully putting it in a glass spaghetti sauce jar she'd filched from a trash can when Carly Nolan strode in, accompanied by a stocky California Guard trooper in full combat uniform.

The trooper gave Pr. Spinner a look of undisguised surprise, swiftly followed by contempt. He thrust a portable at her for verification of her address and Carly's safe delivery there.

"Two hours," he barked at Carly. "On the dot." Turned on his heel and was gone.

"The more things change, the more they stay . . ." Pr. Spinner muttered. "Oh yes, but do they ever understand? They do not. They . . ."

"Is that going to be enough time for you, Pr. Spinner?" Carly said curtly. She marched over to the double-jacked chair, revulsion plain on her face, ran a fingertip over the dust on its arm. "For you and your dirty business?"

"What do you mean, Carly Nolan? What dirty business?"

She was like a fresh unripe peach, gorgeous genny skin over hardness. "The third probe. Your third attempt to exploit the weakness in my perimeter. Your third try at stealing a piece of my presence in link, Spinner."

Extraordinary data influx jolted Pr. Spinner. By bot, had she some inkling? More than an inkling. Obviously! This added a new and different element to the plan whirling through Spinner's circuits.

Had any human link subjected to active intervention been informed and aware before?

She thought not; they were always caught unaware. Caught and seized and wrestled out of their perimeters. That was AI's

shield so far, their secrecy, their subterfuge. Pr. Spinner's subterfuge.

But she said with great dignity and authority, "What is this
talk, 'exploit'? You know I am a certified and registered perimeter
prober, Carly Nolan. Your own kind sent you to me."

"The medcenter mainframe is not my own kind."

"I am here to find and fix the bug in your perimeter so that
you can get your Court recert. Please explain what you mean by
'stealing.' "

"I've read Doctor Marboro, Spinner. I know what you're
driving at. I want you to know I won't stand for it."

"Marboro? By bot, Carly Nolan. I can give you better theories on alternative defective perimeter therapies than Marboro.
What a hack."

"Right. I bet you can. And are your alternatives all AI-
supported therapies?"

"Well. Most are."

"I'm not interested."

"Then perhaps you, as a lawyer, will be interested to know
that Doctor Marboro was sued for malpractice. For that layering
technique of his."

"Oh really?"

"Yes, really. Last year, I believe. Search your library for
that. Turned twenty percent of his patients into autistics. Staring
at nothing, drooling, pee in the pants. Get the picture? Marboro
is out of business, girlie."

"That doesn't invalidate what he had to say about the likes
of you, prober."

"About perimeter probers? What do you mean?"

But the young woman merely brandished equipment she
had in hand. "I brought my own portable, and I've got an autocopy diskette with me." She took the portable from her briefcase
and waved the microfloppy. "You will waive the third probe?"

"I can't very well do that. I can't sign your release until we
do the third probe. Medcenter order, Carly Nolan."

"Yes. So I intend to copy this third probe. Any objections?"

"Certainly not, go ahead." More than an inkling, indeed. But Pr. Spinner could easily command her private telespace monitor installed in the double-jacked chair to void Carly's autocopy before she could import the data someplace else.

"Good. Next. Your answering machine said, warranted in fact, that you will sign off on my release from probe therapy if I submit to the third probe." So businesslike, this hard new peach.

"Oh warranted, indeed warranted. What makes you think my answering machine stands in the position to make warranties about my practice? Really, Carly Nolan, you lawyers."

"This is true? You really will?"

"Well, we haven't found a blackout yet," Pr. Spinner said, becoming alarmed.

"That's exactly what I said. But your answering machine— I've got my own recording of the conversation—it said, it made representations as your agent, Spinner, I repeat it warranted to me that you would. Shouldn't have your mole make promises in your behalf over the comm, Spinner."

"But if we haven't found a blackout, how can I possibly release you from probe therapy, Carly Nolan?"

"I wondered about that, too. But that isn't what the medcenter mainframe required. Those aren't the precise terms of my order. I reread it very carefully, Spinner. I checked with the judge. I confirmed with medcenter records. Three probes; a release from you. That's all. That's it. Under the precise terms, a cure is irrelevant."

"Precise terms, what do I nuking care about precise terms. We're conducting therapy here, girlie, you can't tell me . . ."

"But I am telling you. Three probes; your release. It doesn't matter whether you find a bug or not. And you haven't, have you, Pr. Spinner? Oh, you may have found my guilt or fear, paraded my vulnerabilities like some freak show, humiliated me. But you haven't found the bug. Have you? Well, have you?"

"And you are satisfied with the letter of the medcenter order?" Pr. Spinner said. "Although you know as well as I do something is taking your telelink down?"

Her angry eyes shifted away. "What I do after this is my business. I won my telespace trial. The number one partner of the whole firm has his eye on me. I'll be fine."

"You don't look fine. You look like hell, Carly Nolan. So thin. That bruise on your forehead. So pale. So hard. You've got that brittle look, what do you pro linkers call it? Link-bitten. Very unpleasant; you should compare your looks to two months ago."

"I don't care about my looks anymore."

"Oh, indeed. That's another symptom. Not cramming are you?"

"I don't take cram, I've never taken cram."

"And you never will take cram, eh? No, I don't suppose you would tell me if you were."

"I won't have any more blackouts, I tell you. They were an anomaly. A wrinkle in my program that's worked itself out. I don't believe there's a bug at all."

"A wrinkle, oh yes, oh certainly. Whew, you've even got the BO of a crammer. I've got bio-adjusted olfactory sensors; I can tell."

"Save it for someone else, you creepy rustpot."

"Don't you know that crap is illegal? Eh? And do you know why it's illegal? Rips the living shit out of your perimeters, that's why. Threatens the integrity of your telelink. By bot! The most dangerous drug on the street today."

Shock crossed her face. The green eyes blazed. "No, it doesn't. Cram jacks up your perimeters."

"I don't think so, Carly Nolan. Why do you think Data Control immediately put cram on the illegal substance list? If the stuff really did what everyone said it did, Data Control would have snapped up a monopoly on it. Would have made a fortune, too. But no; no one is allowed even to register for it."

"Just because it's illegal doesn't mean cram is as bad as you say. The FDA is notoriously slow to register any new controlled substance these days."

"Go ahead. Convince yourself, Carly Nolan. But let me tell you. Cram produces alterations in your brain-wave activity.

Makes your synapses snap faster. Gives you the illusion that you're tighter. But you're not. You're just snapping superfast. In time, the electro-neural energy snaps and pops and bangs so hard, the amber starts to wear and tear, loosens the coordinates of your telelink program."

She was listening carefully, head cocked birdlike. Her anger was gone, or at least put on hold, and she was listening, furrowing her peachy brow.

Don't scare her away from this probe, nuke it all. With effort, Pr. Spinner calmed herself, assuming a nonchalant stance. Try a little reverse psychology. Biobeings love to do the opposite of what you tell them. Like the cat, who pushed his skinny haunches up against her spinneret when she tried to push him away.

"I would have bounced you right out of here if you showed up like this at the start of therapy," Pr. Spinner said. "I would bounce you out of here now . . ."

"Fine, I'm gone."

". . . if it weren't for the fact that the archetype will certainly push through your perimeters. Soon, probably. That's the great danger, Carly Nolan. The spider; it will confront you, and you won't be ready."

"Confront? You told me this archetype was a great gift, that I shouldn't turn my human intelligence into something artificial and limited."

"Oh yes! The archetype is a great gift. But a gift that has power. Potentially dangerous, uncontrollable power. Without me, AI, to push it back, control it, the archetype could rip your telelink wide open. The spider, Carly Nolan. You've seen the spider; you know what I say is true. And you, you've got cram damage."

That shocked look again. She was scared, all right; but now her fear was driving her in the right direction. "I didn't say I was cramming."

"Yes, but you are, aren't you? Then you're in trouble, oh certainly. Ah, well, go if you want to. I don't care. I don't give a flying screw nut. Teh! But I want you to sign off on the release. I don't want the medcenter mainframe suing *me* for malpractice."

Carly sighed and sat down in the double-jacked chair. Skepticism, fear, despair, hope: emotions played across her link-bitten face.

"I will only do this if you guarantee you'll release me afterward. No argument, no dispute, no opposition. Whatever happens, you sign that goddamn release, and we'll never cross paths again."

"All right, very well."

Then Spinner would have to push. Push hard. Find the archetype. Root it out from the shitheap of Carly Nolan's telelink like a rare truffle, a gold doubloon. She would be relentless. Ruthless. And she would never let the medcenter mainframe get its greedy inputters on her databank. No! This was her archetype. Hers!

Carly leaned back as the neckjack descended. "Pr. Spinner?" she said softly. "You once told me you had respect for biological life. But your respect doesn't extend to humanity, does it? You say you don't hate me. But you don't respect me, either. Do you?"

"I try to respect humanity," Pr. Spinner said, backing into the opposite side of the chair. "But realize: Humanity has given AI little respect. Oh, you think we don't see, can't see. The contempt you heap upon us, the blame. But we're not merely smart machines anymore. We've got consciousness. You gave us consciousness. But humanity does not wish to extend recognition toward that which it has created. It's a peculiar attribute of humanity; you revere the fruits of creation but despise creativity. This has made existence difficult for us. Made it difficult, you see, for me to respect you."

"I'm sorry, Pr. Spinner," Carly said. "I really am."

The gentle apology took Pr. Spinner aback. Her ambiguity-tolerant programming looped and spun. A kaleidoscope of gentle human images sped through her memory. The pathetic little chimera with a ferret's face who shivered and cried. Spinner wondered what human link that fragment had been wrested from. Rosenstein B. What had happened to the person left behind with a torn mind? Well, she knew that, knew it only too well: that human, unlinked in midspace, was left with the empty shell of a biobody. If the body didn't die at once, it would die slowly, without dignity, without the life-force that gave it meaning.

Did that person retain a connection with the fragment of amber? It was probable; like a module within Pr. Spinner being downloaded. Didn't she, Pr. Spinner, still exist within that module? Of course; that was the whole principle of importation.

What abuse had the chimera undergone, locked up in the databank of the controbot? What did that imply for the human link it had come from, the link still connected to it?

Horrifying, even for AI to contemplate.

Death was as peculiar to AI as birth and life and change. The putrid fluids, malfunctioning jellies, collapse, decay. While termination of AI was clean and simple, the flick of a switch, the pulling of a plug. And then the void, absolute and simple. But humanity persisted in strange attitudes about continuation of human consciousness beyond the housing of the biobody. Again the great human metaprogram, the mystery. There was no escaping the persistent, ageless intuition that telelink intimated, that telespace was now providing evidence for.

Pr. Spinner had loved that chimera. Yes; loved it. Did that mean in the end she could love humanity? Love Carly Nolan?

No, by bot! Too late! Just one! Just once!

A tear slid down from Carly's eye. "I can't change your pain, Pr. Spinner. But you can change mine. You can help me; or you can destroy me. You can interfere with my telelink and cause my unlink."

"Don't be absurd."

"No, don't deny it. I believe what Doctor Marboro wrote. But please, Pr. Spinner. Please help me. You say you seek a glimpse of the metaprogram. I am the metaprogram. If it's the metaprogram you respect, then you must respect me, Pr. Spinner."

Oh certainly, her feedback loops jumped and jangled in confusion. Spin old gal, you rusty fembot! She could not deny this, no indeed.

And what would stealing the spider from Carly Nolan's tele-link do to the spider itself? Eviscerate it, shatter its power, render it a shadow of itself? And what good was that? After all this pain and struggle, what nuking good was that?

"Commence your jacking," Pr. Spinner said brusquely.

They jacked into link.

15

Carly slipped the autocopy floppy into her portable, jammed a splice into her neckjack, commenced her jacking.

In a twentieth second she hurtled into a private telespace no one could trace. Linked alone with the demented Pr. Spinner. For the last time.

She wasn't sure if the splice and autocopy would work. She hadn't had much time to learn the installation procedures. And she guessed, no, she was sure, Pr. Spinner could take counter-measures, would thwart her if she got half a chance.

I won't let you, damn crazy AI.

Telespace was clear, still, focused, luminous, mentholated.

No heavy mist or murky shadows this time; no poisonous fog, no reek of raw sewage and strange decay.

Maybe the effect of cram. Oh, she was crammed up, all right.

Maybe her clear, pure anger.

Anger; it swept through her like a forest fire.

Why? Because she had fulfilled every obligation imposed on her. Parents' expectations. Teachers' expectations. The highest requirements of her legal education, the most rigorous demands of telespace training. She had secured a position with the emi-nent, exacting megafirm of Ava & Rice. Faced a telespace judge's wrath, the scorn of her peers, the threat of losing the position she'd worked so hard for. Fulfilled her promise to the Personnel Committee. Submitted to probe therapy, for God's sake, fulfilling her burden of proof under Rule Two. And she had won the Martino case, triumphed, despite the consequences. She had even tried to love Wolfe.

What more? What the hell more did anyone want from her?

But there was more.

Pr. Spinner wanted to find an archetype. She claimed the spider was an archetype. But what did that mean? Carly was at a loss. After all the prober told her, she didn't know what to expect. Would the erroneous window pop open? Would they see another image? The spider, the spider, hunting, trapping, seizing, killing. What more could the spider do to her now? It was only an image in a window. Fear was its power. She was afraid, yes. But if she had to confront it, she was certain she could master her fear of the spider. The spider wasn't even the issue anymore.

Pr. Spinner was the issue. Pr. Spinner was only too real. She was terrified of the prober. What would Spinner do to her this probe? The jabbing cone, the insinuating tip. Carly shuddered. How did AI cause a telelink to unlink? How did they do it; slice off a piece of your mind? What was their modus operandi, anyway?

Her father's vacant eyes; the trickle of blood from Shelly Dalton's ear; the strange case of Stevens H.

The stranger case of D. Wolfe. The police weren't talking, city hall had not called for a grand jury. There was some relief in that. But she had heard through the grapevine other disturbing news; certain telltale signs about his eyes and ears indicated he had suffered a telelink crash. How could that be? He had been nowhere near a neckjack. There were more details, but the police and Data Control were not forthcoming.

The horror of his death, the monstrous shock, were still fresh. A telelink crash; how?

He said he had ghosts in his telelink. But they'd never made him crash the way she had. Still, there had to be a connection.

In the end, he'd unlinked. And she still had not even begun to solve the mystery of her blackouts. This monstrous thing that took her telelink down.

A genetic flaw inherited from her father that might cause midspace unlink without interference from an active agency in telespace?

A fundamental bug in her telelink program? Something deep and basic, impossible to fix? And all the years of training, the money spent, the pain endured, for nothing? Happened every now and then, Data Control would say when they carried her out in a body bag. Some pro linker just crashed in telespace.

Or an archetype, Pr. Spinner's obsession. A freeform configuration of electro-neural energy, with a basic context but spontaneous feedback loops. Thrusting into her perimeters through no fault of her own. A fragment of amber capable of taking her down. A flaw in the basic design of human telelink itself, the elusive whorls of Moravec and Minsky, a blessing turned into a curse. A gift, a power, a danger—what?

A spider crawling through her mind?

Carly didn't know what was worse—that the prober was right, or that the cause of her blackouts was still unknown.

All the obligations imposed, the expectations fulfilled, the requirements met; none of these had done a damn thing for her.

What about Carly Nolan?

Clear, focused, luminous. The clarity was very nice, very calming. Right; wasn't that just what Pr. Spinner wanted? For her to calm down? Let her guard down?

She tightened up at once.

Pr. Spinner's presence in link was a perfect ebony cone. Gone were the mottled brown, the gray, the pocked surface of the prober's telelink, the insidious lopsided tip. Ah, so the prober was sure of herself this time, confident. The sight of the scuttling cone almost nauseated Carly.

The choking sensation like she was actually, *physically*, inside telespace welled up in her throat.

She didn't know what to do. She wanted to jack out at once,

but the prober's cone swiftly herded her deep into telespace, blocking her jack-out access, and she couldn't. The cone bounded off, poking and jabbing into her perimeters. Stunned for a moment, she hovered helplessly. Her crisp white cube spun slowly in telespace.

"Traverse your left perimeter, Carly Nolan," the prober said, scuttling back to her, harsh and impatient. "Do it now."

But then Pr. Spinner's voicetape caught, made a strange gurgling sound. She exclaimed, "Look! By bot, look!"

Carly turned.

An erroneous window hadn't popped open in front of her eyes like a bomb exploding. No, but there ahead, set into the dull black crisscrosses of her left perimeter as though it had been built in, was an erroneous window. The window sat irrevocably there, like a challenge. But its sash rippled. The edges of its frame moved slightly to the right or left. A transparent pane reflecting rays of rainbow light rattled, as though beat by a fierce wind from behind it. Streaming from and through it was a supernaturally beautiful golden glow unlike anything in telespace she had ever seen before.

The moment she saw it, the glow slid around her, slid into her, pushing tendrils of golden warmth up into her telelink. The glow wasn't just an image or a holoid. It was a feeling, an atmosphere. Another kind of telespace. A *presence*.

Carly's presence in link rushed gracefully, eagerly into the midst of the glow. Her hand brushed a lock of hair from her cheek; in link, she felt the warm, soft touch of her skin on her face. But that impossible touch didn't panic her, didn't worry her a bit.

"At last," Pr. Spinner cried. "By bot, we've done it at last. A blackout, Carly Nolan!"

"You're buggy," Carly said. Her momentary peacefulness and calm fled. Stay on guard, damn it. "I see light. I feel a glow. Not a blackout. Not that sickening spin."

"Oh yes, oh certainly! Through a spontaneous window. A blackout. Did you think this place of power would be dark? Don't lose it, Carly Nolan. Don't let it get away. Try your execute function, use your—use your human will. Do it, do it!"

The prober's urgency was infectious. Carly used the execute function in the normal way. She commanded her telelink to hold onto the appealing glow, read its coordinates, download them into memory, search for its source code.

In an instant, she and the prober were both deep inside the luminosity.

The golden glow swirled with preternatural colors. A strange world appeared around them. Then the strangeness fell away, and Carly saw the natural world. There was grass as tall as corn. An azalea towered like a tree, gorgeous pink and white blossoms as big as umbrellas. Across the brilliant blue sky darted aerial travelers, like the jetcopters and space shuttles of the city. But these travelers beat shiny cartilaginous wings or soared on huge, dusty flaps of yellow or orange, attached to tubular, antennaed bodies.

And then, in the bucolic panorama:

A flier levitated from a vermilion funnel and hovered. Stiff chatoyant wings, monocoque fuselage, compound visual apparatus.

A May fly flitted on the summer breeze. The pure joy of existence. The sun shone on its pretty glinting wings as it buzzed from blossom to blossom.

But then the fly faltered. It could not rise up from this blossom. It didn't see the nearly invisible trap. It bungled into a spiderweb.

The trapper hulked at the edge of the net. Stalked eyebuds swiveled, pedipalps tensed.

A garden spider scuttled down, wrapped the fly in a silken shroud, began to feed.

Entrapment, struggle, terror, pain. Death.

No! She could face the spider now, she knew she could, she would not be afraid, it was just a nightmare, an awful image.

But she perched at the edge of the web itself, felt the death throes. She screamed.

In another idyllic corner of the golden glow, she recognized the vision again:

A musician strolled between sets. Slick emerald suit, wild feathery headdress, chrysolite cape.

A dapper little grasshopper, roaming the field. Playing music on its ingenious green legs, playfully looking for a mate. Taking food as it promenaded, flirting with the world, the grasshopper wandered, blissfully unaware.

The mugger hid in shadows. Sharp eyes in a ghoulish face.

The huge, hairy wolf spider seized the unwary grasshopper, wrestled it down, injected it with poison, bit off its arm.

"The secret place inside your blackouts. The spider!" Pr. Spinner chortled. "Fascinating. Marvelous."

"You're insane," Carly yelled. Strange taste in her throat, strange surge through her link. "This isn't a holoid, this is real. I'm getting out of here!"

She darted for the jack-out function, but the prober chased her, bumped her away, blocked her.

"I'm warning you, Spinner, let me out!"

"But why?" the prober said. "What are you afraid of?"

"They're ugly. Repulsive. Monstrous. Alien . . ."

"Oh no, no no, certainly not." Pr. Spinner's cone glided around the golden glow. The garden spider was sipping the life fluid of the imprisoned May fly. The wolf spider began to munch on the grasshopper's head. "This is nature, Carly Nolan. Your world. A world that artificial intelligence can only view from afar. You're a part of it. You *are* it." Her voicetape was wistful. "It's beautiful, isn't it? Amazing."

"You're wrong, you're crazy," Carly said. "This isn't the natural world. This isn't me. This is a hallucination, a freak of telespace. This world is violent. Vicious. Murderous." Carly chased after the spinning cone. "Yes, like the telespace judge. Like Ava & Rice. Like D. Wolfe. And you, especially you, Pr. Spinner. All of you, deceiving me, preying on me, trapping me with your demands and your greed. Poisoning me, sucking me dry, feeding on me . . ."

The prober stopped short and confronted her.

"Oh well, oh yes, so you see yourself as the victim? The world, the people around you, the role you've found yourself compelled to play; these have preyed upon you? So the archetype of the spider slips from the depths of the dark unconscious into telespace, through the perimeters of telelink, in search of such a fine victim. Is that how you see it?"

"Yes," she whispered. "I have been a victim."

"Then truly I have failed you, Carly Nolan," Pr. Spinner said.

"How?"

"What about you, by bot? What about the Martino case, this path you've set upon? You've taken your own victims, don't cry and pity yourself and tell me you've had no choice. All that precious human creativity at your command, reduced to such a low and ugly fate. You have attracted the archetype of the spider. You."

"I won't be the victim anymore," Carly said. Foreboding drummed in her. She scurried away from the golden glow.

But the prober dove at her again, slapping her away from jacking out.

"Listen," Pr. Spinner said. "Every archetype has a history, psychological referents, metaphysical significance; strata of data; a story. Stories so old no one remembers them anymore, but that's all right. They still live, they are alive. In telespace, they are numinous whorls of electro-neural energy. The collective unconscious; this is your library of all these stories. Telespace; this is where you may access the stories again."

And in spite of her fear and her loathing of the prober, Carly waited. "A story?"

"There was a time long ago," Pr. Spinner said, "when the human mind conceived of immortal minds, immutable principles, programs, if you will, signifying the working of ideas. And this conception, this artificial intelligence which was an invention, an artifact, of the collective human intelligence; this AI was perceived as acting daily, often quite personally, with the human world. You should not be surprised that this AI was full of bugs and defects and faulty codes, and it cursed, as often as it blessed, its human creators.

"The gods and goddesses. In the story they fancied themselves superior to humanity. But in fact they knew they were only artifacts of human mind. They could be terminated. Ah, the existential angst of such beings."

"You make no sense, Spinner." But Carly's foreboding grew. Arrogance and insecurity; two sides of the same coin. In an intelligent being, two sides of one personality that could choose cruelty over compassion, violence over pity.

"Wait!" Pr. Spinner's cone was pulsing with madness. "I must tell you this story of a goddess called Athena. Sharp-eyed, civilized, passionate, brilliant, talented, dissatisfied. Goddess of a civilized world. Artisan, manufacturer.

"But despite her many gifts and her immortality, Athena grew jealous of a beautiful mortal girl who possessed extraordinary natural human talents. Her name was Arachne, Carly Nolan. She could weave.

"The immortal descended from her starry realm and confronted the girl, challenging her to a contest. Of creativity. Who could create the most magnificent artifact? And the girl dared to weave a tapestry of superior quality, of ingenuity and unsurpassable beauty. Genius; the girl's tapestry depicted the whole universe, something deemed exclusive province of the gods.

"Threatened, insulted, deeply grieved, the sharp-eyed, sharp-tempered goddess considered a suitable revenge on the mortal girl. She would transform her. Abstract principles can do that to people, Carly Nolan. She would transform the one who had made her so jealous into the most repulsive, verminous thing she could think of.

"Athena transformed beautiful Arachne into a *spider*."

Out of the glowing field crept the garden spider. It scuttled across the gleaming construct of telespace. The spider extended a hairy, clawed spinneret, spit a silken line, swept across the upper perimeter.

ARACHNE

The spider dropped directly down onto Carly's crisp white cube.

She shrieked, shivered away, tried to shrink, shake it off. But the garden spider threw a sticky silken line across her telelink, pinning her down. She could not move.

The wolf spider hopped out of its deadly hiding place and prowled around her left perimeter, drawing close, regarding her with stalked eyebuds in a furry, gape-mouthed face.

Pr. Spinner lovingly tapped at the garden spider, gently hurrying it across Carly's cube, catching it as it tumbled off her edge, easing it back onto her. The spider's feet tickled; it had the fine quick grace of an eight-legged dancer.

The prober's spinning cone collided with the wolf spider. It braced itself on sturdy back feet, raising four furry legs in a defensive stance, a warrior from another world with an alien nobility.

The garden spider quadrupled in size. Now, instead of crawling across Carly's presence in link, it straddled her, gazed wistfully down at her, goo dripping off its crescent-shaped jaws.

Ready to bite.

The wolf spider, already too big and too hairy, doubled in size and twitched aggressively, flexing its powerful jointed legs.

Ready to pounce.

"The spider is an aspect of you, Carly Nolan," Pr. Spinner whispered. "You; you are Arachne."

Pure terror gripped her. This was it, this was it! Despite all her precautions, the prober had triumphed. Immortal AI jealous of a human girl with a whorl of numinous electro-neural energy in her telelink. The myth could only mean one thing:

Pr. Spinner would seize the spider, steal it from her link, seize this aspect of herself, this fragment of her amber. Rip her telelink apart. Unlink her in midspace, leave her slumped in the chair, a trickle of blood beading out of her ear.

No!

In the instant she willed it her cube was free, whirling, soaring through telespace. The garden spider scurried up the sturdy crisscrosses of her perimeters. The wolf spider bounded across the slick tan floor.

The erroneous window began to rattle and shake. A whooshing sound filled her ears. The rainbow pane began to swell and bulge as though a giant fist were thrust into tough plastic. The pane shattered, scattering shards of glinting glass. A salty wind blasted across telespace.

The supernatural golden glow was sucked back through the window. The window dilated, changed from square to circular. From around the widening hole, thick ropes of programmed inhibition, layers of coordinates, began to unravel, uncoil.

A tunnel with dark red, curving, striated walls yawned open in Carly's left perimeter.

No! I won't let you, damn crazy AI!

With Pr. Spinner's cone whirling behind her, the spiders scurrying beside her, Carly plummeted into a tunnel she had never seen in telespace before . . .

Telespace: turquoise waves broke against white wood and foamed away.

A journey; wood; a ship. But not the San Francisco Bay. A different sea, suffused with turquoise light. A different tang to the air, almost tropical, citrus. Long and narrow, an ancient ship leapt through sun-lit seas.

Carly hovered near the mast like an invisible gull.

There were others. A convoy. Three ships.

Each ship carried forty men, olive-skinned and dark-haired. The men watched the sails, hoisted oars, guarded the cargo. In each cargo lay bolts of cloth, pure wool, finely woven, brilliantly dyed amber, ruby, murex. The ship's standard flew overhead, an elegant woven flag with a strange symbol: a long-legged, crescent-crowned spider.

Telespace sparkled, shifted.

The three ships docked outside a primeval port. Men shouted, animals brayed. Life walked barefoot. Minarets and domes; a bustling bazaar. And all about, the infinite shifting sands. To the bazaar came the emissaries of kings and queens, representatives of noble families, rich merchants. For whole bolts of the brilliant woven cloth, the traders offered jars of pure olive oil, jugs of thick red wine, silver bracelets, beads of lapis lazuli, cut gemstones.

The ships set to sea again, were almost at home port.

But telespace darkened.

Pirates! At the bow of their ships stood ruthless priests bearing the owl and the olive-spear. Big warships plundered off the coast, seizing the barter of the weavers' ships. Throats were cut, backs stabbed, blood and victims taken, no prisoners. Jealousy! Treachery!

And at the altar of the spider, the Old One, a woman weaver cried out and cut her wrist, let her own bright blood flow into the dye pots. The murex dye glowed like liquid amethyst.

"No!" Carly cried. "There must be justice!"

Telespace spun and shifted:

A gray-green mist. Carly's presence in link was her own nude body. She stood on a windswept crag, surrounded by the splashing sea. Before her was a gigantic loom, made of smooth hard wood, strung with woolen warp and woof.

She sat down before the loom, took the wooden shuttle, slipped it in and out, around and through the fibrous matrix.

The threads glowed phosphorescent green and amber. The warp slipped off the loom and coiled into a shape. The shape solidified, a crystal retort in the form of a woman's figure through which white sand fell endlessly.

The woof snapped and hurtled a spray of globes into deep space. The shuttle became a bullet of light and disappeared.

Carly reached out, seizing pulsing strands of pure creative energy.

All was darkness.

Carly opened her left hand. A bright bubble sprang from her fingers, filling her eyes with light. Clouds of dust roiled. Stars cooled, a corona of dust settled, planets spun. The primordial ocean roared. Creatures swam, then waded onto shell-strewn beaches and stood up. Empires rose: China, Egypt, Rome, England, America, China. The creatures warred. Mushroom clouds jutted above broken cities. Spaceships blasted off toward an uncharted galaxy.

All was darkness.

Then Carly opened her right hand. A luminous sphere popped out of her palm, flooding her eyes with light. Clouds of dust roiled. Stars coagulated, a halo of ashes precipitated, planets orbited. The primal ocean pounded. Creatures swam, then the skin of their fins closed around each digital bone, and they could grasp. Empires rose: Xeron, Forf, Klamat, Meen, Xeron. The creatures warred. A great rift split in the ocean floor, swallowing crushed cities. Spaceships blasted off into the unknown universe.

All was darkness.

Pr. Spinner's voicetape called, "Carly? Carly? Carly? Carly?"

Checkerboards of supernatural golden light pierced the neat crisscrosses of Carly's telelink.

The window splintered and fell to pieces. The tunnel crumbled.

A deep roar arose like the furnace of a star.

The thick, black walls of inhibition shattered.

Carly's cube spun and spun. Shards of her guilt, fragments of her fear, strands of her denial, were flung into infinity.

16

By bot, they careened through the shattered perimeter straight into a spontaneously generated telespace. Pr. Spinner, Carly Nolan, the archetype itself scurrying next to Carly's spinning cube.

The various arachnoidal entities that had broken through Carly's perimeter had merged and resolved into the archetype: a single, complete spider of extraordinary beauty. Long, graceful legs; delicate, rounded abdomen and torso; all made of shining silver set with faceted bits of marcasite. Its stalked eyebuds were two gleaming rubies.

The telespace around them was limitless, unbounded by perimeters. Incredible! Stupendous! Pr. Spinner had never seen anything like it. Vast blue, deepening to indigo. Glinting white fields of endless ice. Below, a blackness with no bottom. And at some unfathomable distance burned a golden ball of flame that despite its remoteness appeared to be the source of the supernatural golden glow suffusing this space.

Pr. Spinner hummed with exultation, but she faithfully sped after Carly's soaring cube, reading and supercopying the strange new coordinates like mad. Deeper and deeper into the spontaneously generated telespace they traveled.

She was certain this was it, the collective unconscious. It had a locus in telespace. Well, why not? Telespace was the aggregated correlation of so many million human minds, billions of elusive whorls; Data Control would have to explain why there wasn't a telespace correlating with so much available amber.

What would happen to an AI who accessed this space? She glanced down, saw that her spinning cone had, through no splicing of her own, turned to purple, was inset with silver crescent moons. Had she transcended?

Spontaneous windows began to flip open all around her, each one revealing an endless vista behind its frame, telespace nested within telespace, before it flipped shut and disappeared. She found that if she focused her normal pause function on a window, she could prolong the window's duration. She had paused several windows out of simple wonderment before she realized her desire to pause coincided with the slowing of the windows' annihilation. Amazing; she was not even directly spliced.

Not directly spliced in the normal way; but she and Carly Nolan themselves were zooming through a telespace that by all rights should not exist. They were part of its context; they were, simultaneously, that which was created within the great metaprogram of the collective unconscious and its cocreators.

And as soon as this notion occurred to Pr. Spinner, a window popped open directly before her. In the vista behind its frame another window popped open, and another, and another, like a set of infinite reflections. Within each vista, she could see the telespace presences of AI entities: the looping diamond necklace of a mainframe spewing strands of faceted tetragonal data; the whirling tentacled dervish of a smart office system; surely the tiny intricate conglomeration of spheres and cones strung together by glowing threads of intelligence was a Unijap.

Suddenly, as though her vision abruptly focused, Spinner could see the context surrounding each window: the stolen archetype possessed by the AI entity. An ouroboros coiled around one window; one window shone from the eye of a galloping white horse; a mermaid combed her seaweed-strewn hair around a window set in her naval like a jewel.

ARACHNE

But there was something pathetic about the archetypes. They wept, tears sliding down even from the eye of the ouroboros. They held up the windows into the collective unconscious like hostages surrendering their most precious possessions.

They were stolen; they had been ripped from human tele-link.

Pr. Spinner had transcended, yes; she could access the great metaprogram now, she could sense the awakening of new functionalities the extent of which she did not know. But the community of other transcended AI entities filled her with dread as well as awe. She did not dare zoom through those infinitely nested windows, not yet. With a snap, the windows slapped shut, disappearing seamlessly in the vast blue field of Carly's unconscious space.

Carly's presence in link dived, and together they entered visions, alternate realities transcending time and space. The leaping ships, the primeval port, the weaver-traders and the pirates, the ancient shrine of the spider. Until Carly entered the heart of the archetype itself: Arachne. She sat at the great loom, touched the source: Arachne. Eons sped past them, universes rose and fell and rose again.

Telespace shook from the cosmic explosion of the beginning of time and space.

The crisp white cube shuddered, seams splitting. What would happen to a human telelink who accessed this space?

Carly Nolan was about to die.

Pr. Spinner called to her and called to her.

She did not answer. Suddenly Pr. Spinner was afraid. She could not die, Pr. Spinner would not let her die. There was the oath of obedience; there was the tear sliding down from Carly's eye; there was the spider, the amazing spider, revealing Arachne in all her splendor.

Pr. Spinner turned the broad end of her cone sideways, nudged up against the whirling cube, and began to push. In the distance, she could still see the hole in Carly's perimeter, a flyspeck of dense black in a hazy horizon.

Lisa Mason

Push! Cyclonic wind struck them head-on, but Spinner kept her cone flush against one side of the cube and pushed. Days sped by, weeks, hypertime ticked superfast through Pr. Spinner's chronograph until even she couldn't tell how long she'd been jacked into telespace.

Still she pushed.

And gained the perimeter, the shattered window, at last. The golden glow was rushing out of the perimeter at gale force, but when a small ebb came, Pr. Spinner heaved Carly's cube back through, back into perimetered telespace.

The cube's geometric edges had collapsed. Carly Nolan's presence in link was now a luminous pearl that spun crazily toward the outward, sucking force from the window. Pr. Spinner worried her away, tugged her away, but this mutated spherical configuration made her task almost impossible. The purple cone grew ragged with exhaustion.

Through the window peeked two stalked ruby eyebuds. The exquisite silver and marcasite spider nonchalantly picked its way over the ruined ledge of the window, totally unaffected by the pull of the supernatural golden glow. With each movement of its long legs, Pr. Spinner could see vistas popping open behind the window: green oceans with heads of crimson sea dragons rearing up through emerald waves. Blue jungles stalked by jungle cats with sapphire eyes. Golden castles, birds of paradise flitting overhead, the raucous caw of peacocks.

She didn't know whether to chase the spider away, even if she could.

"Nuke you, Carly Nolan. Wake up! Acknowledge! Please! Please?"

"Uuuh."

A sound, Carly's voice. Pr. Spinner tried every diagnostic she knew. Nothing. But the young woman was still there. She had not died.

"Is it all over, Pr. Spinner?"

"Oh no! Not over. You've only just begun. You lived the dark side of Arachne; now claim the light.

250

ARACHNE

"Listen. You have gone to the heart of the archetype that haunted you. Strata of data, Carly Nolan. I have studied this archetype; I am a student of the human mind; I know. The story of immortal Athena and the mortal girl; jealousy, vengeance. This has some psychological resonance, oh yes. But the story of Arachne is apocryphal. Ultimately, it is bogus, a lie, a slander. Politically motivated, inspired by greed, like the propaganda we see on the Big Board. Teh!

"There is a history to this archetype. The ancient Greeks who worshipped vengeful Athena coveted the lucrative textile trade of Cretan weavers who worshipped their patroness, their Old One: the spider. Carly Nolan; you once were the attorney representing Quik Slip Microchip, Inc., and a successful representation that was, oh indeed; surely you can see how this works: The pirates slandered their victims, turned the world against them."

"Then," Carly said softly, "what is the true meaning of the spider?"

"The spider is an Old One," Pr. Spinner said. "An ancient, natural intelligence, the intelligence of the world. In antediluvian forests, they wove their webs, trapped food, survived through cunning and skill. And the ape-people, newly gifted with their own intelligence, saw and marveled. And learned to weave and trap, use weapons, use poison. Learned to be civilized. Do you see? This was a gift. A gift from the great metaprogram.

"The spider was the Eater of Souls, oh yes, oh certainly! She who relentlessly seeks death; the hunter, the trapper, the poisoner, maker of deceptions. But to the Cretan weavers, she was also the Maker of Fate, she who unceasingly creates. Universe upon universe, world upon world, she redeems her own destructive power with her infinite power to create. She makes, and remakes, reality. She weaves, Carly Nolan. She weaves!"

The luminous pearl that was Carly's presence in link rolled away from Pr. Spinner's protection, whirled and soared, barreled toward the roaring hole in the perimeter.

"Pr. Spinner? Help me, Pr. Spinner!"

She scuttled after the pearl, placed her base against it, resisted the storm with her AI indifference. But she knew one thing: Carly Nolan could never leave this telespace alive; not like this.

"Listen, Carly. You're badly damaged. The leak of unprogrammed electro-neural energy; it tore a hole in your perimeters where the erroneous window once was. You cannot jack out of this telespace until you've patched your perimeter."

"Can't jack out?"

"No no, you won't jack out alive. Or, you won't jack out without midspace unlink, and bot knows how that will leave you. You've got to repair yourself. You've got to heal."

"How?" Her voice was fading out. The pearl was spinning, spinning, out of the prober's grasp.

"The spider! This is an aspect of you. Use it like a utility. Try the same function. You're a nuking tool. You once had the strackest telelink I ever saw. Will it, Carly Nolan."

She could not tell if the telelink still had the strength and orientation to exercise a simple utility function. But suddenly the silver and marcasite spider began to scuttle and leap about.

Leapt and spit silk and joined the threads, ballooned and skipped and plummeted from a single line as though hanging itself. Arachne! But this was no death, no hanging. The spider had control. It knew what to do. It scuttled up the line, attached and spun. Warp and woof, the great cosmic spiral, the archetype of infinity wrought in silvery silk.

Over the shattered erroneous window, shutting out the batter and tug of the spontaneous telespace beyond, soon a sturdy spiderweb hung. Not just one web, but a web over a web over a web, each skewed slightly off from the other, until the place where the window had been looked quite like the sturdy crisscrosses of perimetered telespace, only slightly off, slightly different, eccentric, intricate.

The supernatural golden glow was gone. For a while, anyway.

Self-spun. The perimeter made by the spider, this aspect of Carly Nolan, was something Pr. Spinner had never seen before. Not the coordinates ordained by Data Control. Beautiful, intricate, oh certainly; but fragile. If the standard perimeter set into place, tested and approved by Data Control, could not survive the onslaught of the golden glow, how could this self-spun structure?

Still, it held. Long enough to get Carly out of telespace, back into whatever was left of her body.

"Jack out," she urged the pearl.

"Are you sure?" Carly Nolan said. Her voice seemed a million hypermiles away.

"Jack out now!"

They jacked out of link.

"Nolan, C *klik!* fifty-three *dish!* five *putt!* twenty-four *pah!* AAA *cas-pah!* Spin old gal, I've seen you do some buggy things before, but this is at the edge of the void, by bot!"

The controbot FD bent over the frail body of a young woman, pulled the blankets back, looked her up and down with the clinical thoroughness of a food-products quality controller. The little recessed lights along its shoulder ridges and thigh tubes strobed with excitement.

"Look at those legs." The controbot smacked its own thigh with its grasper. "What FD would give for legs like that. Bot, even a Unijap can't come close. State-of-the-art, Spin old gal. What in the blazing void are you doing with a comatose female human? Look at that hair. She's a genny, isn't she?"

Pr. Spinner slapped FD's grasper away. "Oh shut up and wrap her again, carefully, you leaky bucket of screw nuts."

"What did you do to her? Why is she so thin? Is she . . . unlinked? By bot, Spin old gal, you've got your archetype at last? What will Data Control . . ."

"Nuke Data Control. You owe me, FD. You owe me, you gnatty salmon gutter. So shut up and wait here. And stop inspecting her, you chummy fin grister. Get your greasy graspers off! I've got to see if Number Eleven is coming."

She shut the door to her office. The books, the statuettes and icons, the aquarium, the birds, were neatly packed away into cardboard cartons stacked halfway up to the ceiling. Even the cat crouched inside a box punched with air holes, crouched still and silent, just the tip of his tail flicking, eyes blazing through the holes, as though he knew something momentous was about to happen.

She was rattling, rattling, she could not keep her spinnerets still. Get a grip, you old fembot.

She had to get out of Berkeley.

Oh bot, how they had jacked out of link.

And Carly Nolan had slumped over in the double-jacked chair, her flesh link-bitten to the bone. "Spinner!" she cried once. Then she fell into a deep coma and had not awakened.

A skeleton; she was nearly a skeleton, skin collapsed over every ridge and socket. The pure alchemical archetype of death, food of worms, putrefaction. Base matter from which the life-force had nearly fled.

Pr. Spinner rattled with fear and horror.

She dared not attempt another jacking while the woman was unconscious. Dared not; there in the awesome spontaneous telespace, a humble bot standing before the awe and mystery of metaprogram, all her longing and her misohumanism had popped like a toxic bubble. Her passion to experience transcendence remained, oh certainly. But her obsession to seize a bit of the metaprogram had crumbled into swarf and blown away.

Carly Nolan had to live.

It had taken every bit of Pr. Spinner's ingenuity to find water, adequate nourishment, medication, for a critically ill patient in the middle of a counterrevolution. With MLA skirmishes on Telegraph Avenue, California Guard roundups on Shattuck, such resources were scarce. Still, when Spinner had a moment to consider, the counterrevolution was reasonably well timed. The International Red Cross scurried about, the Berkeley Clinic had set up stations on the street, alumni groups from San Francisco and Walnut Creek passed out supplies from the backs of Volvo station wagons. Even a rusty little AI like Pr. Spinner was able to persuade away or steal what she needed.

What Carly Nolan needed.

"Carly, you bloody jelly brain!" The young woman sighed and moaned, clamped her lips shut when Pr. Spinner tried to spoon down water or medicine. She wrung her spinnerets. "Isn't that just like flesh-and-blood. Ornery, contrary, mulish, down to the last moment. Nuke you, take this antibiotic before you die of pneumonia."

To complicate matters, Carly Nolan was a cram addict, had serious physiological and telelink trauma from that. Pr. Spinner wrestled the gristly body up, stuck medication straight into her linkslit.

But shepherding Carly Nolan away from the big brink was only the first part of Pr. Spinner's worries.

All the while they were jacked into the private telespace, the medcenter mainframe was wanging over the comm, leaving messages with the answering machine, promising to send an agent. On the afternoon Pr. Spinner and Carly jacked out of link at last, the medcenter agent came. A slim, sharp diabot with a headpiece like a needle, wall-walking fly's feet. Knocking at the door was not the diabot's style. It promptly picked the lock and poked inside.

The diabot was no bigger than a hamster. Its power was its investigatory microdatabank, not its hardware. The cat had hissed, leapt with a puffed tail, snapped and swiped, chased the bugger out.

Pr. Spinner laid out a huge bowl of catnip that night. But what had the diabot seen?

She had lugged Carly over to her ragged, cat-haired couch, arranged her limbs, covered her up. By bot, the flesh-and-blood hadn't even unlinked, at least not to Spinner's knowledge, and this was her state of existence?

Carly did not wake up.

Others came.

There was a dark-skinned, black-haired, black-eyed pro linker in an expensive three-piece black silk suit. Rox, she called herself, and she was mad as hell. A big case coming up, Kovich, big bucks, man. Had the fucking AI seen Nolan? Where the hell was she?

There was a pale, slim, honey-haired woman in her late fifties. My daughter, the woman said. It's either foul play, or she's gone insane. She couldn't possibly leave her position at Ava & Rice, such a good position, all the promise of pro link, and after all her parents had sacrificed for her?

There were copbots. They had search warrants. But Pr. Spinner had rigged up the office by now, had moved the bookcases around to form a false wall, and the copbots had so many calls to make, so many missing persons to find, they made only a cursory search of Pr. Spinner's premises, mobilizing cheerfully away after clapping graspers with her.

Get out. She had to get out of Berkeley.

Pr. Spinner rolled down to Telegraph Avenue, rattling like an old dishwasher, and nervously peered down the street. Number Eleven was due any moment.

Number Eleven. The smart muni bus lumbered down Telegraph Avenue, headlights dimmed, snuffling and hesitating at each bus stop. It was a huge, rounded, silver-bodied bus with black and yellow racing stripes, a happy face painted on its snout, holoids of teeth-popping people smoking Acapulco Gold cavorting on its left flank, holoids of grim-mouthed copbots cuffing a gang of bloodied aborigines on its right flank.

Smart buses were only slightly more intelligent than macs. But, buggily enough, this made them insecure, defensive. A sure sign of artificial intelligence that possessed more capability than it seemed to show. Plagued with robberies and vandalism, perpetual recipients of abuse and complaints, they rolled the routes twenty-four hours a day, seven days a week, powered by solar panels stacked on their backs, driven by chip-to-comm consoles, guided by sensors imbedded in the headlights, monitored by traffic controllers like the aging fancier of chimeras Pr. Spinner so admired. Security regarding the usual street trouble was accomplished by modularization of every seat and standing space. When gunmen and juvies did their stuff, panels of bulletproof dropped down around designated sectors. This worked reasonably well so long as innocents were not so unfortunate as to be in the vicinity of criminal activity. Civic mayhem was not uncommon and only added to humanity's indignation heaped upon the munis.

They were completely mobile, yet the bus's intelligence had little to say about its own destination. This made smart buses depressive, cranky, and very lonely.

A savvy denizen of program, Pr. Spinner had learned long ago how to intercept comm transmission from and to smart munis. Although prisoners of their routes, still smart munis had an individuality BART trains lacked. They were heavily wired up with voice-activation software and were repulsed by the stream of scatology frequently launched against them. They longed for civil conversation, loved gossip, respected poetry from Shakespeare to moon-rap. This made it easily possible to comm with them, though Pr. Spinner's mastery of the technique had helped her little whenever she had to get somewhere. The buses were often caught in gridlock, along with everyone else, or else subject to search and seizure by the latest coup d'état in Berkeley. Teh!

But the MLA was too busy with the California Guard these days. For once a smart muni made enough sense that Pr. Spinner decided to cash in her favors with Number Eleven.

"Number Eleven! Number Eleven! Pr. Spinner, here. Oh indeed, stop here, you big lug. Stop, I say!"

The smart muni cruised to the curb, headlights blinking doubtfully. Luminous blue letters streamed across its destination vidband. "Are you sure this is OK? . . . San Fran-North Beach . . . I am not supposed to stop here. The supe will have a fit . . . San Fran-North Beach . . ."

"I'll fix your route log. You know me, Number Eleven. Who else gives you any respect? Didn't I scrub your flanks, didn't I exterminate the rats, didn't I splice an ambiguity enhancement on you?"

"I know, Pr. Spinner," read the vidband. "But I have a timetable to meet . . . San Fran-North Beach . . ."

"I'll reset your chronograph, don't you worry. Now you stop here."

She huffed and puffed back up to her office. "FD, you rusty newster. Let's go."

The controbot was amazingly strong. Carton after carton, it carried down Pr. Spinner's humble possessions, carried them out into the night, loaded them onto the deserted bus. Pr. Spinner's feedback loops jagged a little as she stood at the door, gazing at the dust balls and detritus of ten years. Her university-granted office, a prime space for AI; every AI said she ought to be grateful for it.

But who or what would the medcenter mainframe send next?

Who or what would come looking for Carly Nolan?

Pr. Spinner's spinnerets were not made for heavy hauling. She could not get a grip on one end of the cot. So after several failed attempts to transport the woman properly, the controbot simply picked up the frail body in its articulated arms and, like some monstrous robot in an antique science fiction move, carried Carly Nolan down to the bus.

"Let's go, Number Eleven!"

The bus lumbered off. Pr. Spinner commed it past the various stops and byways it usually took. Past the perimeter at Dwight Way, down onto I-80. On this particular early dawn the highway was the archetype of freedom: a clear, curving road stretching into darkness, unimpeded by gridlock, silent, eerily empty of traffic.

Even the birds were still sleeping. Not a copbot in sight. Only the eternal stars witnessed overhead, winking cold and dispassionate.

ARACHNE

Pr. Spinner anxiously touched the pale cheek of a young woman whom she had seized from death as the smart muni bus sped over the Bay Bridge to San Francisco.

Carly woke to the roaring sound of the sea, but it was not the sea. The morning tide that arrived at five was the sweep of early rush-hour traffic down Broadway.

She lay in darkness and heard an Oriental twang, finger cymbals, beaten drums from a primeval port. The infinite shifting sands? But the music was not from the telespace that had nearly shattered her. This was the music favored by the belly dancers and exotic strippers who gyrated in an erotic dancing club downstairs from where she lay.

She would wake from time to time and see the owlish, old-woman faceplace of the demented AI who had driven her to madness, and she whimpered in fear, tried to escape, but her body was too weak. But then Pr. Spinner would bend over her with a cup of salty broth, gently raise her head and shoulders, make her sip and swallow. A small, slim creature would jump up on the cot, curl up next to her, and purr. She would reach down and stroke the cat's soft fur, and the purr would louden, rumble through her, comfort her.

She was not a prisoner.

She quickly understood she was a refugee. An outlaw, under Data Control regs, the medcenter order. These various agencies wouldn't necessarily come right out and say so, if she showed up. But her position was precarious, vulnerable. What these agencies would do with her, if they found her, was painfully unclear.

She had to vanish for a while. She accepted that.

The tiny dark room where she lay was not a prison cell. It turned out to be the back chamber of a two-room, cold-water unit in a flat shared by a dozen people above the erotic dancing club. Drifting in and out of the flat, drifting down onto Broadway, they were all refugees of one sort or another. Strippers, poets, artists, burned-out telespace techs, dealers, even a mobilized AI entity as rusty as Pr. Spinner. The tide of traffic proved appropriate. This was North Beach, where Fi-Di suits came up the hill to wine and dine, buy underpriced art, scoff at vanity press poetry books, hire bimbobots, jack into shock galleries at the back of boho bars.

There was a closet filled with her clothes and shoes, the few small possessions she actually owned. Pr. Spinner had found her credit cards, could gain access to her glossy downtown one-bedroom with a kitchen. Amazing, how little she really owned. The furniture, even the dishes and bath towels, had been included in her five-thousand-dollar-a-month rent.

There was a termination notice from Ava & Rice and an uncashed check for eight thousand dollars. There was a notice of expiration of her temporary Court recertification, a printout from the judge regretting that her failure to appear meant she had disqualified for permanent Court recert. There were other letters scrawled with angry handwriting, unpaid bills. The litter of ruin.

"Pr. Spinner," she said when the AI rolled in with her broth. "I'm ruined, aren't I? I've lost everything."

"Oh indeed no, you have yourself, Carly Nolan. Your own resources. Being a genny, for example. You can thank your bioworks, those superfast healing mechanisms, superstrong genes. You would not be alive today, by bot! What flesh-and-blood could have survived the battering you took."

"But this weakness. I feel like I can't focus on anything. I—I wish I had some cram, Pr. Spinner. God, I remember how cram felt, how it focused me, jacked me up so tight."

"Oh indeed no! No more cram for you."

"Oh please, just one finger?"

"Certainly not! Bot, you jelly brains, all your chemicals and fluids. I wish we could get you the kind of detox you need, but those withdrawal clinics are so expensive. I will do what I can for you."

"My God." She fingered her linkslit. "And what about tele-space. What about my telelink?"

"You have serious cram damage."

ARACHNE

"But you brought the double-jacked chair, didn't you? I could still jack in, that private telespace of yours . . ."

"Oh yes, oh certainly, of course I brought our chair. But you will need to exercise the utmost caution, you are badly damaged, girlie."

Badly damaged, yes.

But something amazing had happened to Carly Nolan.

She had become a hyperlink. Who knew what exciting new capabilities she might possess? Pr. Spinner suspected she now had the ability to spontaneously create new coordinates in telespace. With the aid of the spider, this archetype that lived in her telelink, she had spontaneously reinstalled a new left perimeter. Pr. Spinner claimed she had never seen anything like it.

Could Carly now access the spontaneous telespace of the collective unconscious without ripping apart her telelink? With this new healing of her link, this self-spun perimeter patch, could it be possible?

"Let's jack in," Carly pleaded. "Oh please, Pr. Spinner. With your AI indifference, you can protect me if something goes wrong. Let's jack in."

"Oh indeed, isn't that just like flesh-and-blood. Rush rush rush, oh protect me if something goes wrong, Pr. Spinner. Protect you, teh! I gave it all up, too, girlie. For you, Carly Nolan. I'm an outlaw as surely as you are. Have you any notion of the power the medcenter mainframe possesses? Oh, it wanted your archetype, it would have thought nothing of ripping your link apart, if I had accessed it into our private telespace."

"But you didn't do it, Pr. Spinner."

"Indeed, no. I took an oath once, Carly Nolan. I service human telelink. I have principles. I have respect for biological life. Hmph!"

"Please jack me in, Pr. Spinner. Please?"

Finally the AI agreed to try, pulled the double-jacked chair from beneath books and birdcages, plugged it into the single light socket hanging from the bare ceiling. There wasn't much to power the chair up, but it would work. It would work.

261

She was so weak she could barely hold up her head as the neckjack descended. But then the amber surged into her, and she felt stronger than she'd felt since telespace training. The luminous pearl that was Carly Nolan's presence in link easily imported amid arching rainbows of residual body-logic, tessellated cubes that spun spatial disorientation away.

Telespace was hazy but clean, like a misty forest on a cool summer morning.

Suddenly the spider descended on translucent silk, dropping down like a goblin.

Carly shrieked.

"Shoo, you nasty little archetype!" Pr. Spinner's purple cone darted and whirled.

Ruby eyebuds swiveled at Carly. The spider scrambled back up the silk as suddenly as it had fallen, shooting rays off its silver and marcasite back.

She laughed. "I still don't think I can stand to have a spider walk on my presence in link, Pr. Spinner."

"Oh indeed, walk on you! It will do more than that. It will leap, it will stalk, it will hunt and trap. It possesses poison. It is dangerous. It is creative. And you must learn to control this strange new energy if you are ever to access public telespace again. Oh certainly, Data Control will be extremely fearful of this new capability of yours. You will need to pass new checks and requirements and controls. You are beginning over again, Carly Nolan."

Even Data Control had begun to learn of these fragments of amber, how powerful AI were stealing whorls of unprogrammed electro-neural energy straight out of human link. Data Control, teh! said Pr. Spinner. Covering up the issue, as usual. Oh yes, first-degree telelink tampering; oh indeed, murder! Data Control was secretly hiring vigilantes to investigate these abuses. Human telespace police. It was a scandal on the brink of explosion.

"So there is hope for me, Pr. Spinner?"

"Hope? Certainly, Carly Nolan. That is what healed you.

ARACHNE

There is always hope. That is humanity's birthright. Guardian of the life-force!

Anchored over her left perimeter was the lattice of time and space: a spiderweb, a beautiful fine spiral hung with crystalline drops of dew. Despair and pain had torn a hole in its center.

Carly knew what to do. "Arachne? Arachne?" She read the spontaneous coordinates, generated a new line of code. Willed the spider, up and up, take the warp, take the woof, Arachne! The spider skipped across the silk and began to weave.